R

To Low. Th... Support. Enjoy The Book

Rap Star

By Tony Clincy

Tony Clincy

Printed June 2013, First Printing August 2010

HoodLife Books

Seaside, California

Copyright Anthony Teague 2009

ISBN-13:9781461086628

Printed in the United States of America

10 9 8 7 6 5 4 3 2 1

Rap Star

This and all my books are dedicated to the memory of Troy (Locco) William Hill, who rolled over on his rack, looked at me with that big ole smile of his, and said. "Nk you should write a book!" then went on to explain simply that. "I'm telliing you. All you gotta do is write it, and if it's cool they gotta fk wit chew!"

The rest is history. I'm at this chit, lil homie and I swear I wont stop. How right you were when you told me a few weeks later that God had put you in there in that cell with me for a reason, and you could see how writing would change my life.

Such wise words from such young lips.

I love and miss you my nig, and I promise I won't quit till I get that penthouse in Manhattan like I told you I would.

And then I'm gon' go harder.

MOB! (never) Lol.

Love you man.

Rest in Paradise.

P.S.

When I blow with this, I got Tatiana. On mommas!

Tony Clincy

For, my mother, brother, sisters, nephews, and nieces, whom, it seems, have taken onthe job of bringing smiles to my face,

and warm fuzzy feeling to my heart.

Love y'all to death.

And for Eric Moberg, my mentor and friend

JUST DOING IT...

THE RINGING PHONE woke Spits from a deep sleep and he snatched it off the nightstand barking "Hello!" into the mouthpiece.

"I thought you said you were coming at two" Mash started. ",and look at you. Still sleep!"

Spits wiped the sleep from his eyes and looked at the Dallas Cowboy wall clock above his bedroom closet and shook his head sighing. "Man it's only one o'clock and you-"

"-And like I said." Mash put in, cutting him off. "You butt's still sleep." he let out a long , frustrated breath and asked. "Man, is you comin' or not 'cause if you ain't then let me know so I can let these other Nk's come through and finish up their CD."

Though mad at having gotten woke up, Spits couldn't help but laugh at the whine in Mash's voice. "Shut up and stop cryin', punk. " he told him. "You sound like a lil beezie I just faked on or sumptin, boy. Man up my nig, 'cause the begging don't even look fly on you, chief."

"Whatever." Mash said and waited.

"Give me a minute." Spits told him after a moment. "I gotta shower and dress first, and then I'll slide through your lil raggedy studio and rip that thang up."

"You better, with all the woofin' the homies been doin about you." Mash told him before disconnecting the call.

Spits laughed as he hung up. He then climbed out of bed yawning, and headed for the bathroom.

"Deandre are you hungry?" His mother called out from the kitchen when she heard his door creak open. "I cooked some of that fish you brought home yesterday."

"Yeah mom. Make me a plate to go." He called out before closing the bathroom door shut. After emptying his bladder, he went to the sink and looked up to return the smile of the tall and handsome, cocoa-complexioned young man

5

smiling at him in the mirror. "Just do it!" he told his reflection, reciting the motto which he lived by. "There aint nothin' to it but to do it, so go over there and show the homie what's up wit you and dis rap thang."

Ever since he'd gotten out of San Quentin six months ago, Mash had been pestering him to come to his studio and lay down some tracks, but Spits had come home with money on his mind, and had told him time and time again, that he was on his paper chase and could give less than a care about rap music. But Mash had kept at him, finally getting him so tired of being sweated, that he'd agreed to drop by and lay down a track or two if Mash promised to leave him alone afterwards.

Spits had a smile as big as Christmas on his face as headed for the kitchen. All was right in his world and from the looks of it, were about to get a whole lot better too.

When they let him out of Quentin with his $200 gate money, he'd caught the bus to Salinas and headed straight for Chinatown where he'd copped a quarter ounce and set about getting his money back right. That was why he had been ducking and dodging Mash these past months, because he was just too busy getting his weight up to be sitting up in somebody's too-hot garage rapping.

When he reached the kitchen he found his mother standing at the stove with her back to him a mischevious grin lit up his face as he started sneaking up behind her with his arms wide and ready to hug.

His steps were soft-footed and slow as he made his way across the kitchen tile with his long arms wide and ready to hug. "Good morning, beautiful lady." He said as he wrapped her up in his arms and hugged her close.

"Hey you." She said with a contented sigh as she leaned back into her only child's loving embrace. sighed and leaned back into, content there in her only child's loving embracer.turned towards him with a smile and saw the sparkle in his eyes. "What's got you all excited this morning?"

"Nothin'. I'm goin' to my patna's house to record a couple of songs."

His mother knew how much her baby loved to rap so upon hearing this, she smiled and hugged him. "Oh baby, I'm so happy for you!"

"Dang Mom." He complained, pulling away as if he were too old to be hugging his mother. "It ain't nothin'."

She gave him a look and waved him off. "You forget that I raised you boy. I know how important music used to be to you and I know that cool front you be puttin' up for everybody else is just that. A front. So don't be actin' all grown on me when I wanna hug you and share your happiness."

When Spits was done eating, he got dressed and left for the f+ve minute drive to Mash's house and parked in front. He climbed out and headed to the back garage door on the side of the house like Mash had told him to.

As he walked to the door, he heard the heavy bass banging inside the garage and stopped walking suddenly nervous. He let out a deep breath and pounded his chest.

"Just do it." He told himself again and knocked on the door. Mash opened the door with a smile. His *Seaside CA* and seahorse tattoos on his bare chest and stomach were on full display.

"I didn't think you was gon' come." Mash said waving him in and stepping to the side so that he could pass. Mash nodded his head toward the booth. "D-Boy and Carlos is laying down their verses."

Spits stepped into the dark, blue-lit garage and stared at the dimmed soundproof booth at the front of the garage where the two familiar faces stood.

"How long y'all been at it?"

"Man," Mash let out a heavy breath and continued. "I been bangin' out beats since three this morning. They just came through a couple of hours ago though."

Spits looked at his watch and shook his head. "All that money out here and you been posted up in here playing

DJ all night?" Spits shook his head again. "I can't see it homie. I'm trying to get paid. Forget all that extra stuff."

"Once I blow up, you gon' see what paid is, chief. Watch what I tell you." Mash said.

"I heard that."

The tone of Spits voice caused Mash to laugh. They'd already had this conversation before and he knew Spits wasn't buying his spiel.

"You just make sure you don't come up in here with no weak raps, boy." Mash warned him before sitting down at his control panel to tweak the sounds blasting from the speakers.

Spits was sitting and checking out the posters of the deceased artist hanging on the walls, and he noticed that someone was missing and asked. "Where's Pac at?" He saw Biggie, Easy, Mac Dre, and Nate Dog, but Tupac was nowhere in sight.

Mash laughed and answered, telling him. "He ain't make the wall of fame up in here, chief. Only real cats get up on the wall of fame." He shook his head, no, and explained. "Pac was a set-jumper. We don't do that out west."

"You need to be trying to put a picture of ya boy up there though." Spits said and pointe to a blank spot on the wall. "Yeah." He said. " Pac or none of them cats can see me at this here rappin'."

Mash rolled his eyes, certain he was putting extras on it. "You puttin' it on way too thick, chief. And like I said, you gotta be legend to get your face up on my wall, so until you prove yourself a legend, you can miss me with the small talk, chief!"

Spits nodded his head with a self-confident smirk on his face and rubbed his bald head as he turned to the booth. Mash lit a blunt and the blue snake-like smoke climbed to the bare blue bulb above them with potent indigo fumes.

"Pass the tree's, chief." Spits said and reached for it. He hit it hard and the California sticky relaxed him, erasing the nervousness he felt at being back in the lab after so long.

This was the first time in years that he'd been in a studio. Now he was anxious to get on the mic and hear himself spit on some of that west coast gangster funk.

In his heart he knew that he wasn't to be messed with when it came to rapping. And if it wasn't for the fact that he had to be out here in the streets chasing a dollar, he'd probably be posted up in this blue ass garage all day and night just like Mash. But just like he just told the homie, he couldn't see it.

"How long you gon' stay?" Mash asked, anxiously watching the boys in the booth. He couldn't wait for them to be done so he could see what Spits had.

"I got a couple of hours. Then I got to bounce." Spits told him. "Some cats in Salinas owe me some bread and I got to go pick it up."

The two wannabes came out of the booth smiling and the taller of the two asked. "How did that sound?"

"It was cool." Mash said unenthusiastically. He looked to Spits with a smirk. "You know D-Boy and Carlos?"

"I seen 'em around" Spits responded and put a fist out to give them dap. "What it do homie?"

"What's up Spits?" Carlos said.

"Hey." Replied D-Boy

Mash was busy typing commands into his computer as the three talked about what was going on in the hood they called home.

Mash turned to Spits when he was done. "Let's get your ass on the mic so I can see what all the hype's about." Spits smirked. He knew Mash still doubted him by the tone of his voice.

"Just throw on an old school beat and I'll show you what the hype's about ." Spits promised before walking into the booth and putting on the pair of the headphones.

"How about a Biggie beat?" Mash asked through the mic.

"That's cool" Spits told him and immediately heard the sounds of Biggie's "Juicy" in his ears. He smiled and nodded his head to the beat with the blue bulb casting its light into the booth and falling on his feet, leaving the rest of him standing in a dark blue silhouette.

With his hands pressed firmly to the headphones, he stared at the smoke snaking its way to the ceiling. His was mind empty of all things except the bass heavy instrumental pounding into the headphones.

"Turn down the bass a little and I'm at it." Spits requested. Mash leveled the bass out and Spits could see the cherry of the blunt Mash was puffing glow bright red through the blue smoke clouds. He closed his eyes and gave himself to the beat.

'It wasn't all a dream I weighed up thirty six on a triple beam.
Slid a sack to baby girl, told her to move the cream.
These haters mad but ef em all.
Stay smiling at these suckas, ice grill like Paul Wall.

I let my glock pop till they talk stop.
Aint sweatin' hood rats' cause Spits a pimp, just like his pops.
Way back. When I had the blue and black lumberjack,
With the rag to match.

Remember Cash Money, bling-bling bling-bling.
Neva thought you'd see Spits in da booth doin' da damn thing.
Be stayin' out the limelight' cause them cuffs tight.
I'm tryna get paid, blow up like Lebron James…

Mash was sitting at the edge of his chair with wide eyes.
"You hear this!" He asked aloud and turned with a smile to Carlos and D-Bo, smiling as he waved his hands in the air. "Y'all hear that ? That boys killin' that thang up in there.!" He clapped his hands together and rubbed the palms together

10

like he was about to get his grub on, saying. " Now that's how you do it, boy! That's what I'm talking 'bout right there!"

He spun back around and stared at Spits as he ate up the instrumental.

This is it! This is who I been looking for right here! He thought and saw all of his dreams coming true.

Having gone to school in Florida for music production, Mash had an excellent ear for music. He was one of the best producers of hip-hop in Northern Cali though few outside of his Seaside hometown knew it.

As a youngster, he had discovered a love of music and in spite of the mean streets of the Hood Life Projects that had raised him, he had kept his passion alive.

A few years ago when a gang war broke out in Seaside between Hood Life and their cross town rivals, one of Mash's closest friends had gotten killed.

Fearing for her son's future, Mash's mother had taken out a mortgage on their home, begged him to leave Seaside, move to Florida and enroll in the music production school he'd often told her he dreamed of attending.

Eventually his mother's tears won him over. After four years he'd graduated and to his mother's horror, returned to Seaside.

When she asked him why he had come back when here were so many other places he could've settled, Mash told her that he wanted to blow up using local talent. What he'd always known and tried to make his mom understand, was that there was a lot of talent in Seaside and Salinas. He wanted to reach his dream of putting the Central Coast on the map and needed to be back in Seaside to do it.

Now as he sat listening to Spits go for his on the Biggie instrumental, Mash knew that he'd found just the person to blow up with. In Spits, he heard the swagger of a great rapper.

With his ear for music, he could tell the difference between the average and the exceptional M.C. He knew that most of these wannabe rappers could get on the mic and say some half-assed slick verses like it was the easiest thing in the world. Sadly most of them really believed that they were the best thing since Jay-Z. But what Mash heard when he listened to all those rappers was a lack of confidence and a weak delivery in most cases.

Mash compared rapping to mackin' at females because just like when you pop game at a female, you had to sound confident and sure when you rapped or you'd come across as sounding bootsy.

The raw arrogance in Spits' delivery, made Mash want to nominate the boy for the mack of the year award right this second.
Spits soon finished his third and final verse and came out the booth.

"Play that back so I can hear how it sounds." He said as he took the chair beside Mash. He smiled at the awed look on Mash's face. Mash clicked the *play* icon and the song came blaring out the speakers.

As the song played, he began making adjustments to the bass so that it complemented the vocals rather than competed with them. Spits nodded his head at the difference it made.

"Yeah, that sounds better."

When the song ended, Spits looked expectantly at Mash.

"So did I live up to the hype or what?"

The look on Mash's face said that he knew that Spits flow was on point.

"You already know that was gas." Mash smiled and gave him dap." When did you write those verses? "

"I didn't." Spits said with no hesitation. "I don't write no more. I'm Spits , I spits mines off da top of the dome, Chief, you aint know?"

Carlos laughed behind them when he heard this. Hearing this, Carlos laughed behind him.

12

"If you don't stop it." Carlos told him and elbowed D-Boy. "You hear this clown? He think he Jigga or somebody." He looked back to Spits and said. "You putting way too much on it, homie."

Spits spun around in the chair to get a good look at him with his lips curled and a look of disgust on his face.

"Who is you that I gotta be lying to? Ain't nobody in here I'm tryin' to impress." Spits laughed. "Y'all the ones who up in here trying to be Run-DMC, not me. This is just a hobby for ya boy. I'm 'bout getting money, not trying to be your friendly neighborhood rap star."

"I'm just saying, though." Carlos answered still not convinced. "You don't expect us to believe that you free-styled them verses do you? Cause if you do, you can take that somewhere else. I ain't goin' for it."

Spits smiled at this. He turned to Mash whose eyes were alight with eagerness as he watched the drama unfold. Turning back to Carlos, Spits stood, reached into his pocket and pulled out a "knot".

"I tell you what. Let's bet some money on this 'cause it's nothin' for me to do the it again."

He started counting out bills. "I got five hundred dollars that say I can go back in there and freestyle about anything you tell me to. I'll step inside, and when Mash starts the beat, you give me the topic, and I'll rap about it. It's nothin'."

Still not convinced, Carlos was smiling as he took out his own money, counted out five hundred dollars and set it on the table next to the bills Spits had put there.

"Bet." Carlos said and shot D-Boy a knowing look. "We fixin to be smoking and drinking on ole boy tonight homie."

After shooting Mash a knowing look, Spits headed for the booth. He stepped inside and took off his T-shirt to show off his buffed, dark, and heavily tattooed six foot, three inch, 210 pound frame. Again he put the headphones on and spoke into the mic.

"Give me another old school beat Mash."

Mash's heart was pounding so hard with excitement that he thought it would jump out his chest. He searched his files for the right beat and settled on Whodini's 'One Love'. When he pressed play, he saw Spits smile and nod his head to the beat.

This boy aint playin' no games with this beat. The homie's was right, he do go hard in the paint wit it. Listen to him! He gettin' on this beat like it done did sumptin to him! Mash was thinking as he sat listening. He sat up straight in the chair, rubbing his hands together like he was about to tear into a tasty dish. This is the one I been waiting for, right here! Everybody thought I was woofin' when I told em I'd put the hood on the map if I found one of the homie's who's raps were up to par, but as he listened to Spits go for his, he knew that he would soon be proving himself right. That if he and Spits went hard in the studio for a few months, they'd set the music world on its ear with the music

his Mashed Out Productions Mash thought and sat up straight, rubbing his hands together as he listened to Spits kill the instrumental.

When Spits opened his eyes he saw their blue silhouettes staring at him through the soundproofed glass. He closed them again, allowing himself time enough to get all the way into the beat as he mentally prepared himself to ride it, leaning into the mic and asking Carlos. "What you want me to rap about?" when he was ready.

"Say somethin 'bout how the streets be killing all our dreams out here."

Spits laughed and asked him. "Is that it?" His voice was thick with sarcasm. "I'm livin' that, boy. . You just lost your little five hundred dollars."

He shot D-Boy a look and told him. "You better get your money together if you wanna get messed up today homie 'cause your boy just donated his."

Rap Star

Was it the love of the money or the hustle, was it only a dream.
Am I stuck on these streets, prayin' that the games just a dream.
Slept in cell as I dreamed. Lived in em when I 'cause I was sleep.
'Cause of crack sales, and no bail I was in cells wit da sneaks.
But nowadays, I'm havin bigger dreams when I'm woke.
Of movin these flows, no longer tryna ball of the coke, cause we through movin coke.
I swear that's why they stay bein' mad. 'Cause they stuck in the streets.
It's crazy, da homie's still bangin rags. Shits kinda of sad.
Just think of all the time we be wastin'.
Fell in love with hustle, so we chase after chips.
I'm a made figure.
All my beezies paid figures.
Tryin' to run from these streets but I swear they be telling me to stay, but I can't.
I'm dyin', the game's been killing me slow. I sent pro's to the stroll and packed heat when the streets got too cold.
Can't wait to parole, and kill em with these flows that he gave me.
Flip the script, trick I'm Spits.
I'll make this rap game pay me.

'Cause this is my life, it can't be a dream, it can't be a dream, cause hard times done killed my dreams. But I still be dream.
Won't let nobody stop me from dreamin'. You'll probably catch me dreamin' sometimes.

'Cause this is my life, it can't be a dream, can't be a dream cause hard times done killed my dreams. But I still dream.
Won't let nobody stop me from dreamin. You'll probably catch me dreamin' sometime..

On and on he went, telling the story of how the streets had corrupted him and others and how it had made them give up their dreams to chase money in the streets.

Mash was smiling when he turned around to tell Carlos. "I think you just lost your money, homie." .

"Yeah, ya boy did that." Carlos admitted with a defeated look on his face as he started putting on his jacket. "We outta here though. I'll get wit you later homie." He promised, heading for the door.

"Yeah. Y'all hit me up and we'll finish working on your album." Mash told him before turning back around to face Spits.

Spits eyes were still closed and he had a look on his face like he was in a place that only he could go as he told the story of the game stealing his dreams while he chased a dollar in the streets.

When the track ended, Spits came out drenched in sweat. He laughed at finding that Carlos and D-Boy had left, asking Mash. "What happened to your little patnas?" as he picked up the money off the table.

Mash dismissed the question with a wave and a smile and asked him. "Why you don't be in the studio recording? You should be putting out CD's?. You're the truth, Chief. And if you was to take this rappin' serious you'd blow up."

"Like you be doing?" Spits asked him as he look the garage over with judgmental eyes. They fell on the scattered crates and boxes laying here and there, the tangle of cords snaking along the floor, and finally came to rest on the washer and dryer, where he saw empty pizza boxes full of crusts, ashes, and empty soda cans. He curled his lips in disgust and shook his head no, telling Mash.
"Naw, I'm good. I think I'll pass on the rap career. Ain't nobody out here making no money rapping. I'm getting big boy money moving works in Salinas, and I'll be damned if I be stuck up in this raggedy garage with your broke butt." Again he shook his head. "Naw, homie, I'm cool with all the

dreaming stuff. It's real true to life situations jumping off in these here streets and ya boy out in these streets dealing with em.?"

Undeterred, Mash asked him. "Why you think aint nobody making no money rapping out here?" and watched him close, curios to hear his opinion. He had his own ideas as to why nobody had blown up out here yet, and was pretty sure he knew the solution to the problem, but wanted to hear what Spits had to say before speaking.

"I don't know. You tell me." Spits replied, turning the tables on him.
Mash wasted no time in answering. "aint nobody making it out here in the music game because cat's don't know how to play their positions. Everybody wanna be a rapper but it takes a team to break an artist though." He grew excited as he spoke, becoming animated, waving his hands for emphasis. "All we got to do is put together a team and get your music out there and we'll blow up. Your lyrics is so tight we can't miss. We can put the hood on the map."

Spits shook his head as Mash spoke. He held up his hands for him to stop. He wasn't trying to hear it.

"Man I been quit trying to be a rapper. This stuff is just a hobby. I'm trying to eat right now. Like today. I'm in the game and ain't no part-time positions on the block I play on. Y'all can have this."

Spits went on to tell how he had started rapping at the age of twelve with his homeboy Bull, and how for four years, the two of them would battle each other every day.

"But when I caught a gun case at sixteen and they sent me to CYA, I was in there bangin and the whole, wanting to be rapper thing was out. It was all about survival from then on, and so here I am now and aint nothing changed. It's still about survival out her so I'm getting my money right like I'm 'pose to."

Upon his release from the Youth Authority, Spits had come home to find a lot of dudes putting out their homemade mixtapes. Although he had known that he was better than everybody he'd heard, he also knew then, just like he knew now, that there wasn't any money to be made rapping on the Central Coast.

Faced with this, he had jumped back into the game without a second thought. Six months later, he was sitting in San Quentin State Prison with a four year sentence. Mash listened to Spits' story and felt where he was coming from. But he also knew in his heart that Spits had what it took talent wise to make it big and the two of them could put Hood Life on the map.

The problem was that in a way, Spits was right. Life was real, and it took money to live out here. So unless Mash could find some way to get enough money to make Spits back away from the game, then this chance of a lifetime sitting here staring him in the face would most likely end up back in prison for the same thing he'd just gotten out for. And Mash would be stuck here making beats for these same stale rappers just like he'd been doing.

As Mash sat there with these thoughts running through his mind, Spits was watching him. He knew what Mash was thinking and thought it was funny because as far as he was concerned, Mash and the rest of his friends were just wasting their time. Although he too shared a love for music, he'd be damned if he sat up in a garage broke and chasing pipe dreams.

Spits looked at his watch and saw that it was almost two. "You wanna record another track before I bounce up outta here?" He asked snapping Mash back to the here and now.

"Yeah." Mash said. He reached for the mouse next to the computer and scrolled through his menu of beats. "I want to hear you flow on one of my beats real quick."

QUESTIONING THE GAME...

AS SPITS DROVE north along the scenic highway 1, he couldn't stop himself from dreaming again as he listened to the last of the three tracks they'd recorded. He sounded good, no, better than good. He sounded great.

When Mash had started going on about how tight his lyrics were Spits had thought it funny because he'd been hearing the same stuff for year. Even if nobody were to tell him, he knew in his heart that couldn't nobody see him.

While in prison he would give rappers the business out on the yard whenever they'd be out here rapping. The funny thing was that everybody in there use to tell him the same stuff Mash was screaming about leaving the game. But just like Mash, couldn't nobody tell Spits how he was supposed to eat out here in the meantime.

He thought now about all of the of O.G's he'd met in prison who'd been playing the game for so long that most of them were stuck and unable to turn off of the dead end road they'd been driving down all their lives. He also remembered how it had scared him to realize that most of them didn't even want to.

The fact that a man could accept it as being natural to go in and out of prison was somethin' that he couldn't wrap his mind around. So he vowed to himself then that he wouldn't allow himself to wake up one day and find that he had accepted prison as being a natural part of his existence.

He came up with a plan to make sure that he wouldn't end up like the O.G's he'd met. He'd would go home and hustle hard for his first year out and then use the money he saved to get an auto dealers license. With that, he would be able to buy cars from auctions and sell them for a nice profit. So for the last six months since his release, he'd been driving to Salinas and hustling in Chinatown. He had just over twenty thousand dollars stacked so far and had just started moving weight last week.

As he headed to Salinas now, he found himself wondering if maybe they were all right about giving the music industry a shot. At one point in his life, his every thought had been of one day becoming a famous rapper. And back then nobody could convince him that he wouldn't be. But with life being life, he'd found himself travelling down a road he'd had no intention of ever going down. He was stuck in the game just like everybody else in the hood.

At sixteen, his best friend Bull had started gangbanging and selling dope. With his boy having chosen that route, Spits, the ever loyal homeboy, had followed suit and rapping became an afterthought. But listening to the track pounding through his cars speakers now, he couldn't help but wonder that since he was a little older and better able to control his destiny, if this would be the time for him to give it a shot. Back then, he hadn't known his ass from a hole in the ground. But now he wasn't so easily influenced.

"I could do this stuff if I wanted to." Spits said aloud. He knew that since he was such a hustler, if he was to tell Mash that he wanted to give this stuff a shot, he would sink or swim based on how much effort he put into it.

And I ain't no loser. He thought to himself. His phone ringing snapped him back from these thoughts.

"Hello." Spits answered.

"Where your slow ass at?" His homeboy Loco asked. Laughing, Spits turned down the music and told him that he was just pulling in to Salinas.

"Is you still at your grandma's house?"

"Yeah, chief." Loco answered. "Hurry up. There's a grip of money on the block right now. My cousin just came back and he said it's crackin'."

"I'll be there in a minute." Spits promised and hung up. He had met Loco when he first started going to Chinatown and the two had got tight real quick. Whenever

Spits hit the block, he'd pick Loco up and they'd watch each other's back while they hustled.

When Spits turned onto Cabrillo Street where Loco's grandmother lived, he called to let Loco know that he was pulling up. Loco was soon outside and climbing in the car.

"What's up homie? " Loco said offering his fist which Spits pounded.

"What up." Spits said as pulled from the curb and made a U-turn, heading for the block. When Loco turned the volume up on the stereo and the instrumental came blaring out of the speakers, he began nodding his head to the beat.

"Oh, you on your old school crap in here today."

"Listen though. That's some new stuff right there." Spits said. He watched Loco from the corner of his eyes, wanting to see his boy's reaction. Loco was a northern Cali rap aficionado and so his opinion definitely carry weight with Spits.

When Spits' vocals came on, Loco realized that it wasn't Biggie. He liked what he heard and turned the volume up more.

"Who's this? This boy got gas!" Loco said turning it up even more.

"That's me." Spits told him with a smile while nodding his head up and down. "I just left the homie Mash's studio."

He watched Loco and couldn't help but smile at the shock on his face.

"I ain't know you was this tight, chief. Aint none of these rap cats in the game seein' you at dis. You killin 'em boy!"

When Loco held a fist out and Spits dapped it. Just like Mash, Loco had also heard that Spits had major gas on the mic. But this was the first time he'd heard his boy get down. He turned the volume down and looked at him sideways.

"What you doing selling dope doe?" Loco asked while shaking his head at Spits' stupidity. "You killing these other rap cats. You should stay your non-hustling ass in somebody's studio and get some real money." Loco smacked his lips and shook his head. "You hecka stupid."

He sounded like Mash and Spits laughed. But at the same time, he couldn't help but ask himself again if he was doing the right thing by sticking to his one year plan rather than give the rap game a shot.

"I can't do that stuff homie." Spits said and went on before Loco interrupted. "I got a plan and it's going just like I saw it all them nights I laid in my bunk at Quentin thinking about it."

"You stupid. Fools is stuck out here in the game 'cause they asses can't do nothin' else and your retarded ass got talent but rather sell dope to a bunch of homeless cats. What kind of crap is that?"

He knew Loco spoke the truth. But the money he was making *now* made him turn a blind eye to the future and what *might* happen.

Spits shook his head and said "Man ain't nobody trying to mess with us out here on the music tip. The Central Coast is way too small for a major label to mess wit it. And I'll be damned if I stop getting this money to chase a pipe dream." He shook his head again. "Forget all that."

Loco smiled. "Sounds like you trying to convince your damn self of it homie."

Spits laughed because he knew that he was right. "Forget you chief."

Spits took his phone out to turn it off before turning into Chinatown.

"I know these smokers better have my money or I'm gon' beat they faces." Loco said when they turned onto Soledad Street.

"Shut up and quit woofin'. You ain't gon' do nothin' but talk a bunch of stuff." Spits teased. He knew damn well that Loco would do exactly what he'd just said. As he drove down the dirty street, Spits felt his stomach turn like it did every time he came here. This was the bottom of the bottom and the people who hung here were the worst of the worse. All the money in the world couldn't quiet the small voice in his head that liked to tell him how wrong he was for coming here and taking advantage of these drug addicted homeless people.

Soledad Street, where a majority of the drug activity took place, was cracking. Spits could tell right off that Loco's cousin hadn't been lying.

Ignoring his guilty conscience once again, he parked and sat watching the block. He told himself that it wasn't his fault that people was out here tore up on drugs and homeless. If he didn't get the money, then the next cat would and he'd be broke. But still he felt guilty.

"I'm 'bout to get this money, chief." Spits told Loco and started to open the door then stopped because he felt Loco's heavy stare on him. "What's up?"

Loco let out a loud breath instead of answering right away. "You hecka stupid." He reached out and turned the music up. "I'm fixin' to post up and listen to the rest of your stuff. I'll be out there in a minute."

Loco's words only made him feel even guiltier about being here. And yet, here he was. Exactly where he knew in his heart he shouldn't be. Doing exactly what he'd done to go to prison in the first place.

"I'm going inside Dorothy's to look out the back for the police." Spits said and got out. He walked across the street to the shelter and soup kitchen.

"Hi Spits." A voice called before he made it across the street.

"Spits, you got anything?" "What's up Spits!"

Voices called out as he crossed the street. He ignored them and headed inside. The strong odor of unwashed bodies, feet, and alcohol hit him with an uppercut to the nose as soon as he stepped into the crowded and noisy front room. He was forced to stop in his tracks and focus on breathing through his mouth. The place was as busy as the street outside. It was full of the less fortunate, who'd come to eat, take showers, sleep, or just hang out.

He walked through the maze of chairs and noisy conversations that cut through the air and headed down the dim, semi-filthy hallway leading to the back alley. He stepped outside and looked to the next street over where the police liked to park in the cut and catch people slippin. Finding that the coast was clear for the time being, he stepped back inside.

"Spits will you help me with these boxes?" A feminine voice called to him. He knew it belonged to Margarita who was one of the shelter's volunteers. He turned to find her standing with a hand on her hip staring at him.

"What's up Margarita?" He asked the dark olive toned Latina goddess who volunteered here five days a week. His eyes went from the smile on her face, to the baggy slacks and tennis shoes she wore then back to her eyes.

"Look at you making them unsexy clothes look sexy as heck." Spits said. Standing 5'10 with long, lustrous black hair and green eyes, Margarita was one of the most beautiful women that Spits had ever met in his life. And the fact that she seemed to be totally unaware or unconcerned with her beauty only made her even more so in his eyes.

Margarita laughed and waved him closer. "Boy quit playing and help me take these boxes to the office." She pointed to the stack of boxes in the closet. "I need to take all these out. When we finish I need to talk to you about somethin'."

"You need to be talking 'bout us going out. All this extra stuff you got me doing up in this dirty ass place." He told her before bending down to pick up one of the boxes.

"You don't ever stop do you?" She laughed and grabbed a box herself.

"Nope. I don't. You might as well go ahead and let me take you out so we can get to know each other better." He answered. "Every time I ask you out, you be acting like I bite or somethin'."

"You're crazy. I don't be acting like you bite. I just don't have time for boys right now." She told him. They moved the boxes to the office and stacked them in a corner. When they were done, she asked him to have a seat.

"What is it Margarita?" He asked as he took the seat across from her curious as to what it was she wanted. He was hoping that she was finally ready to let him take her out. He'd been getting at her from the moment they met. But all she kept telling him was that he needed to try and get his life together because he was on a dead end road leading to nowhere.

"What's going on with you man?" She asked him. "I see you out there every day doing your thing, and I'm worried about you. You're smarter than that and there's so much that you could be doing with yourself."

"Like what?" He asked smiling. "What do you want me to do? I gotta eat and ain't nobody fixing to give me no job with my record. Everybody keep telling me the same stuff but ain't nobody told me how I'm supposed to eat out here though. Life's real right now and time is hard."

"So you're just gonna give up and throw your life away?" She asked. Her huge expressive eyes were sad suddenly. "Why don't you go back to school and get a degree or somethin'?"

"Because I'm addicted to money, that's why." He answered. Then he went on to tell her that he liked the finer things in life. He wasn't about to be running around broke while he chased after a degree which wouldn't guarantee him a job once he got it.

"Naw, I'm cool on the school thing ma. I know you don't like how I make my money but I'm eatin' good out here and I ain't about to stop no time soon."

"But there's so much more to life than money Spits. Isn't there anything that interests you besides trying to get rich?"

"Yeah. But every time I ask you out you start preaching." He answered with a flirtatious grin. For a few minutes, she continued trying to get him to admit to wanting somethin' more from life besides money and he went on trying to get her to go out with him.

Margarita caught a sudden movement out the corner of her eye and turned to find a group of people standing at the front window staring outside.

"Somethin''s going on." She said in a worried voice and stood up. Spits stood also and rushed for the door knowing that it was probably Loco who was causing all the excitement.

"We'll finish talking later." She called to Spits as he rushed ahead. Stepping outside, he saw Loco across the street holding somebody in a choke hold, and instantly Spits knew that he'd caught one of the smokers he'd been waiting for.

Spits ran across the street and grabbed Loco around the waist. "Let him go homie. This is my homeboy's uncle from Seaside."

"Then you better tell your homeboy's smoked out ass uncle from Seaside to give me my ten dollars before I beat his ass for realz." Loco told Spits and threw the wide eyed man to the ground. "His ass been owing me for two weeks already. Ain't nobody playing with his ass."

Looking to the O.G who he'd known for years, Spits asked him if he had the ten dollars. He said that he didn't so Spits paid Loco the money himself because he knew that Loco wouldn't let it go.

"You need to stop getting stuff on credit if you can't pay it O.G" Loco warned him. "'Cause aint nobody out here playing 'bout they money."

As Spits and Loco walked away, Spits couldn't help but question his plan again. This was just another example of the crap that he was involved in. He knew that anything could go down out here in these streets on which he ate.

Those tracks we recorded were hecka tight. Maybe I should give it a shot. I'm gon' think about it for realz and see what's up, 'cause this ain't cool.

Rap Star

IF IT MAKES DOLLARS, IT MAKES SENSE...

MASH PACED BACK and forth in his garage with the last of the three songs he and Spits had recorded blasting from the speakers. Ever since Spits had left an hour ago, he'd been trying to figure out a way to get Spits to focus on music and chase his dreams with him. In his heart, Mash knew that if he could talk him into it, the world would be theirs for the taking. Most of the rappers who came through Mash's studio would kill to have a rap career. Talent like Spits' was a rarity and it killed him that he'd finally found someone who had what it took and he'd rather push rocks in Chinatown.

The only reason that Mash wouldn't give up on Spits was that he knew in his heart that for him to posses the level of talent that he did, he had to still have a love for music beneath all that cool stuff he was talking.

Yet it all came back to the money. Without it he really couldn't argue with Spits because all they'd be able to do is hustle mixtapes in the hood. Eventually they could blow up doing that, but it would take years. Years that he knew Spits wasn't about to sit around and wait. Not when he could be getting his money out in the streets like he'd been doing.

A thought hit him suddenly and he stopped in his tracks.

"My uncle!"

His uncle Dame was the biggest drug dealer in Seaside. Mash knew that he had more than enough money to finance his record label. Although the two didn't talk much, Mash figured since Dame was money hungry in the worse way he could convince his uncle to help him put out Spits' music. All Mash had to do was show Dame how much money he could make in the music business and he would be with it. Especially after he heard Spits rap.

Mash grabbed his phone and dialed the number.

"Unc...I'm good...Naw, ain't nothin' the matter...Mom's is cool, she's still at work...Naw I don't want no money. I just need to holla at you about somethin' real quick. It's important…Okay. I'll be at the house waiting for you. Just come around the back, I'm in the studio…Bye."

Mash hung up and smiled. His uncle said he'd be over when he finished handling somethin'. Mash thought for sure that he would be able to convince him to invest in his label.

He sat in front of his equipment and began working on the tracks. He wanted to have it mixed right when his uncle arrived. This was the moment he'd been waiting years for and he was determined to make this happen before Spits messed around and got caught up.

As he worked on the tracks, Mash got so in to what he was doing that he lost track of the time and didn't hear his uncle come in and take a seat behind him on the couch. Dame sat there listening to the song Mash was tweaking and was surprised at how good it sounded.

My nephew done stepped his game up. That sound like it should be on the radio.

Dame had heard a few of the mixtapes Mash had put out since returning from Florida. But what he heard now was far superior to anything he'd heard before.

"That slapped right there nephew. Who was that rapping?" Dame said when the tack ended.

Surprised, Mash spun around smiling. "That was the homie Spits. We just recorded it a little while ago."

"I see you been up in here handling your business. That sounds like it should be on the radio." Dame told him.

"That's what I'm saying. I been in here putting in sixteen hours a day and now I finally found a cat who I can blow up with." Mash explained. "We fixin' to get rich as heck if I can put this together Unc."

"I hear you. You know I don't listen to too much rap, but I think you might be right. Your boy Spits is the real deal. I ain't heard too many dudes who messin' with his flow. He on point."

"Exactly!" Mash said suddenly animated and his light brown eyes sparkling. "He's the one I've been waiting for."

Mash grabbed the mouse and clicked the *play* icon on the computer. "Listen to this."

When the Biggie instrumental came on, Mash watched his uncle closely. Dark skinned and huge, Dame was known to wear a permanent stony and unreadable mean-mug on his bearded face. Outside of him nodding his head to the beat, Dame's expression told Mash nothin'.

"Yeah nephew, your boy goes hard in the paint." Dame finally said halfway through the song. "I like that right there."

"The cold thing about it is that he freestyled it. All three songs we did came off the top of his head. He don't write his stuff no more. He just spits it like it's nothin'."

Dame's usually unreadable face registered surprise at hearing this. "Get outta' here." He looked at Mash like he had lost his mind. "Can't anybody go like that off the top of they head."

"Real talk, unc." Mash assured him. "I couldn't believe it myself but I sat here and watched the dude do it. We 'bout to get rich with this music."

Dame looked at the gold and diamond studded watch on his wrist signaling that he had to leave soon. "Okay Mash. I hear you, but what did you call me for? You said that you had somethin' to talk to me about."

Now Mash grew nervous. Although he knew that he had a good plan. He also knew that his uncle was real tight with his money. Growing up, Mash and his uncle had at one time been tight. But with age came understanding, and Mash started wondering why he and his mother were struggling while his uncle, his mothers only sibling, rode around town spending money like it grew on trees.

This had made Mash pull away from his uncle and though they still were on good terms, Mash was hesitant to ask him to put up the money. But since he wanted this too much not to, he took a deep breath and said "Unc I need your help."

"My help with what?" Dame asked and sat up with his elbows resting on his knees.

"I wanna get Spits to record a few mixtapes and flood Northern Cali with his music." Mash said and then went on to outline how this would whet the public's appetite and create a street buzz. As he spoke, his nervousness left him and he grew more confident.

"We can't lose unc. All we need is the money to promote him and press up the CD's. Once we get everybody talking about us, we'll hit em with a radio single then an album. You heard how tight he is unc. We gon' blow up."

Dame was impressed. He could tell that Mash knew what he was talking about. He also knew that there was millions to be made in the music industry. Having stacked close to three million dollars hustling in these Seaside streets, he was ready to go legit and had been searching for a way to do it.

During the past two years he'd tried his hand at two business ventures which had both failed. First had been the barbershop that had lasted all of three months. Then he opened a clothing store, which only lasted six. So he was open to what Mash was hollerin' now. Plus he too believed in Spits' talent. The boy had it and if Mash's plan worked, Dame knew the money they would make would make the money he'd made selling coke look like peanuts

"What's Spits say about all this?" Dame asked him. "Is he with it?"

Mash tried not to let his face show the panic he felt at question as he spoke. "He's got his mind on getting his money now and not later. He be out in Salinas movin' works. I got at him but he said that he wasn't about to be broke out here chasing a dream. But if he knew there was some money behind us, I think he'd be with it."

Dame sat scratching his beard as he thought about what Mash was saying. He looked around him at the soundproof booth, the table with all of Mash's equipment, the tangle of cords snaked on the floor, and the posters of dead

30

artists then asked himself if he could really be a music exec.
He knew that it was a whole different ballgame than the one
he was use to playing. After a moment, he came to a decision
and nodded his head.

"Check it out nephew. If you can get Spits to do this,
then I'm in for a million." Dame said and laughed at seeing
the huge smile on Mash's face. He held his hand up and
added. "But I want half ownership of the label though."

"You got a deal." Mash said as he stood to offer his
hand which his uncle shook. "Let me call Spits and get him
back over here so we can talk."

He pulled his phone out to dial Spits number and
frowned when he got the voice mail. Mash left a message
telling Spits that he needed to talk to him about somethin'
and could he call him back. Dame said that he had to go but
he would be waiting to hear from him.

"Get at me as soon as Spits calls and I'll swing back
through so we can all sit down and talk."

"I will." Mash promised. "He's supposed to stop by
tomorrow to record another track anyway. So if I don't hear
from him today, we can get at him then."

When Dame left, Mash sat at his equipment grinning.

"We 'bout to put Hood Life on the map." He said
laughing. He was sure now that his dream would come true.
"It's on now."

LIFE CHANGERS...

"DAMN HOMIE! I'LL be there in a minute!" Spits said into the phone with a voice full of irritation. This was the third time Mash had called him since he woke thirty minutes ago and it was starting to get on his nerves. He'd blown his phone up yesterday, calling every thirty minutes and leaving messages asking Spits to call him back. He knew Mash was still on that 'give the rapping a chance' crap.

Spits hadn't answered and wouldn't have this morning either if he hadn't already promise to stop by and record another track before heading to Salinas.

"Alright homie. It's important though. That's why I keep blowing you up." Mash explained.

"Yeah okay. Give me ten minutes and I'll be there." Spits said and hung up. When the phone rang again two minutes later, Spits thought it was Mash and answered with an attitude.

"What!" He yelled. "I told you I'll be there in a minute didn't I!"

"Shut up punk." Loco said on the other end laughing. "Who you yelling at like you gon' do something' punk?"

"Oh, what's up Loco" Spits said and laughed too. "I thought you was that fool Mash. He been sweating me to come to his studio and make another song."

"You need to take your dumb ass over there and quit playing then." Loco told him. "But since you too dumb to do that, you better get out here and get this money. There's a drought out here. Don't nobody got works in Salinas except for my Pisa connect."

"Ain't nothin' out here neither." Spits replied. "I called everybody I know last night and I can't get nothin'. I was just gonna go to Mash's till somebody called me back with some weight."

"Didn't I just tell your dumb ass that my connect got works?" Loco asked him.

"Call and see if I can get a quarter bird." Spits said.

"Okay. Let me get back at you in a minute." Loco said and disconnected the call. Spits finished dressing and walked out to his car with thoughts of making a killing running through his head. To be able to cop works during a drought was every hustlers dream and he wasn't about to miss this chance. Forget what Mash was talking about. He was fixin' to get this money if Loco called him back with good news.

"If Mash's ass wanna sit in his garage broke, that's on him. I ain't the one though." Spits said as he pulled up to Mash's house and parked. Climbing out of the car, he noticed Dame's black Benz parked across the street.

I bet his ass got plenty works. He thought as he walked up the driveway. He didn't know Dame personally but he knew him by reputation. Everybody in the hood knew that Dame only sold keys and if you weren't balling then you couldn't cop no works from him.

Mash opened the door before he could knock and Spits walked in. He stopped in his tracks surprised to find Dame sitting on the couch looking like a well-dressed grizzly. He looked to Mash with raised eyebrows and walked to the couch to shake Dame's hand.

"What's up Dame?" Spits said.

"What's going on with you lil homie?" Dame asked as they shook hands. "I see that you know who I am. That's good."

Dame watched Spits as he sat and thought that he had seen him somewhere before. He studied his model handsome face with its high cheekbones, generous mouth, intense light brown eyes and his solid broad shouldered 6'3 frame.

He looks like a star already. This lil big-headed boy got swagger like a mug. Dame thought, noticing that Spits kept looking at his watch.

"You got somewhere you need to be?" He asked Spits.

"Maybe." Spits said and checked his phone to make sure that he hadn't missed any calls. "There's a drought and my boy trying to get me some works from his connect."

Dame threw back his head and laughed at hearing this. "A drought huh?" He looked at Mash standing next to Spits' chair. "You hear that nephew? He think there's a drought' cause he can't get no works."

Seeing the look of confusion on Spits face, he explained that there wasn't a drought. Everybody was just waiting on Dame to serve them.

"But I'm here waiting for you to show up. So everybody on hold waiting to cop because you act like you can't answer your phone."

Spits face was still a mask of confusion as he looked up at Mash.

"What's up Mash?" He asked then turned back to look at the bear-like Dame. "Why y'all call me over here? What's this about?"

Rumor was that Dame had killed a few people out here in these streets and it was a well-known that he wasted no time messin' around. So if Dame had anything to do with it, it must be serious. Mash sat down and turned his chair to face Spits.

"Check it out, homie." Mash began and then went on to tell him how he felt that Spits had what it took to make it in the music industry, saying to him that, "Can't none of these rap cats see you rapping, chief and I already told you I'm trying to fk with you. You killing every rapper out there. Me and my uncle want you to get at this music money with us."

Spits was shaking his head as Mash spoke but let him finish before he said anything.

"We already talked about this yesterday chief, ain't nothin' changed. Just like I told you then, I ain't fixin' to be chasing no pipe dreams with you. It takes money to make it in the industry. *Big* money. And as much as I like rapping and would love to mess with the stuff, it's just not gon' happen for me.

"We don't have no major label money behind us, so we'd just be wasting our time. I got too much I'm trying to do right now. I'm getting paid out here. If I wasn't, then maybe I would mess with you homie. But it ain't cool right now."

Dame was silent as he listened to Spits and found himself liking how confident and sure he sounded. He seemed to know what he wanted and how to go about getting it.

"What if I told you that we had a million dollars behind us?" Dame asked when Spits finished speaking.

"What!" Spits exclaimed and jumped to his feet. His face was full of surprise at what he'd just heard but he had a hard time believing it despite knowing that Dame wasn't with the game playing.

Spits had been prepared to hear some bull when Mash called him over there. But hearing Dame say made him see a change in his future. Big time.

He listened to Dame explain how he would finance the label as long as Spits would agree to give it his all. As Dame spoke, Spits mind flashed back to the squalor and hopelessness he'd been hanging around in Chinatown and how it made him sick being there sometimes.

"If you want to do this, then we can." Dame said. "But I'm warning you now." He pointed a finger at him. "I take my money serious. So if you agree to get down with us then I expect you to come hard or don't come at all.

"I heard the songs you and my nephew recorded yesterday and I think you got what it takes. We can go legit and get some real money selling music. I don't know about you, but I'm tired of selling dope."

Spits stood there with his mouth open as Dame spoke. This was it. The chance to see his dead dream become a reality. The game he'd been playing since the age of sixteen had taught him he needed to be ready for all that life would throw at him and time stood still for no man. So he realized that this chance they were offering to him would not come again.

If he wanted to do this then he couldn't hesitate to take them up on this. Yet he knew that there had to be a catch because this just sounded too good to be true. These two were sitting here telling him that he could live his dream but he wasn't naïve enough to believe that they were doing it out of the kindness of their hearts.

"Is Y'all serious?" He asked looking from Dame to Mash, who was smiling, and back to Dame.

In answer to this, Dame reached into his pocket and withdrew a stack of hundred dollar bills. He peeled off ten of them and set them on the table in front of him. He told Spits that if he agreed to do this, he would pay him a thousand dollars week just so that he'd have a little pocket money.

"That way you don't have to be out there hustling. Just focus on making music and when the money starts coming in, we can all eat." Dame said then asked. "Is that serious enough for you?"

Spits stood there quietly staring at the money. The fact that Dame was offering to pay him a thousand dollars a week told him that Dame was expecting to get that back and then some. Spits wasn't a dummy he wasn't about to let no punk ass thousand dollars make him forget that if they did blow up they would be making way more than that.

After thinking on this for a minute, he asked Mash what label would they sign with. Mash told him that he had his own label so Spits knew for sure that there would be more than enough money to go around. He wouldn't allow either of them to get rich off him unless he too was getting his equal share. Having heard all of the music industry horror stories, he vowed to not join the long list of artists who were broke after selling millions of records.

"Okay." He said after making up his mind to give it a shot. "I'll do it on one condition."

"And what's that?" Dame asked him.

"I want one third ownership of the label." He said while looking Dame in the eyes. "If we gon' get rich we gon' do it together."

As soon as the words were out of Spits mouth, his phone rang. He looked at it and saw that it was Loco calling. He answered and Loco told him that his connection had what he wanted.

"Hold up a second Loco." He said and looked to Dame for an answer.

"You got a deal lil homie." Dame told Spits and stood to shake his hand. "It looks like we 'bout to get rich 'round this place nephew." He then said to Mash.

Tony Clincy

WHO'S THE BOSS...

THE LUNCH CROWD in Chili's was in full swing. The whole restaurant was filled with the noise of dozens of working class people eating. Dame sat at a window seat lost in his own thought as he waited for his best friend Tracy. He was oblivious to the chinking of silverware and the buzz of many conversations around him. As usual, his mind was on money.

After he and his nephew convinced Spits to get in the studio, he'd found himself unable to think of much else besides the millions he would soon be making and the lifestyle he'd be able to live. Money was Dame's passion and motivation and he made no apologies for it. He had loved the finer things in life since the first time he touched big money and his devotion to it made him willing to do anything for it. He didn't even lose sleep over the things he'd done in his pursuit of it.

But music was a completely different tune and he was confident that it was one he could play. He was a shark that felt capable of swimming in any sea he found himself in. In his mind he figured that the music biz was nothin' if not another hustle. And if there was anything he knew how to do it was hustling.

Looking towards the front of the restaurant, he saw Tracy making her way through the crowd. The crème colored Donna Karan pantsuit and Jimmy Choo shoes she wore complemented her fresh manicure, and honey complexioned, well-proportioned figure to perfection. Dame stood with a smile and stepped around the table to give her a hug as she approached.

"Hey girl." He said and pulled out her chair for her.

"Hey Dame. How you doing?"

"I'm cool. Just trying to get this money." He said and smiled because he knew that she would start preaching about the dangers of the game. Shaking her head, Tracy indeed told him that he needed to find himself another way to get money.

38

"These youngsters out here ain't got no respect for nothin' no more Dame. The game ain't the same as it was back in the days."

Holding up his hands in surrender, Dame laughed. "Okay Trace. I get you. Don't start on that stuff again. I'm trying to make a move out of the game as we speak."

He looked past her and waved the waitress over.

"Yeah right." She mumbled and picked up the menu sitting in front of her. "I'm hungry. Let's order and then you can tell me what it is that you wanted to talk about."

"Sounds like a plan." Dame said and grabbed his menu just as the waitress approached. "Can we get a couple of drink's while we decide what we're gonna eat?"

He ordered a double shot of Hen for him and a long island ice tea for Tracy. Having known each other since childhood, Tracy and Dame were as close as any two friends could be and trusted each other totally. When Dame tried his hand at going legit, it had been Tracy whom he'd called upon to manage his businesses. Although his attempt failed, he knew that it hadn't been for lack of effort on her part. Tracy was a people person and had a natural instinct for business and making connections. Now he was determined to convince her to quit her court clerk's job to help him run the record label.

The waitress soon came with their drink's and they placed their orders. When she left, they drank and talked about the latest goings on with the people they knew as they waited. When the food came and they finished eating, Tracy pushed her plate away before rested her elbows on the table.

"Now tell me what's so important that you made me cancel my lunch date boy." She demanded.

"I'm gonna try my hand in the music industry with my nephew and his homeboy." He blurted out and went on to explain how Mash had called him two days ago asking for his help. "You should hear this boy Spits, Trace. You know I listen to Jazz but this boy ain't to be messed with. We all fixin' to get rich."

Tracy cupped her chin with her hand as Dame spoke and waited for him to finish. "Let me guess, you want me to help you?"

"Yeah." He admitted with a boyish grin and held up his hand before she could say no. "I know you told me after the last time that you wasn't about to drop what you're doing to help me with one of my little ventures again but this is different."

"Different how?"

"Different in me putting up a million dollars different."

Tracy dropped her hands and her mouth fell open at hearing this. She, better than anyone knew how wolfish Dame was when it came to his money, so to hear him say that came as a shock to say the least.

"Are you serious?" She asked but sensed that he was.

"Yep. This is my way out Trace." He told her. "If this works, I won't even have to *see* nobody who sells drugs again if I don't want to. Ain't you always telling me that I need to find another way to get my money? I have now. This is it, but I need your help Ma."

"Uh-Uh Dame. Don't try to run that one on me." She said shaking her head. "I'm happy for you and everything, but I got bills to pay. I got a good, stable job and I'm not about to give it up. No. Uh-Uh." She shook her head again. "Definitely not."

"Not even if I give you fifty thousand dollars as a bonus?" He asked. "Plus I'll pay you a thousand a week to start."

She didn't speak and so he went on.

"Look. You already know how I am when it comes to my money. So if I'm willing to risk putting so much of it up to finance this label, what does that tell you? It should tell you that I *know* I'm fixin' to be making that back and then some. This boy Spits is the real deal and you'd be a fool to miss out on this chance I'm offering you. *"

"I admit that you putting up so much money surprises me, but still, I can't just drop everything I'm doing to help you. My job is my security blanket Dame."

He smiled across the table at her as she spoke. He knew despite what she was saying, she would help him out anyway like she always did.

"Stop smiling at me like that." She told him. "I'm serious this time Dame." She looked away to the parking lot then back at him. "Why you always do this stuff boy? You and your crazy ass ideas."

Dame threw his head back and laughed. "Let me take you to meet Spits and if you still say no after that then I'll leave you alone."

He pulled out his phone to call his nephew. When Mash answered, Dame told him that he and Tracy were on the way over to talk to him and Spits. Dame gave Tracy a triumphant smile as he put the phone away and stood.

"Come on, let's go. You can follow me in your car." He told her and led her to the parking lot. Pulling up to the house, Dame called and told Mash to open the front door. When the door opened and Mash found Tracy there, he grinned and gave her a hug.

"What's up Tracy?"

"Hey you." Tracy said with a smile as she stepped back to look him over. "Look at you getting all grown on me. Last time I saw you, you were a lil bad teenager who thought you was hot stuff."

They hadn't seen each other since Mash left for Florida four years ago and she was pleasantly surprised at the handsome young man he'd become.

"I bet you got these little teeny-boppers going crazy."

Mash blushed at the compliment

"You know it." He said and turned away. Tracy had always had this effect on him since he was a child. "Come on."

He waved them in and led them to the garage with Tracy giggling behind him at his embarrassment. When they

41

stepped inside the dark blue garage, she saw a man lying across the couch with his eyes closed and puffing a blunt as he vibed with the instrumental pounding from the studio's speakers.

Mash went to the computer and stopped the music causing Spits to open his eyes. Seeing Dame, he swung his legs down and sat up.

"What's up Dame?" Spits said before looking at Tracy and nodding his head in greeting. "How you doin' Tracy?"

"So you're the famous Spits huh?" She asked him. Her eyes took in his strong handsome features and well-muscled arms in the white wife-beater he wore.

"I ain't famous yet but I'm about to be when we drop this mixtape series on em." He answered with confidence.

Tracy smirked and looked to Dame. "Well he definitely ain't lacking in confidence." She pointed out.

"Cause its true Ma. We about to the blow up." Spits promised her.

"I'm trying to get her to manage you and to help me get the label up and running." Dame explained.

"Dame seems to think that you're a sure thing and he wants me to quit my job to work with you guys." Tracy clarified. "He wanted me to meet you since I wouldn't tell him yes."

"You better get on board then." Spits told her. "We about to do this. We're gonna rewrite the book on how to get this music money." He counted off on his fingers. "I got the gas, Mash got the beats and Dame got the cash."

As he spoke, she watched him closely and found herself drawn to his magnetic swagger. While he went on telling her how they were preparing to take the rap game over, she noticed that he had this strong presence that dominated the room. It was like he was already famous. She turned to Mash and asked him to play some of the music they'd recorded.

"Let me see what Y'all been up in here doing that done got Dame all excited and Spits thinking that he's the next Fifty Cent." .

Mash laughed as he turned to search his files. After finding what he was looking for, he pressed play. The sounds of another popular song was soon blasting from the speakers and when Spits' vocals came on, she understood why the three of them were so confident.

In his lyrics she heard that same cockiness that she had detected when she walked in. Tracey smiled and looked at Dame, nodding her head.

This boy knows he's good. She thought. Though she couldn't put her finger on it, there was somethin' about Spits which told you that he was a force to be reckoned with. It was as if somethin' within him was demanding better for himself. Like the good in him was determined that it be set free to experience all he was worthy of. She looked at Spits who was staring back at her with a look that screamed 'I told you so'. Even though he was big headed and conceited, she believed in his talent.

She laughed and said. "Okay. I'm in. But I want you all to know off the top that I'm the boss and what I say goes."

A TOAST TO THE FUTURE...

THE PARTY AT the table next to theirs started clapping and the four of them looked to see what all of the commotion was about. They found a waitress carrying a birthday cake with candles burning as the people broke out singing 'Happy Birthday.'

"Come on you guys." Tracy said and stood with her glass held up. "Let's make one of them toasts like the white folks be doing on TV."

"Tracy sit your ass down." Dame told her and waved his hand in dismissal. "We black. So we don't toast until we drunk, not before."

Spits and Mash laughed at this. She shot Dame a look and ignored the laughter.

"Come on you guys. It'll bring us luck. Let's start this off right." She insisted and looked to Spits for help. Spits nodded his head.

"Okay." He said and stood holding his glass towards hers. "I ain't never been one to turn my back on a little lady luck."

He smiled at Tracy and she mouthed her thanks. Left with no choice, Dame and Mash stood and raised their glasses too. With their glasses touching, Tracy toasted to their future success and health. After taking a drink, they sat down with Dame teasing her about her being so superstitious.

"You ain't gon' think I'm superstitious when it works and we blow up, is you?"

It had been her suggestion that they come to A.J Spurs and celebrate the beginning of their foray into the music industry. They were Paper Chasin' Records and tonight was their official jump off. Having only met Spits earlier today, Tracy thought it was a good idea that they take this time to get to know each other better. She reached into her hand bag and came out with a digital camera, then slid out the booth and stood.

"Okay you guys. It's picture time." She announced. "I want to remember this night so start striking some poses in here."

Smiling at her pushiness, Spits looked to Mash who lifted his shoulders as if to say 'what can I do?'. Spits had a phobia about cameras from going to jail and having the pictures he took put on his wrist. He hadn't liked to take them when he was a kid either.

"I ain't trying to be taking no pictures right now. I'm hungry. We can do that later."

She gave him a look before said speaking. "Boy quit playing and let me see some teeth."

Tracy stepped back and knelt for a better angle before she started snapping away.

"Scoot closer to Mash and strike one of them baller poses like rappers be doing." She coached. Mash posed and Spits looked uncomfortable. She stood up and held the camera down while looking at Spits like he was foreign.

"I know you ain't camera shy." She said and gave Dame the same look. "This boy's camera shy Dame."

"Girl stop messin' wit folks. You just met the boy and you already trying to boss him around."

"Whatever. I *know* what I'm doing. You just get your big butt into them books I bought you." She told him and looked back to Spits. "I can see now that the first thing we gon' have to do is get you over your camera-shyness. You're our star and we can't have that."

She sat back down and looked at him with her eyebrows raised. "You don't get stage-fright too do you?" She asked and noticed how Spits avoided her eyes.

"Awww, poor baby." Tracy teased then assured him that he would get over it with a little practice.

"Shoot." Mash said. "I don't know what you trippin' on homie. I can't wait to do a photo shoot and show off my Seaside tats."

Tony Clincy

He pulled up the sleeves of his shirt and showed them his forearms. "I'm gonna have the homie Mar-Mar hit up Hood Life right here."

Mash boasted about how he was going to keep his shirt off whenever the cameras were rolling so that everybody would see his tat's and get up on HoodLife. "It's 'bout to go down. Watch."

"Boy you so 80's." Tracy said dismissively. "Ain't nobody thinking 'bout your hood or nobody else's." She turned back to Spits. "So tell me. Do you got a girlfriend? What's her name?"

"You're a trip you know that." Spits said smiling. "And nosy too." He added.

"So what? Answer the question." She insisted.

While he was usually standoffish with those not close to him, he found himself drawn to Tracy and her bossy ways. He got the sense that though she was meddlesome to the extreme, her heart was in the right place. He felt like he could trust her.

"You're a trip." He repeated.

"What?" She asked and giggled while batting her lashes dramatically. She back handed him and demanded that he tell her all about his love life. "I'm the one who's going to be out there representing you. So I need to know all about you."

"Tracy you always be up in everybody's business." Dame said and shot Spits a sympathetic look. "Why don't you leave that boy alone and let him enjoy his food."

"Naw it's cool." Spits told him. He knew what Tracy had said was real and that if they were going to be working so close together then it would be best for them if they got to know each other. He shook his head and told her that he was single.

"I ain't had time to get in a relationship since I got out of prison. I've been hustling trying to get my money right from day one."

"What else?" She probed. "Tell me about your life."

"There really ain't too much to tell." He answered. "You know the drill. Sold drugs, gang banged, went to prison and all that."

Tracy shook her head and told him that wasn't good enough. She didn't know the drill and she wanted to know what he was really about.

"What kind of person are you? What makes you tick? What do you want out of life? Who is Spits?"

The questions caught him a little off guard and he looked away. If someone had asked these same questions just yesterday, he wouldn't have hesitated in saying that he just wanted to stack a couple hundred thousand dollars by the end of the year and go on to sell used cars.

But with Dame now paying him four thousand a month to do what he'd wanted to do more than anything else in life at one point, he was forced to see the lifestyle he'd been living these past years for the waste it truly was. He wanted a future he was worthy of.

"I want power." Spits said finally while nodding. "All my life it seem like circumstances just boxed me in and I didn't have no choice but to do some pretty messed things just to survive. But now that I've decided to go on this paper chase with you guys, I have a chance to get so much power that I won't ever have to worry about being in such a helpless place again."

Hearing the sincerity in his words, Tracy reached over and affectionately rubbed the back of his head and thanked him for being so honest.

Looking to Dame and Mash, she told them that once this thing started happening and they got their first taste of success, there would be a lot of pressure on them.

"There's gonna be a lot of different people trying to come between us and if we're not careful, we'll be at each other's throats fighting about money and a bunch of other stuff." She warned them all. She then looked to Spits. Her emerald green eyes were full of love and concern for the three of them.

Dame, who was a little tipsy and choked up from Tracy's little speech, told them that this wouldn't happen because they were going to keep it real and remember where they came from. He told Tracy that she was, and always would be his best friend. He told Mash and Spits that as co-owners of their label, to have each other's back to the fullest. And most of all to enjoy the ride they were about to go on.

"We ain't gonna let this crap come between us." He promised. "As a matter of fact," he said as he stood to raise

his glass. "let's do one of them toasts to this."

When they all stood, Dame toasted to their Paper Chasin' family and told them that from here on it would them against the world. Mash was smiling the whole time. It was the first time that he'd ever seen his uncle get emotional and he thought it was funny.

"Dang Unc, you must be drunk. I ain't never heard you say no stuff like that. When did you start getting all sentimental?"

Spits laughed at the embarrassed look on Dames face and saw Tracy smiling over at him. He winked at her. Spits loved this situation he now found himself in and for once he felt comfortable with what his future held. He liked the camaraderie at the table and knew in his heart that if they all played their positions then this would be a long and successful journey.

"Since you done asked me all kinds of questions, why don't you tell me about yourself Tracy." Spits said suddenly catching her off guard as he wanted to. Laughing at his shiftiness, she told him that all he needed to know about her was that she was a doer and that she wouldn't quit on him once she was on the job.

"I don't fail well. Once I start in on somethin', I'm not happy until I accomplish my mission. And my mission now is to make you a bona fide rap star."

"Do you got a man? If you do, I know he got his hands full for realz."

"Well one thing's for sure." Tracy answered with a frown. "Your little young ass ain't got nothin' coming. So if that was supposed to be one of your little lines then you can save that weak crap."

Dame threw his head back and laughed at this. "Don't nobody want your old ass Tracy. This boy's fixin' to be famous. He ain't thinking 'bout you."

"Who you calling old?" She asked while twisting her face up.

"I can't wait till we get famous" Mash broke in and said. "We bout to have all kind of groupies on our nuts after we drop the mix tapes on they ass. It's about to go down."

Spits agreed with a smile.

"I'm gonna holler at that V.J Sweet from Rap Down as soon as I get my foot in the door." He promised. He was referring to the host of a popular T.V show. All Tracy could do was shake her head as Spits and Mash went on about all of the females they'd have when they were famous.

We're really about to do this. Tracy thought to herself. She noticed how they all seemed to speak as though their success was inevitable and she liked that very much.

Tony Clincy

OFF TO THE RACES...

TRACY USED THE money Dame had given her to
turn the spare room of her condo into a temporary office. The
two of them would use it until Dame found somethin' more
suitable. The two matching desks sat face to face littered with
legal documents, trade magazines, notes, and dozens of other
papers they'd been working on the past three weeks.

A Picture of Big Sur's Bixby Bridge hung on the wall
behind Dame's empty chair and Tracy sat staring at it as she
talked on the phone with the Fox California's manager. She
was trying to book the historic Salinas Theater for Spits first
concert which they planned on having in three months.

She loved the meetings with industry insiders,
working the phones and making the contacts which would
allow them to get Spits proper exposure along with the
thousands of other things she found herself doing every day
in pursuit of their label's goals. The work was proving to be
harder than her and Dame had imagined it would be but just
knowing that they had the best rapper in the game was all the
motivation they needed to kept at it day after day. So far they
were more than pleased with the progress they were making.

From the start, they'd been hard at work learning all
they needed to know about the nature of this industry. Tracy
bought two copies of 'Everything You Need To Know About
The Music Industry' by entertainment attorney Donald
Passman so they'd have a clear understanding of what they
would be dealing with as label execs. But as the saying goes,
experience is the best teacher and they were finding it to be
true.

There was much to be done in order to get the label in
position to drop the 'Legend In The Making' mixtape series.
The plan called for them to release the mixtapes one week
apart for two months. This would whet the public's appetite
and insure that Spits had a strong following by the time they
were ready to drop the radio single and album in three
months. This would also give Dame and Tracy enough time

to get the label on solid footing so they wouldn't be overwhelmed by the success they were all sure Spits' album would bring when it came.

So far all was going according to plan. Mash and Spits were hard at work in the studio at least sixteen hours a day building a catalogue of material. True to his word, Spits was putting his all into this. He focused all his energy on becoming an even better rapper. He displayed a work ethic that was out of this world and it forced everybody else to try and keep up.

Dame handled all things legal and Tracy dealt wit with everything else including doing things that would help properly introduce Spits and his music to the masses. With the drawing up of contracts, promotions, planning of shows, interviews and the search for an assistant, they had little time for much else outside of work. And Tracy loved it.

"Okay Dave. If we can't get the first of March, We'll have to go with Friday the eighth." Tracy said as she penciled the date in on her desk blotter. They agreed on a time for her to come drop off the deposit and she disconnected the call with a triumphant grin on her face.

"Yes!" She yelled with a fist pump. "Paper Chasin' is in the house." She picked the phone back up and dialed Dame's number. "I booked the Fox for the concert!"

"You did?" He asked. His voice was full of surprise. "How you get them to do that when we ain't even put no music out yet?"

"I turned on the charm, that's how." She told him with a girlish laugh. "When are you coming back to the office?"

"Later on." He said in an uneasy voice. "You know I don't like that damn office Trace. You won't let me smoke my cigars and you got all them plants in there. It smells like a garden in there."

She laughed at him. "If you don't like it then hurry up and find us an office. And you need to find Mash some studio space. We can't have them boys making music in that dark garage forever."

"Yeah I know. I'm on it." He promised. "I have a call coming in. Lets meet at Chili's in an hour and have lunch."

"Okay. See you then."

After hanging up she showered, dressed and headed to Chili's. Lunch hour traffic was heavy and she found herself crawling along Freemont St. at a snail's pace. It was while stopped at a light that she felt a sudden chill along her spine and had this uneasy thought of Dame cheating Spits and Mash out of their money. As quickly as it came, the feeling of dread went away leaving her feeling muddled and wondering what the strange premonition meant.

Tracy knew Dame better than anyone and loved him in spite of his greedy ways. She watched him stunt on everybody in Seaside for years and had always felt that he probably would be a better person had he not had money which he allowed to be a barrier between him and those who didn't have as much as he did. Since she knew that money made Dame anti-social, she could only hope that this new money wouldn't bring out the worst in him.

Pulling into Chili's parking lot, Tracy found a space and parked. She walked inside and spotted Dame at the bar drinking what she knew would be a double shot of Hennessey. As she made her way to him she couldn't help but notice heads turn as both men and women took in her figure hugging black pantsuit. Standing 5'6 with a pale yellow complexion and emerald green eyes, Tracy knew that she was bad and took pleasure in the complimenting looks of the restaurants patrons as she headed for the bar.

"Hey ma." Dame said greeting her with a peck on the cheek and a hug.

"Hi Dame." She said and sat on the stool he'd pulled out for her. Noticing his gaze sweep over the length of her body, she scowled. "Boy you better stop that."

"Stop what?" He asked with a mask of innocence. "What did I do now?"

"Stop looking at me like you wanna sleep with me! That's what." She told him.

Laughing, Dame told her that she'd mistaken his look and that if he would've been really looking at her like that then she wouldn't be complaining.

"Tracy you know you still got a crush on me." He added casually. She didn't even bother to respond to this, instead she shot him a look which told him how stupid he sounded. Any chance of them having a relationship outside of being friends had ended in high school when Tracy caught him cheating on her. Never one to be disrespected, she had lured him to her house when no one was home and hit him in the head with a wrench. Forty stitches and Tracy's attitude had ended all romance between them and they'd been just friends ever since.

"Are you two ready to be seated?" The hostess asked at Dame's elbow.

"Yes." Tracy answered and shot Dame another sour look before following the pretty blond waitress to their table.

"I just got off the phone with an agent about seeing a couple of office spaces." Dame informed Tracy after sitting. "She's got two places for me to look at. One's in Seaside and one's in Marina."

"Get the one in Monterey." Tracy said. "We're trying to get out of the hood remember? We can't have our office in Seaside. Stop being so damn cheap for once and get us an office worthy of where we're trying to go as a company."

"Okay, I'll do that and I'm on the hunt for someplace to put Mash's studio too."

"Did he tell you to make it big enough for three studios?.

"No why?" He asked her not understanding why they'd need three studios.

"When I stopped by the studio yesterday he was telling me that once we blow up we should sign some more producers to work with the artists we sign." She explained. "I've been so busy working the phones that I hadn't stopped to think about signing other artists. But he's right. We need to start looking beyond Spits while we're doing everything to put him in position."

Dame nodded his head in agreement. "Okay I'm on it."

"And we need to hire a publicity firm to work with Spits. He's too damn shy and standoffish when he's not on the mic. That looks cool and everything but he can't be shy when the cameras start rolling."

"And what about the assistant you wanted to hire?" He asked.

"I'm interviewing her later on after I stop by the studio to see the boys."

Tracy turned to look out to the parking lot as she wondered what Spits was doing right now. Most likely he was in the booth being as cocky as he wanted to be while pouring his heart out to the music. She smiled at the thought. She'd found in him the little brother she'd always wanted but never had and felt that the two of them would have a beautiful lifelong friendship.

"I saw this new Maserati I think I'm gonna cop." Dame announced bringing Tracy back to the here and now.

"What?" She asked him with an annoyed tone.

"I'm gonna cop me a Maserati." Dame repeated again missing the irritation in her voice. "I saw it in the Robb Report. It's burgundy and white."

"You and your damn grandstanding. You always got to show off don't you?" She said and shook her head. She recalled the premonition she'd had at the light and told herself that she had to keep an eye on him to make sure that he didn't let this money make him any more selfish than he'd always been. Tracy vowing to herself that she would keep Dame honest with Spits and Mash.

AS NOSY AS EVER…

"YOU KNOW HOW cats be sitting around arguing about how much money these rap cats got?" Spits asked Mash from the couch as Mash tweaked the sounds of their latest 'Spit's Sopranos' as Spits now called his raps. "Once they hear this one here, they fixin' to be talking 'bout how much money we got."

The first of the "Legend In The Making' mix tape series would drop in two weeks and they were both anxious to hear the fan's reaction to their music.

Mash was in seventh heaven these days because in Spits he'd found a kindred spirit; a workaholic like himself who loved nothing more than pulling twelve hour studio sessions, sleeping on the couch in The Blue Room, to wake and do it all again. The music they were making together was as good as they'd both known it would be and it was getting better daily.

In three weeks they'd built a catalogued of eighty songs, twenty of which were Mashed out Production. It had been Mash who'd suggested that they used the beats from some of the more popular Bay Area rap artists, explaining that since it was the Northern Cali rap fan they were aiming at, it made perfect since to serve them with Spits voice, which would be new to them, over beats which they already knew and loved. "It's perfect, homie." He'd told him with that boyish grin of his. "Just trust me and we gon' blow the fk up 'round dis bootch."

As for Spits, he didn't care at all for Northern Cali rappers. Southern one's either, preferring instead, the lyrical dexterity of their East Coast counterparts over the drug and violence filled lyrics of West Coast hip-hop. drug-glamorizing lu give a half cent about too much care for Northern Cali rappers. Southern ones either for that matter, preferring the lyrical dexterity of his East Coast counterparts instead.

And so they'd compromised. Half the songs on the mix tape would from be to top radio single's instrumentals, So Mash and Spits had compromised. Half of the beats on the mix tapes would be from Northern Cali rappers. And the other half would be from popular radio singles.

"That's crazy how Tracy got KDON to agree to drop one of our songs on the air." Mash said as he turned in his chair to take the blunt Spits held out. "We ain't leaked no songs over the internet or nothin'. How the heck did she do that?"

"She probably went out to Salinas and bullied the program director." Spits said and they laughed.

"We bout to put the Hood Life on the map for real." Mash said. Spits saw a terribleness in Mash eyes which either hadn't been there or he hadn't it noticed the other times he had similar statements.

"We fixin' to get rich." Spits said wanting to keep Mash's head on the two most important things; money and music. And in exactly that order.

I gotta keep an eye on him and make sure he don't get on no dumb stuff. This stuff's too real for us to be on some kiddie crap.

Someone banging at the back door interrupted their conversation.

"Who is it?" Mash called out as he turned down the music.

"It's Tracy. Open up this dang door." She yelled and kicked the door. Soon they could hear her laughing.

"Didn't we just talked to you a few minutes ago!" Spits called as he made his way to the door.

"Yeah but I forgot to tell you that we have an appointment." She pushed past him. "So grab your stuff and let's get moving." She looked at her watch and frowned as if pressed for time. Both Spits and Mash knew better than to argue.

"Dang Trace." Mash mumbled and turned to his equipment.

"Dang what?" She demanded. "Y'all been living up in this blue garage like some dang vampires." She playfully slapped the back of Mash's head and turned to leave. "That's why Spits is so camera shy now. You need to get out and start socializing more."

With Spits sitting quiet in the passenger seat of her car, Tracy took Broadway and headed to highway one, to the picturesque Pacific Ocean to the west of the scenic route. Soft Jazz played low on the car's stereo while Spits stared out the window thinking about all of the changes his life had taken over the past weeks and all that his future now held.

"Why you looking all thoughtful.?" Tracy asked him.

"I just got a lot on my mind right now." He told her. "I mean, here I am about to be rich and famous all of a sudden and I wanna make sure that I make all the right moves."

This was the perfect situation for him and he knew it. The music industry would allow him to live a life of wealth which few others would ever experience. And the confidence he had of their being successful was laced with the knowledge that if he wanted to reach the pinnacle of the industry, he needed to be sharp on his business too. Because when it was all said and done, big business was where the money was, not rapping.

Tracy nodded her head that she understood. "Do you want a suggestion?" She reached over and squeezed his hand. "Just be yourself boy. You're already a star and you know it. You think you're a star wherever you are so just be one."

Spits smiled and turned to the ocean still squeezing her hand. "Just be myself huh?"

"Yeah. Just be yourself." She repeated. "I see that same 'I'm a Boss' look that I've been seeing in Dame's eyes since high school."

He laughed at that. "You're crazy." He said and turned to her. "It's crazy you said that because I think me and Dame are interested in some of the same things."

"And what's that baby." She asked him.

"Business." He told her simply. "When I hustle, I like to stay on top of my business and this ain't nothin' but another hustle. But the thing is, I don't know all the rules of the game yet." He shook his head, frustrated. "I don't like that. I'm in this by myself as far as my business and-"

"Wait a minute baby." She squeezed his hand tighter and looked down at their hands. "You see that." She squeezed again when he looked. "You aren't ever in nothin' by yourself boy. You're my little brother."

Embarrassed and dabbing at the wetness in her eyes, she changed the subject." Now tell me why you ain't got no dang girlfriend with your fine black butt."

Spits smiled.

"I been trying to get money since coming home from the pen." He said before going on to explain to her his one year plan and how he had put it down for six months before agreeing to do the rap thing.

"Females be needing to much attention and I didn't have the time for no needy woman distracting me. And I really don't have time now."

Not buying it, Tracy shook her head. "Don't front like you don't got eyes. I know you done seen somebody you like?"

"I got eyes but-"

"What's her name boy." Tracy said cutting him off before smiling.

Spits laughed. "You crazy, you know that don't you?"

"So what? Tell me her name or we gon' be out her till the moon sets."

She took the keys from the ignition and put them down her shirt, giggling the whole time. She crossed her arms over her chest and gave him a look like 'I'm waiting'.

"Damn Trace. You are crazy."

Spits laughed. He liked Tracy. He'd never felt such deep of a bond with anyone as fast as he had with her and he thought that her pushy personality was cute. So instinctively, he trusted her.

"Her Name's Margarita. She's from Salinas." He said before he could change his mind.

"Margarita!" Tracy clapped her hands happily when she said this. "I knew it! What's she look like? How old is she? Do she got a boyfriend already..."

He just shook his head knowing that he was in for it now. "You're worse than the C.O's in Quentin."

"And?" She smiled.

"Look Tracy. I'll make you a deal okay." He offered. "I'll answer your personal question where you get all in my business but you have to keep me up on all things about label business. You have to be my eyes, ears and mouth when I can't."

"Well that's what I get paid to-"

"No." he stopped her. "I'm talking about as your little brother. If we're close enough to where you can punk me into doing stuff then we're close enough for me to know that you're gonna always have my best interest at heart."

She looked out to sea, to the coast of Santa Cruz Curving from East to West 50 miles away. She nodded her head yes.

"That's fair baby." She offered her hand and he shook it. "You've got yourself a deal."

"Deal." He agreed.

"Now tell me about Margarita." Tracy said and spun around tucking one leg under the other, facing him. "What's she look like."

"She's fine. She has light skin and these big expressive eyes. She purses her lips sometimes when she's trying to figure somethin' out and she's shy."

Tracy had the biggest grin on her face as he spoke and she nodded her head all the while. "Oh yeah." She said when he finished. "You got it bad. You described that girl like she was a damn poem." She put a finger to her temple as if thinking. "Now what we need to do is get Y'all together. You need a girlfriend baby. She'll stop you from stressing about this fast paced life you're about to be living."

59

"Naw I'm cool Trace. For real. I want to focus on my music and business. That can wait a year at least. There's too much that I need to learn right now."

"Yeah you're right." She said a little too quickly. "We need to get you to this publicity firm I'm talking to. We should have an agreement by tomorrow. And You need a daily planner. I'll get you one. If you want to be on top of your business then you got to start writing down your commitments."

"That makes sense."

"And once the publicist gets done with you, you might be able to say somethin' slick to Margarita." Tracy giggled.

Who is this Margarita? She better be as perfect as he's making her out to be. Tracy thought and vowed to find out. Spits too was thinking about Margarita and how the main reason he hadn't really pursued her as hard as his heart wanted was because he was ashamed. In his heart he understood that Margarita must have felt that same ugliness he felt while hustling in Chinatown. She must have a deeper aversion for the place than he could imagine. And because of this, he felt a shame that he'd never felt before. He'd known all along that he was wrong for preying on the less fortunate all for money's sake. Yet had done it anyway.

SOAKING UP GAME...

SPITS WALKED IN the morning fog, still coming down from the high he got every time he and Mash were recording. It was four in the morning and he was on his way home from the studio after having pulled a thirteen hour marathon. He was beat. He couldn't remember ever working so hard in his life as he had been these past weeks and he knew that this was only the beginning. It would get even more hectic once they started dropping the mixtapes and he was looking forward to it.

As he did most nights, or mornings, after finishing up at the studio, he would go home and read for three hours before he slept. He was set on learning all that he could about the industry. He was giving himself a crash course in Music Business 101 by spending hours studying the workings of the industry and business law whenever he could steal the time to pick up a book.

In his street wisdom, he compared the music game to the dope game by understanding that in the dope game, a hustler wanted to cop works which he would then turn into money. In the music game, an Exec wanted to cop contracts with signatures stating that people owed you money for services and he planned on making sure that Dame and Tracy copped those signatures.

As usual, the walk home and the instrumentals he listened to on his Zune, invigorated him as he headed to his mother's house.

It's about to be lovely. Spits thought yet again looking to the future and seeing the limousines, the bodyguards, the screaming fans and all that would come with it. He understood that this was the perfect situation for him.

The rap game's mine. He thought and smiled, imagining this meteoric rise and seeing it in 3-D. What he found funny was that he had forgotten just how passionate he was about music. The game had blinded him to his love of it all those years he'd ran the streets. But now that he'd reawakened his passion, he found he was more alive than ever and these new found feelings had begun coming across in his music as he put his thoughts and emotions to song.

His phone vibrated in his pocket and he knew that it couldn't be nobody but Loco who liked to call him at all hours of the day trying to catch him in between studio sessions.

"What it do boy?" Spits said upon answering

"Shoot." Loco said. "What's up with you?"

Spits could hear females laughing in the background. "Where you at? And what Y'all doing up so late? Who's them broads I hear?"

He knew that Loco was somewhere acting bad.

"Me and Choc is over some broad's house he know. We over hear blowin' trees." Loco explained. "I'm 'bout to put you on speaker, hold up."

Spits heard him telling the girls to watch and see somethin' and knew that Loco was acting a fool.

"Hello? Spits, can you hear me?" Loco asked.

"Yeah I hear you. Who you got me all on blast with."

"Just these beezies Choc know." Loco said. He could hear the girls being upset at being called beezies. "Shut up! I'm tryna talk to my homie."

Spits laughed. "Loco, what you got going on?"

"Man, these broads talking 'bout Messy Marv and Hustla like they hecka hard. I told them you the hardest out there and they think I'm woofin'."

"So what you calling me for at four in the morning for?" Spits asked laughing. "The sun ain't even woke yet and you got me on speaker phone."

"Just shut up and listen for a minute and I'll tell your square butt." Loco said as if speaking to a child. Then he spoke in a more serous tone. "Just say a rap so they can hear you got gas!"

Spits shook his head as he smiled. "You is burnt. I ain't fixin' to rap on the phone at dark-thirty in the morning walking in the fog. You stupid."

"You hecka scary." Loco said to him. Then Spits could hear him talking to the girls. "My boy got gas. He just shy."

"Ain't nobody shy." Spits said with a laugh. "Y'all don't listen to Loco."

"You is shy. That's why you can't knock Margarita wit yo scary butt."

Spits changed the subject quickly. "When I get to the house, I'll e-mail you a new track you can play for your little friends."

"Alright. That'll work." Loco said then added "You bet not start acting all funny style when you blow up."

"Never that."

"I'm tryin to go on tour with Y'all and get at me some of them groupies chief. That's gon' be the bomb."

"Yeah, I got you. Don't even trip." Spits came to his house and told Loco that he would get with him later. "Hit me tonight." He told him before hanging up. Spit's mother was sleep and the house quiet. He made his way to his room and stretched out on the bed with a smile on his face.

I'm fixin' to be rich as heck! He thought for the thousandth time this week. Through it all, He was driven by the fact that he would soon have enough money to escape from the dead-end lifestyle he'd grown accustomed to. He wanted to put as much distance between him and these Seaside streets as possible and vowed that he would take this chance he'd been given and run with it.

A Seasider through and through, he loved the small hilly town. This is where he got his game from so it would always hold a special place in his heart. But he had always known that his future lie elsewhere, that he was destined to see bigger and better things than what he'd seen so far.

Rolling off the bed, he went to his desk and e-mailed Loco a new track before grabbing the book he'd bought on entertainment law. He stretched out on the bed again and focused on the text as he soaked up as much game as he could.

Tony Clincy

I'm gon' take the music industry by storm. They ain't even gon' see me comin'. He thought to himself as he read till he fell asleep.

SHUT UP AND PARTY...

"COME ON Y'ALL! Why you actin all funny style like you can't have no fun." Tracy complained to Spits, Dame, and Mash, who sat silently angry while taking in the club.
 They didn't want to be there.
"Don't pay them no mind girl." Tracy turned and told the new assistant named Janet that she hired earlier.
"It's okay." The light complected and mousy Janet assured her. "I'm sure we can get to know each other later. There'll be plenty of time."
"Uh-Uh." Tracy said shaking her head. "Forget that. We here now and we about to have some fun."
Dressed to the nines in a crème colored Vera Wang pantsuit and pumps, Tracy wasn't hearing nothin' outside of what she was saying right now.
"Ain't nobody even want to come here." Mash mumbled. "We was busy and you come busting in talking 'bout we going out."
"Forget all that." She snapped. "Y'all been living in that blue cave like a couple of vampires." She nodded her head that she was right as she said this. "Y'all need this. So drink up and stop sulking!"
Dame sat watching the exchange, his face a mask and his mouth shut. He and Spits knew better than to talk and get went off on. She had went to Dame's house first, storming in and telling him to quickly get dressed so they could go out.
"We partying tonight. I'm tired of all this, 'all work and no play' stuff." Tracy had announced to Dame at the time. Left with no choice, Dame dressed and stuffed his big frame into the back seat of Tracy's Camry and was forced to listen to her telling Janet how much fun they were all gonna have tonight. From Dame's she had drove straight to the studio and punked Spits and Mash. So here they were and the guys were mad about it too.

"I'm not about to be working with you boring guys if we can't enjoy this together." She told them with a little less anger, hoping to appeal to them. "We all been working our behinds off you guys. Let's just have a few drinks and relax for a minute."

Calming down some at the plea in her voice, Spits looked to her and somethin' in him broke. He threw his head back laughing and gripping his sides.

"What's so dang funny?" Dame asked annoyed. He could think of a hundred things he could be doing right now besides sitting here in this club. Still laughing, Spits pointed at Tracy.   "Tracy. She's skitz. She just came to the spot, punked us, and now she trying to make us have fun."

Mash looked at Tracy and the stubbornness he saw on her face proved too much. He started laughing too and so did Dame.

"You gotta stop bossing us around like we some little kids, Trace." Spits told her.

"You be punkin' us like you're the Queen of Sheba or somethin'."

"Forget all that!" Tracy answered. "Y'all be on some crap half the time." She turned to Janet. "These guys need to be pushed a little but most of the time they're alright."

With the mood lightened, Spits offered Janet his hand. "It's nice to meet you Janet." He said and apologized for not properly introducing himself earlier. "Tracy be having us hot sometimes but don't trip. We're like a family most of the time."

"Yeah and I'm the Queen Bee around here." Tracy said and giggled as she took a sip of her drink. "You guys drink up. I ain't pay for them drink's so they can sit on the table."

"How long have you been in the industry?" Mash asked Janet after introducing himself.

"I started singing when I was five and signed a deal when I was fourteen. I stayed in the studio trying to build a following for four years before my label dropped me. When that happened, I begged for a job, got hired as an A&R rep and I've been doing that for the past five years."

"Janet knows most of the D.J's in Northern California." Tracy gloated. "And since we're building our fan base from the ground up, those are connections that we're gonna need."

"I told Tracy that I think we should start shooting footage of you two recording in the studio. When we drop the mixtapes, we can put the footage up on YouTube. That will give the fans the opportunity to connect with you."

"Heck yeah!" Mash agreed picturing himself and Spits being filmed in the Blue Room. He would have his shirt off so he could expose his Seaside tats'. He smiled and looked at Spits. "You gon' have to get over that being scared of the camera stuff homie. We fixin' to be on the world wide web with it."

Dame, suddenly in a festive mood, waved over the waitress and ordered them two bottles of Hennessey "Forget it. We might as well get lit since we here already."

"Tracy let me hear some of your music earlier Spits." Janet told him. "I think that you're definitely hot."

"Yeah he is." Mash said proudly. "We fixin' to blow up. With his lyrics, and my beats, they ain't gon' know what hit em. We got like twelve songs we could release as singles already."

Spits looked away. He liked the material they'd recorded so far but he hadn't heard anything he thought was single worthy yet.

"Where are you from?" Spits asked Janet.

"I grew up in Monterey but when I got signed, my parents moved us to L.A so that I could be closer to my label." She looked him in his eyes as she spoke and Spits thought that she might not be as shy and mousy as he'd thought at first. "We just moved back to the area three months ago and I've been going crazy missing working in the industry."

Spits could hear the passion she had for music in her voice as she spoke and saw why Tracy had hired her.

"Well I'm glad that you're a part of our family now." He told her. "I hope you're ready for this wild ride we about to go on."

She smiled at this and assured him that she was. "I'm looking forward to the fast pace."

"Well then, let's have another toast." Dame said and stood with his glass of Hennessey held high. They stood also and toasted the newest member of the Paper Chasin' family, laughing as Mash started talking about all the groupies he and Spits would run through once they dropped the first mixtape.

Rap Star

A STAR IS BORN…

"I'LL BE THERE in like ten minutes." Spits promised Loco.

"Hurry up slow poke." Loco said laughing. "Your girlfriend's sitting here waiting for you."

"Be quiet Loco!" Spits heard Margarita shriek and he laughed.

"Let me get off this phone before I get a ticket. I'll be there in a few."

He disconnected the call as he turned onto Blanco Road and the floor of the Salinas Valley, a portrait worthy landscape stretching from the brown-green Gabilan Mountain Range to the east and west to the tan sand dunes that held the turquoise-blue waters of the Pacific ocean. He was driving Dame's Benz on his way to kick it with Loco for the day. It was his first day off since going into the studio last month. He'd told Loco two weeks ago that when he took a break he would come to Salinas and kick it with him. Loco was his best friend and he missed him and all the laughter.

Loco was real quick to do just what his name said, Go Loco. Nine times out of ten, when they went somewhere, anywhere, Loco would go bad on someone. As annoying as the drama was and as long as Spits could stop him from beating somebody up, it was funny. Spits couldn't count the times he had saved somebody from getting whooped on.

He turned left onto West Alisal, heading towards Old Town Salinas where the Fox Theater stood.

We fixin' to have Old Town lit up! He smiled thinking of the event Tracy and Dame were putting together for his album release party. He pulled into Chinatown and his stomach turned at its ugliness.

These cats ain't gon' never leave this place.

Seeing the busy junkies, crack heads, depressed homeless and mean drunk's, he knew what he was thinking was right. Dame's Benz had the whole block watching him as he parked across the street from the shelter. The junkies began hounding him soon as he stepped out the car.

"Spits you got a fifty?" "What up homie?" "You got somethin' man?"

"I don't get down no more." He told the small group who'd rushed over. "I'm messing with this music now."

"What's up chief?" An approaching voice called out and he looked up to see Loco's cousin Scooby.

"What's up boy!" Spits smiled and hugged him.

"Loco let me hear the CD you gave him. That was fire." Scooby said nodding his head. "He told me how Y'all out there in the Side putting it down. That's cool."

"Who you tellin. I'm so cool on this block stuff homie." Spits looked around them and shook his head. "This ain't even the business no more."

"It never was." Scooby said then told him that he had to go get his money. "I gotta go but I'll holla at you later."

Spits walked into Dorothy's and saw Margarita smiling through the office window. He smiled also. Loco was sitting next to her smiling with his arm around the back of her chair and leaning close, trying to make it look like they'd been cozier than they were. Spits just shook his head. Margarita came out into hallway and hugged him.

"I'm so proud of you. I knew you were better than this man." They walked into the office and sat down. "I'm so happy to see you. Loco told me about your music and how all of a sudden you're part label owner."

"Yeah, it just happened out of the blue."

"Yep! And he got gas too." Loco boasted and slid his arm behind her chair leaning in to her.

"Stop it Troy!" She shrugged his arm off and slapped his chest. Loco just laughed. "You play too much Troy."

Loco looked Spits up and Down.

"Why?" He asked Margarita. "Spits ain't gon' do nothin'. If he don't step his game up, you might as well let me stab 'em."

"Loco!" She gave him a look and then turned to Spits, ignoring him. "Anyways. He played the CD for me and you're good. Better than good actually."

"Yeah he is." Loco agreed refusing to be ignored. "We about to be famous as heck. Watch." He nodded his head. "When the homie blow up, I'm fixin' to be all in them camera's faces throwin' up the MOB." He said while throwing up his gang's hand sign and grinning.

"How have you been Margarita?" Spits asked as he stared at her black hair laying on her back. "I see you're still happy."

"Yeah, you know me. Just working and going to school." She smiled and nodded her head. "I am happy."

"Yeah, that's what's up." He said seeing a sense of peace in her black, bright eyes and hoping that the music industry would be the road which led his eyes that shone like hers. "I want that too." He nodded and she smiled.

"That was hecka corny." Loco laughed and put a fist to his mouth. "See, that's why she ain't messin' with yo' lame butt. You be sayin' some real corny stuff. 'I want that too'. Who says that to broads?"

"Troy shut up dang!" Margarita shot him a look.

"Uh-Uh." Loco shook his head and stood. "He came out here to see me so we out." He looked to Spits. "Where my CD at? I know you ain't brought your no game havin' butt out here without my CD"

"It's in the car." Spits said. He and Margarita stood. "You wanna hear the CD I brought him?" He asked Margarita.

"Sure." She smiled. "Just let me get somebody to watch the office and I'll be right out."

Spits and Loco went outside. Loco stopped and turned to him when he saw the Benz. "Is that your whip? Let me drive that thang."

Spits laughed. "Naw, that's Dame's. He just let me use it since I been in the studio for five straight weeks." They

71

climbed in the car and he put the CD in the player. "We just finished this track last night."

Mash's beat started knocking and Loco nodded his head while smiling. "Did chief make that beat? That thang slaps."

"Yeah. That's all Mash right there. Listen to it though."

The vocals came on and Spits was rapping about the Black and Hispanic gangs of the Central Coast. When he reached Salinas, the first hood he gave it up to was Cabrillo St. and Loco went wild.

"MOB!" He yelled and threw up his hand sign. He turned the volume up and climbed out the car. "MOB! My dude got gas! Ain't nobody seeing this cat." He told the block. Spits saw Margarita walk out and turned the music down before climbing out the car.

"Is this your car?" She asked with wide eyes.

"Naw, this Dame's car. He's the one who put up the money for the label." He said walking her around to the passenger side where she sat while he found another song. "Here, I know one you'll like."

He had chosen a "gangsta love song" with a strong R&B flavor and saw from her smile that she liked it.

He is good. She thought while nodding her head as she watched the looks of pleasure on the faces that had crowded the sidewalk. "That's good Spits. I'm so happy for you. You have a lot of talent and I'm glad to see you do somethin' with it."

"You guys should do a duet together." Loco suggested. "Yep. Y'all can be like J-lo and Ja-Rule. Margarita be singing her butt off. They had open mic at Dorothy's last week and she was singin'.

Spits cocked his head and looked at her. "You sing?"

"No. Not really." She said and began blushing and staring at the ground.

Loco gave Spits a devious grin and nodded his head towards her. "Stop lying Margarita. You was up in there sounding like a Mexican Sade."

"I didn't know you could sing. What kind of music do you listen to? You sing Spanish music?"

"Naw chief. She sang this song she wrote and it was like Sade music." Loco told him. "Sing a song for the homie Margarita."

"Yeah Margarita." Someone in the crowd said. "I heard you the other night, you're good."

The last thing in the world she wanted to do was sing now. She was too shy to sing in front of people. The other night was the first and only time she'd done it. And she couldn't do it now.

"No I can't. I have to work."

"Come on Margarita." Spits said and touched her hand. "I want to hear you sing."

She sighed knowing she'd be more embarrassed resisting everybody than to just sing a quick verse. "Okay, I'll sing part of a song I wrote."

She looked to the ground again and closed her eyes for a moment before she began humming a slow and sensuous, bohemian type rhythm. She swayed slowly from side to side and it was as if all of the beauty which she went to lengths to hide came from within her.

Spit's mouth dropped and he looked at Loco, who was staring at her smiling. She began singing in a soft, husky, blues-tinted voice, singing of a love she yearned for yet could never find.

I know just the song I want her to sing on. Spits thought as he and Loco shared a grin.

HOOD LIFE DAYS...

MASH WAS STRAPPED while wearing a black hoodie, jeans, and steel toe Timberlands. He was on his way to the PJs. A thrill seeker in the worst way, he only loved music more than he loved running these hilly Seaside streets. The Hood Life Projects was his home and these were the streets which had taught him to hustle. They also taught him how to be a man. These were the streets that gave him his heart and he would represent them until he died.

Alert, his eyes scanned his surroundings for danger. People had been known to come up short out here and he was determined that he wouldn't be the one. Especially not before he hit the big time.

Truth be told, he knew he was wrong for being out there strapped like he was but with this being his first break in five weeks, there was nothin' on earth that could keep him from the projects today. And knew better than to go unarmed.

They ain't gon' catch the Mash monster slippin'.

He rubbed the gun through the pockets of the hoodie as he thought. Part of him wanted someone to try somethin' so that he could give them the business. The brown brick PJs sat at the top of Seaside on Yosemite Street. Mash smiled as he walked up the hill and entered the first lot where the homies were scattered around doing their thing.

"PJs!" He called out as he stepped into the lot.

"All day!" Someone responded from between the first two buildings. Mash walked to the pathway and stopped when he saw his homeboy F standing against the wall holding a forty ounce.

"What's up chief! Where you been at?" Mash asked as he hugged his short, dark, and heavily tatted homeboy.

F laughed. "Naw, where you been at? I been out for a month and I'm up here twenty-four seven."

"I been at the house making music." Mash said. F passed him the forty ounce and he took a drink. "You been out for a month? How long was you gone for? Like three years or somethin' wasn't it?'

"Yep. They gave me five. I did two and a half on it." F told him. He and Mash had gotten jumped in together and had been tight ever since. F was a rider and well respected in the hood and he respected Mash's gangsta.

"I been out here getting my money right. It's all good. I done stacked a few racks already. I'm good."

Mash took another drink and handed the bottle back. "In a minute you ain't gonna have to even do this stuff chief." He promised. "Me and the homie Spits is fixin' to put the rap game on lock."

"Spits?" F asked with raised eyebrows. He'd been in CYA with Spits and didn't remember him ever rapping. "When the homie start rappin'?"

"He been rappin'. He just wasn't tryin to do nothin' with it. But the boy is tight as heck. My uncle put up the money and we bout to do it real big." Mash explained.

F was smiled. "That's right homie." He dapped him. "I know you gon' put the hood on the map"

"You already know." Mash started pulling his sleeves up to show his newest tattoo. "I got a picture of the PJs right-"

"What you talking to that scary fool for F?" A voice called out from the other side of the lot. Mash spun towards the voice, his light brown eyes full of fire.

"What you say?" He asked the pigeon-toed and smiling D-Boyne as he approached.

"I asked the *real* homie what he was doing talking to you. That's what I-"

Before he could finish, Mash had pulled the gun from his waist and swung it catching D-Boyne on the cheek knocking him to the ground. D-Boyne was out cold and Mash kicked him repeatedly in the face.

F stood there laughing. "Stomp that fool out chief! Jack that mark up!"

He stopped cheering Mash on when he noticed he had brought up the gun ready to shoot. F dropped the forty and grabbed him from behind in a bear hug.

"Naw homie. There's too many witnesses chief." He felt Mash relax and look around at the people watching him. "Get his ass later or somethin'." F said and let him go.

"Good looking out chief." Mash said and spit on D-Boyne as he tucked the pistol back into his waist. He stood quiet as the storm inside him calmed.

"I'm tired of fools talking that stuff because I went to Florida during the funk." He said knowing that that's why D-Boyne had called him scary.

"Forget what they takin' bout. Cats know you was out here putting in work before you left. I heard about how you was ridin' with the best of 'em when I was in the pen."

Mash heard F but his words didn't make him feel any better because he knew that people were still gonna talk no matter what the truth was.

I bet don't none of these fools say that stuff to my face though. I ain't playin' wit people out here. They all can get the business.

"You better get out of here before the police come." F warned. "You know one of these snitches done called them."

Mash smiled and asked F if he wanted to come to the studio and hear some of the songs him and Spits had made.

"I got some trees and some beer up in there. We can get messed up and call some girls over."

"Let's go." F said and led the way.

CHANCE OF A LIFETIME…

SPITS AND LOCO sat in Dame's Benz waiting for Margarita to walk outside.

"She's gon' sound tight on my song. Did you hear her voice?" Spits beamed. He still couldn't believe that she could sing like that. "That girl got pipes on her."

"I told you to come chill with your boy." Loco told him while smiling like he'd known it all along.

"You know what it is with me and you homie. I'm always gon' come hang wit you."

Spits was thinking about a few tracks that needed female vocals and there was one in particular that he knew Margarita would sound great on. He called Mash and he told Spits that he was at the studio with F watching Auburn and Oregon State play for the Bowl Championship. Spits responded by saying that he was coming over with a singer.

Spits stared across the street to Dorothy's and nodded his head. "Loco, I'm telling you. I did this one song where I'm talking about how I was hustling on the block and I'm getting at this female, telling her that I'm not a bad guy. Margarita's perfect for it."

He knew in his mind that if Margarita sang on the track, they'd have their first single. When they saw her coming out, they got out the car and surprised her.

"What are you guys doing out here?" She asked them as they crossed the street.

"Waiting for you." Loco said. She had been expecting them and smiled internally.   "Waiting for me? What are you waiting for me for?" She asked growing nervous.

This is it! Yes! I knew it! I knew I was good!

"I need you to sing on one of my songs." Spits told her as he stepped onto the sidewalk. "I called Mash and he's waiting at the studio for us now. It won't take but an hour."

"No." She shook her head but wanted to nod more than anything. "I can't. I have to go home. My mom's expecting me. She'll worry."

Loco laughed at her.

"You act like you're twelve, or somethin'." Spits laughed. "Come on Margarita. Just call, and tell her you'll be a little late." He handed her his phone. "I really need you to do this for me."

She looked at him and knew that he was living her own dream and that this was her chance to get a taste of what she'd only imagined before.

"Okay I'll do it." She smiled as she'd never smiled before then took the phone and followed them to the car.

"Call ole boy and ask him who's winning the game." Loco told Spits as they left Salinas. He'd bet five hundred on Oregon to win the championship and wanted to check on his money. Margarita sat quietly staring out at the Gabilan mountains as they headed for Seaside half believing that she was dreaming.

She'd been singing since she was seven but only to herself. By the time she was ten, she'd stopped singing other peoples songs and started writing her own. Few people outside of her family had known that she could sing until she'd pumped herself up to perform at the open mic night she'd organized at the shelter. She was glad now that she had done so.

I can't believe this is happening to me. She thought with a secret smile. They reached the studio and found Mash and F sitting on the couch with beers watching the game.

"What's up F!" Spits smiled at seeing him. He shook F's hand and pulled him into a hug. "I ain't seen you since I got out of Y.A."

"Yeah, I just got out the pen my dang self." He looked Spits up and down. "You looking good homie. Mash let me hear some of the music Y'all recorded. You bout to blow up for real."

"Yeah, you know how we do. This is my homie Loco though." Spits said and turned to Loco "Loco, this is F and Mash."

"What's up chief." Loco said and shook their hands. "Let me get one of them beers."

He went to the washer where the case of Heinekens sat and grabbed two, handing one to Spits.

"Margarita, this is Mash. He's the one I been telling you about." Spits grabbed her elbow and pulled her away from the door where she stood nervously checking out the studio.

"Hi Mash." She shook the offered hand. "It's nice to meet you. I heard some of your music and I liked it a lot."

"Yeah, we doing our thing up in here." Mash said as he sat at his laptop and brought up the track list. "Spits told me that you had a good voice."

She smiled and looked at Spits. "I guess I do."

"Listen to this and tell me what you think."

"Okay. Can I have a beer first." She smiled at seeing the shocked looks on Loco and Spits faces. "What? I'm twenty two. Why you guys looking all surprised?"

"Cause you be actin like you mother Theresa that's why." Loco told her making her and Spits laugh at the truth of his words. The instrumental that Mash had selected was more horn than bass, giving it an R&B flavor. When it came on she smiled and nodded her to the beat, noticing that all eyes were on her. When Spits' verse came on and she listened to the lyrics her eyes darted to him. He looked away.

He's talking to me. She thought knowingly.

Closing her eyes, she pictured the two of them in Chinatown. Her working in the shelter and him hustling and sometimes coming inside to flirt with her.

I like this song. It's good. Better than good actually and I think I could write to this beat too.

When the track ended, she opened her eyes to find them still staring at her. She laughed and looked to Spits. "Dang. I'm already nervous and you staring at me isn't helping any."

"What do you think?" Mash asked her.

Tony Clincy

"I can do it." She said with a smile. "Do you have a pen and a note pad so I can write?"

"Yep. Right here." He handed her the paper and pen as she told Loco to scoot over so that she could sit next to him on the couch. The boys gathered around the washing machine to watch the game. It was the end of the third quarter and Auburn was up 19-13.

"I told you Cam Newton was gon' make it happen." Spits told Loco who was riding with the West Coast team all the way.

"Oregon gon' come back though. Watch what I tell you." Mash said and F agreed.

"Spits, you a trader."

"Naw. I'm just going with the money. Y'all better get off that crap." He answered and thought how true his words were in more ways than one. Though he had been speaking about the game, he knew that Mash needed to stay focused on them making music and get his mind off of that 'putting the hood on the map' stuff.

That fool better be trying to get his priorities straight. I'm trying to get rich.

\

Rap Star

BREAKING DOWN BARRIERS...

THE MORNING AFTER the late night studio session found Margarita in pure bliss. Sitting in the Dorothy's office staring at the papers on the desk, she replayed the nights events in her mind with a secret smile on her face. It had been her love of music that caused her to see a brighter future for the homeless whom she had dedicated her life to helping. So being there working at the shelter that day just seemed to mean so much more.

After writing and singing the hook and verse for Spits' single, Loco had opened his big mouth and told Mash about her own song she'd sang at the open mic night and also the one she'd sang for him and Spits.

"I'm telling you chief, Margarita got some tight songs." He'd said. Of course they all ganged up on her and she'd ended up recording the two songs to the beats Mash made after having her sing them a capella. In all, it had been the best night of her life and she'd gotten little sleep for laying in her bed thinking about how wonderful it had felt recording her songs.

She looked to the wall clock to check the time for the eightieth time, anxious for Spits to come and bring her a copy of the songs. She couldn't wait to let her family hear her singing on CD. She knew they'd be proud of her. She smiled picturing the smile on her mother's face when she played it for her.

"Excuse me Mija." A voice gravelly male voice called from the office door waking Margarita from her daydreams. "Can you put me on the shower list?"

She looked up smiling and found an older Hispanic man standing there. "Yes I can." She grabbed the clipboard off the desk and went to him. "I just need your name."

"My name is Juan Flores." He answered with flourish, bowing dramatically. The oversized and weatherworn coat he wore touched the floor. "And what is your name beautiful young lady?"

81

She smiled sweetly. "My name is Margarita."

"Aww. A lovely name for a lovely young woman."

"You got that right." Another voice added.

"Spits!" She jumped in excitement at seeing him. "Did you bring it?"

She checked his hands and they were empty so she looked to the pockets on the brown leather jacket her wore trying to see if she could spot the impression of a disc.

"Where's the CD?"

"It's in the car." He said and laughed at the confused look on her face while thinking that she looked as beautiful as ever with her lips pursed like that.

"What's so funny? Why is the CD in the car?" She asked then looked to Juan who stood there with a knowing look on his face. "Juan I'll call your name when it's your turn for the shower okay?"

"Not if she wants the CD she won't." Spits said winking his eye at Juan.

"Spits what are you up to man? Stop playing." She swatted his arm. "Go get the CD so I can listen to it."

He shook his head. "Nope. It's not gon' happen. You're gonna have to let me take you out for lunch if you want the CD. That's the deal so take it or leave it." He looked at his watch as if he had somewhere else to be.

"Come on man. I know you're not blackmailing me." She looked to him in wide eyed astonishment. "I can't believe you'd do that to me."

"Am I that ugly that you can't even have lunch with me?" He teased. "First you was telling me that I needed to get my life together. I did. And now you still won't let me take you out. What's up with that? I know you're hungry."

Margarita thought about it and knew he was right. It was because he was a drug dealer that she wouldn't go out with him before but he had left that life behind for good. She felt that she should at least give him a chance. She nodded her head.

"Okay. I'll go and have lunch with you but only because I'm hungry and I want the CD. So don't get the wrong idea." She smiled mischievously.

"Whatever. Just get somebody to cover for you so we can go."

As soon as they got inside of the Benz she reached for the CD player.

"Is it in here?" She asked then pushed play and smiled when the beat to their single 'Take A Chance On Me' came on. She got excited when her part came on and clapped her hands.

"Don't I sound good? I think I do. I love this song. Do you think we'll get radio play?"

"I think we got a number one hit on our hands."

He'd known from the moment that he'd heard her sing last night that her voice was just what this track had needed to put it over the edge. While Mash, Dame, and Tracy were all excited about the music he and Mash had recorded so far, he had been a little worried because although they had a lot of good material, he knew they'd need somethin' candy coated and watered down for the radio so they could go mainstream.

In his readings, he'd discovered that the real money in music was got by getting your songs in rotation because radio stations were required to pay the artists royalties for each spin. And with top ten songs receiving some three thousand spins a week while on the charts, Spits knew a lot of money was involved. Margarita had done him an even bigger favor than she knew and he planned on paying her back.

"Do you remember how you use to tell me that I needed to get out the game and do somethin' else with my life?"

"Yeah, I remember."

"Well that was good advice and I took it. Now I'm gonna give you some too. You need to get serious about your music Margarita. You've got a lot of talent. Even Mash thinks so. When I got back to the studio he was working on your tracks and he started talking about how he wanted to work with you on an album once we're finished with mine."

Her jaw dropped. "Are you serious? Don't play with me like that man."

He laughed at the look on her face figuring that he'd looked pretty much the same when Mash and Dame had first got at him about messing with music.

"I'm not playing with you. Why you think I wanted you to sing the hook for my song? You do sound good ma. You got this soft and sensuous thing going on with your voice and it's just sexy."

She blushed and swatted his arm. "You're just saying that."

Inwardly she was overjoyed at this. To hear that both Spits and Mash liked her music so much was a validation for what she'd always known in her heart. She knew she was good enough to sing professionally, though she was way too shy to ever really do it.

"Naw ma. I'm serious. You should think about it. Mash wants you to call him when you're ready."

"Okay. I'll think about it." She told him but knew that she wouldn't call because she was too much of a coward. Spits took her to Red Lobster and once seated, she wanted to know how he liked being a label owner. Margarita noticed how driven he was when they'd first met and she often wondered how he would handle making the transition from drug dealer to legitimate businessman.

"So what's it like being a big time record exec. I bet it's challenging."

"You don't even know."

He told her how he was going crazy trying to learn the ins and outs of the business. "I be so busy in the studio with Mash that I have to steal time to read up on the industry. The music business is all about paperwork and if you don't have your paperwork game up to par then you're setting yourself up for failure. So I'm just making sure that I put myself in position to win."

"Wow. That's great Spits. I'm so proud of you. I hope the music industry is kind to you." She brought a hand to her mouth to hide her smile. "I think you'll do good at the whole being a star thing. You have the being arrogant thing down pat already. When I first met you I use to laugh at how you carried yourself like you were the epitome of cool."

"Oh you got jokes huh?" He nodded his head showing that he could take a joke.

As they ate, he watched her closely thinking how right it felt to be here with her at this moment in his life. He wanted this from the moment he'd first looked into her huge doll-like eyes but hadn't felt confident enough to make a serious effort in courting her because though he'd never admit it, a part of him had felt that he wasn't worthy of her. She was too good for a guy like him.

"So how do you feel about making a video for our song and doing a few shows to promote it once it drops? I'm pretty sure that it's gonna be the first single from my album."

The question caught her off guard even though she'd known that the song was a hit before she even wrote her verses. She couldn't say she was too surprise by his question, she just hadn't thought that far ahead.

"I don't know Spits. I mean- I can't- I." She laughed at herself knowing she looked silly. "I don't know. I'll have to think about that one."

She immediately regretted what she said because every part of her being wanted to scream out yes.

Why didn't you say yes! Tell him you'll do it before he changes his mind!

Spits tried to hide his disappointment and failed. "I really need you to do this for me Margarita. 'Take a Chance on Me' is the best song we've got and it's perfect for the radio."

He looked away and stared at the passing cars along Main Street. He figured that maybe she was hesitant to spend too much of her time doing the whole music thing because she was so passionate about her work at Dorothy's. He understood this but at the same time he couldn't do this without her.

"Look. I know you love what you're doing at Dorothy's but look at it like this. When the song blows up you'll be famous and can use your fame to advocate for the homeless."

Margarita laughed at this. "Oh, you're good."

She thought about what he'd said though and knew that he spoke the truth. But as bad as she wanted to tell him that she would do it, she knew that she was too self conscious to make a habit of singing in front of people. It was hard enough for her to muster up the nerve just to sing in front of him and Mash the other day.

Spit sat watching the changing emotions on her face, hoping beyond hope that she would agree to at least make the video. They could do the live shows without her if it came to it but for the video they'd definitely need her. She read the worry in his face and made up her mind.

"Okay I'll do it." Margarita laughed suddenly full of joy. A music career would be the fulfillment of her deepest inner passion and she would remember this day as being one of the happiest of her life. The day that she finally stood up to her fears and decided to chase her lifelong dream.

HOME SWEET HOME…

"MAKE SURE THAT you don't drop that desk!" Tracy snapped at the two movers carrying the desk into the building. "That's five thousand dollars right there."

One of the movers made a smart comment under his breath and she rushed up to him pointing.

"What did you say?"

"We got this mam." The oldest of the six movers promised. "I know you want everything to make it upstairs and it will. We do this for a living, so just trust us to do the job that you paid us to do."

"Yeah. Just make sure that don't nothin' get broke." She turned away leaving the movers to finish unloading the office furniture from the three trucks at the curb. Last week her and Janet had found the perfect office space for them in the heart of Downtown Monterey and so having already ordered their office furniture, she'd wasted no time getting things rolling.

"Hi Tracy." Janet said from the ladder where she stood painting the Paper Chasin' Records Logo on the reception room wall. She waved to Tracy as she stepped off of the elevator and into their reception area.

"Hey girl." She stopped to look at the logo which was a frightened hundred dollar bill running. "That's nice girl. Good job."

"Thanks."

"Where's Candice?" Tracy asked as she headed towards the back offices in search of the recently hired secretary.

"She went to get somethin' to eat for the movers."

"Are you 'bout ready to go to the studio?"

Tracy had Janet set up a YouTube account last night and had told her to be ready to film some footage for them to post today.

"I wanted to talk to Candice but I'll have to get with her later. We need to get to the studio and get this footage."

"Yeah. Just let me wash my hands and grab the camera then we can go." Janet climbed from the ladder and left down the hall to the bathroom. They were soon in Tracy's car heading to Seaside.

"When we get there don't listen to Spits if he says he don't want to do it. He's just shy. Once you start filming, he'll get use to it."

Janet giggled and Tracy joined her. "Them boys is gonna get tired of you always bullying them Tracy. You know that don't you?"

"No they ain't. They like for me to tell them what to do. Shoot, They *need* me to tell them what to do. That's why Dame asked me to help him do this because they need me to keep em in line."

"I want to thank you again for hiring me. I love working with you guys."

"Ain't no need to thank me girl. You were the best person for the job and the guys love you too."

"I can't wait till we release some of Spits' music. I've been around the music business for a long time and he's the hottest rapper hands down. I mean his wordplay is out of this world. I like how he comes across so cocky." Janet beamed.

"Yeah." Tracy agreed and nodded her head. "Now if we can get his butt to come across as cocky in front of that camera, we'll be alright."

"Do you think it's gonna be a problem?" Janet asked.

"Not really. He's driven and he knows that we have to do this. So I'm betting that he'll be okay."

Tracy thought about telling Spits and Mash that she would be coming through today to film them for YouTube but had changed her mind thinking that it would be best if this were a spur of the moment thing. That way Spits wouldn't have a lot of time to worry about having a camera all up in his face.

"That boy was born to be famous." Tracy added.

When they arrived at the studio, Tracy wasted no time in barging in, turning on the lamp and announcing that they had work to do.

"Where's Spits at?" She asked Mash since she didn't see him in the garage. "Dame told me that you guys were here recording."

"What you up to now?" Mash asked from his chair looking from her to Janet who was standing by the door holding a black duffel bag. "You always coming up in here disturbing our groove and crap. We got an album to finish remember?"

She waved this off. "Where's he at?"

"He's using the bathroom."

"Okay." She pointed to a spot on the floor. "Janet, you can plug up the lights right there. Go ahead and get set up and when Spits finishes we'll get this poppin'."

Mash stood with a big smile lighting up his face when he saw the camera. "What we filming for?" He asked making his way to Janet to take a look at the equipment.

"Janet set us up a page on YouTube last night and we're gonna film you guys working in the studio and post it when we drop the first mixtape next week.

"That's what I'm talking about right there." He took off his shirt. "Make sure you get my tats. We bout to put the hood on the map round here. Watch what I tell you."

When Spits opened the door and saw Tracy standing there with her arms crossed he knew somethin' was wrong.

"Aww man." He complained as he stepped down the steps and saw Janet setting up the lights and camera. "Tracy you always be on some crap."

"Whatever. Just get your black behind ready to be famous. We've got a YouTube page and we need some footage to post up."

She pulled him by the door to talk in private.

"Don't worry baby. You'll do fine. This is what you were born to do. This is your dream and it's time to turn it into a reality." Tracy told him softly. He nodded his head that he understood and turned to watch Janet positioning the lights.

"It's cool. I got this, don't even trip." He told Tracy.

Mash did twenty five push-up's and got up. "Come on Janet, get me while I'm pumped up. Make sure you can see the Hood Life on my arm though."

Spits laughed and told Tracy. "Mash bout to get on his Hood Life crap and everybody gon' think we banging on wax. Let me go do this." He walked to where Mash crowded Janet.

"Wait Mash. Let me set it up first." Janet was having problems getting the camera's battery to fit in properly. "I don't think it's the right one. "

"Here let me help you girl." Tracy took the camera, snapped in the battery then handed it back.

Janet put the camera to her eye. "It's working now." She turned to Spits. "Come on. Say somethin'."

"What it do YouTube? This ya boy Spits and I'm in here chilling up in the Blue Room, my homeboy/producer's studio."

He pointed to Mash and Janet put the camera on him.

"What's up chief?" Mash said and threw up Seaside with his fingers. "Seaside's in the house, Hood Life! Paper Chasin' Records bout put the rap game on lock." He stood suddenly extra hyphy and animated. "Yeah. Y'all the first ones to get a taste of my boy Spits and them Central Coast Spits soprano's we been in here putting together. All you other rappers better take this as a warning, Spits is coming for the rap throne."

"That's right." Spits agreed and waved his hand as if it was nothin'. "A legend in the making. But I don't think they ready for it though Mash. I wouldn't even do it to em but you and Dame stepped to me with a offer I couldn't refuse. So I'm at 'em."

Tracy stood back beaming, her smile bright enough to keep the garage lit when she turned the lamp off drowning the garage into midnight blue.

"That's the homegirl Tracy, changing stuff up like she always be doing." They all laughed at this. "But that's how we be doing it up in the homeboy's studio. We keeps it blue round here."

"Step in the booth and show YouTube that you a beast at this rap thang homie." Mash sat at the computer and started searching his tracks as Spits walked inside the booth with Janet right behind him.

Tracy called Dame with the news. "He did it! I knew that boy wouldn't let us down. I knew it."

Dame laughed hard. "You always be trying to take credit for somethin'. You ain't know nothin' girl. I put you up on it."

She couldn't do nothin' but laugh at the truth of his words. "So what. That's my little brother."

After she told him that they'd be able to move into the office in three days, Dame grunted and mumbled "Good. I'm tired of this damn forest smellin' room you got me stuck in."

"Bye Dame. I love you." Tracy laughed and hung up to watch her little brother put on an Oscar winning performance.

Tony Clincy

THE MOVEMENT...

LOCO POPPED SPITS on the back of his head from the back seat. "This is fixin' to be tight."

Spits turned around and tried to pop him back but Loco blocked the blows while laughing. "Quit playing."

"Shut up square." Loco told him. "For realz though. There's all kinda bad chicks up at San Jose State. I'm 'bout to come up watch."

Tracy took her eyes off the road just long enough to roll them in the rearview at him.   "Troy, don't be acting a fool when we get there. We going out here to work so you can't be distracting him okay."

"Ain't nobody thinking 'bout Y'all. I'm fixin' to shake the spot and go do the Loco. You got me messed up if you think I'm 'bout to be hanging around watchin' y'all."

The three of them were in the Benz on their way to San Jose State, the first stop on their three college tour to promote the release of the first 'Legend in The Making' mixtape. Mash was following in his Chevy along with the four girls who made up their street team. In the trunks of the two cars were 5000 CD's, T-shirts, posters and flyers which they would be giving away during the trip.

One of Janet's contacts had put Tracy in touch with the program directors of the schools radio stations and she'd gotten them to promote the events and schedule 'on air' time for Spits to make guest appearances with the DJ's.

Spits sat staring out at the passing the green grassy hillsides along Highway 101 trying his best not to show his nervousness. He'd *just* gotten over his camera shyness, at least he thought he'd gotten over it, and wasn't as sure as everybody else that he was ready to face the public just yet. As usual, Tracy hadn't given him a choice nor a warning, only charged into the studio announcing that they had business to take care of and they needed to get packed so they could go on a three city promotional tour in the Bay Area.

92

"Come on you guys," She'd said looking at her watch and smiling. "We got paper to chase around here. Turn that stuff off and get it movin'."

Glancing at Spits now, Tracy knew that his nerves were on a razors edge. "You okay baby?"

She reached out and rubbed his head. By now she knew him well enough to be able to recognize when he was nervous even when he tried to pretend he wasn't. But she also knew that once the lights came on, he would go for his like the star she knew him to be. In getting to know him, she'd come to see just how strong his will to succeed was and so had little doubt about him being nervous right now. Spits looked to her and returned her smile with a nod.

"I'm good. Just trying to pump myself up to do this. Why? Do I look nervous or somethin?"

"No. And You'll be okay too. Don't worry, they're gonna love you. Especially the girls with your lil' cute black self." She assured him.

He turned back to look at the mountains thinking about how hectic things had become. Between the marathon studio sessions, filming for You Tube, prepping to film the video for 'Take a chance on me' and rehearsals for his debut concert and album release, this was the last position he would've thought he'd find himself in had he been asked a few months ago. He was still trying to figure this whole 'being a star' thing out but he knew that whatever happened, he would win at this. Period.

His phone rang and he saw Margarita's number on the screen and smiled.

"Hello…How you doing ma?… No, I'm on my way to San Jose and a couple other colleges to promote the mixtape…I didn't know myself. Tracy came through on her bullcrap…We'll be back in-"

"Who's that?" Tracy asked at hearing her name. "Who you saying my name to and trying to sound all sexy for?"

93

"This square probably talking to Margarita. You know he took her out to lunch the other day." Loco said grinning.

This got Tracy's attention. "You did!" She looked at Spits with wide eyes. "Why didn't you tell me? Hi Margarita!" She yelled.

"Can't you see me on the phone? Dang." He complained with a look of annoyance.

"Boy please." Tracy waved him off and reached for the phone. "Let me talk to her."

He switched the phone to his other ear. "Let me call you back Margarita… Yeah. Tracy and Loco's playing right now… okay, bye." He hung up and gave Tracy, then Loco a look which they laughed at.

"You know you gon' have to give me all the details don't you?" Tracy asked with her girlish giggle.

"Don't even trip. I already got the whole scoop." Loco promised to Spits' annoyance. They reached the campus thirty minutes later and found Pierre, the program director along with three of the stations DJ's at a table in front of the student center. The CD Tracy had sent was already blasting from the speakers atop the table. There was a crowd of both teachers and students surrounding the table enjoying the music and awaiting their arrival.

"You must be Pierre." Tracy said to the tall, dark, twenty something year old man with the short afro. "I'm Tracy, and this is our star right here."

Pierre took the offered hand. "It's nice to finally meet you Tracy." He stepped back and look Spits from head to toe. "I was wondering what you looked like. I've been listening to your CD over and over. You guys are about to be big. Ain't nobody seeing you in the rap game right now."

"And this is Mash, our producer." Tracy said pulling Mash's sleeve to get his attention away from the three girls he was flirting with.

"Man your beats ain't no joke." Pierre shook Mash hand and then led them around the table where they would sit.

94

"You like my stuff huh?"

"Heck yeah. I can't wait to see how you guys blow up once you drop an album and video on the public." He told him.

Tracy left Spits and Mash with Pierre and huddled up with the street team to make sure that they understood exactly what she wanted them to do. Loco left to chase females.

The lunch hour saw the front of the student center grow crowded as students gathered to see what all the noise was about. Sitting at the table talking to the students who'd been listening to their music on the schools station, Spits found himself in his element. Seeing the love in the people's faces and hearing them say how much they liked his music gave him a high which he could never have imagined.

This is tight right here. He thought remembering how the CO's in prison use to look at him and the other inmates as if they were less than human.

"What's that say on your chest?" An Asian girl asked Mash pointing to the ink peeking from the top of his white wife beater.

"It says Seaside." He told her proudly smiling as he stood and took off the shirt exposing all his tats to the girls in the crowd. He pointed to the seahorse. "That's where we from and this is the city mascot."

"They call me Spits because I be spittin' game." Spits explained to a pretty light skinned girl who was doing all she could to give him a peek at the miles of cleavage at the top of her hot pink cut off shirt.

"I wanna hear you say a rap right now." She said sexily.

"Yeah!" Someone else put in. "Say a rap for us now Spits."

Spits looked to Tracy behind him and she raised her hands in the air like 'What do you want me to do?' before smiling and walking away leaving him to deal with his fans.

FOR THE WORLD TO SEE...

THE SALINAS POLICE department had Chinatown blocked off for the filming of the 'Take A Chance on Me'. Dorothy's place was closed and the usual homeless who hung on the block had been cleared out except for those who volunteered to be extras.

Spits, Margarita, Mash, and Tracy were inside of Dorothy's along with Eric Moberg, the video's director. After having met with Spits last month to hear his vision for the video, Eric had come here with his assistants to get a take on the layout.

"Look Spits," Eric said. "I think I know just how you want to play this. Like I told you when we spoke the other day, me and my team came down here, took a look around and I got the chance to see the environment you use to sell your drugs in."

They followed Eric outside to the front of Dorothy's. "What I want to do is have you, Loco, and Mash stand over there on the sidewalk." He pointed across the street where two of his assistants were explaining to the extras what they would be doing when they began filming. "Spits will be standing against that building rapping while on the lookout for the police with occasional glances over here to where Margarita's working."

He turned to Spits who nodded that he understood. "Okay. Now Mash and Loco. We're gonna have cars pulling up to the curb and the two of you will be taking turns going up to the cars and pretending to sell them drugs."

Again he walked inside of Dorothy's stopping at the front door and pointing to the ground. "When we film you Margarita, I want you here staring across the street with a troubled look on your face as you sing the hook. For your verse, we'll follow you around the shelter as you assist people."

Tracy sat at the top of the block with Dame and Janet watching the crew work. A look of irritation was etched on her face from Dame's constant complaining about how long this was taking.

"Will you be quiet for a second Dame?" She snapped.

"Heck naw. They need to hurry up with this crap. All these fools getting' paid by the hour on my dollar. Heck naw I won't shut up. Eric needs to get this show on the road so we can get off this raggedy street."

"Come on Janet." Tracy said and stood. "Let's leave this penny-pinching, ungrateful, stupid, dull man by his dang self."

"Yeah, take Y'all butts on then." He yelled at their backs. "You just talking that crap 'cause ain't none of this coming out of your pockets."

Try as he might, Dame just couldn't find it in himself to not trip on seeing his money being spent. Intellectually, he'd known that he'd be spending hundreds of thousands before it began coming back to him but he found the actuality of it to be much harder to accept than the thought had been.

Money meant everything to Dame and he could care less what people thought about it. Money had been good to him and as he came up in the streets amongst snakes, schemers, and shifty people, he learned long ago to trust only in that almighty dollar.

Eric stood across the street in front of Dorothy's watching Spits lean against the one story building and spit his first verse while Mash and Loco stood at the curb looking like they were hustling. He waved to one of his assistance and signaled for him to send the first car down. When the car drove up and pulled to the car in front of them, Loco leaned into the passenger window and handed the driver a package then stood counting money as the car drove off. Three more customers walked up and Mash served them as Spits looked out for the police. When Spits was done with his verses, Eric stopped filming and had his crew set up to film Margarita.

Spits stood outside watching the things going on around him and knew that he was in the perfect position to catch fame by the tail and ride it to the stars. He vowed yet again that he would be the best thing the rap game had ever seen.

Tracy was right. I am a star. And I'm 'bout to shine brighter than a mug too. He vowed to himself. When Eric called it a wrap, they all drove to Margarita's mother's house for the huge dinner she had cooked in celebration of her only daughters good fortune.

"Mom, I did it!" Margarita ran into her smiling mother's arms. "I can't believe it mom! I'm gonna be on TV!"

Her mother had cooked a variety of Mexican dishes which she'd set out on two wooden picnic tables in the backyard. Margarita, with her arm around her mom's waist, led everybody out back where her brothers, nieces and father were.

"Ah, there's my little princess." Her father's smile spoke of his love for her more than any words ever could, as did the proud look on his face when she ran to his arms. Spits and the rest of the team stood watching as Margarita's family made a fuss over her.

"Come meet my parents guys." Margarita said after a moment suddenly remembering her manners. "Mom, this is Spits. He's the one-"

"I know his mother didn't name him Spits." Her mother cut her off while smiling at Spits. "Now tell me what your name is young man. Because we don't use nicknames in this house." She shot Margarita's brothers a look when she said the last part.

"My name's Deandre mam. That's what my mom named me." He stuck his hand out but she stepped forward and grabbed him into a hug.

"Thank you for making my daughter's dream come true." She whispered in his ear before turning him loose.

"Now come on and eat everybody. I know you're all hungry. There's plenty of food and drink."

Dame sat back in his chair with a cigar hanging from the side of his mouth. He was glad that they'd finally finished filming after ten hours. Despite all he was talking earlier, he knew in his heart that he was standing on the brink of having some real money that would make what he had now look like Monopoly money.

I did this. He thought, forgetting that it had been a team effort which had gotten them this far. *They gon' be talking about how I blew up for years. This is goin' down in the hustler's history book.*

He sat there listening to the conversations going on around him with a smug look on his face while mentally spending the millions that would soon be sitting in his bank account.

Tony Clincy

BIG MONEY. BIGGER MOVES...

DAME WAS GRINNING from ear to ear as he reclined in his black Italian leather chair with his feet resting atop his mahogany wood half moon wrap around desk. He had the top distribution company on the west coast, Nationwide Records, CEO Tyrone Hudgins on the phone wanting to do business. A friend of a friend of Janet's had passed Tyrone a CD full of Spits' sopranos and had told him about what Paper Chasin' Records was doing. And Tyrone sounded anxious to work out a deal.

"Look Dame, I'm not gonna lie to you. I like what I'm hearing about your camp and we're interested in doing business with you. As you already know, the business side of this industry is all about the numbers. So why don't you throw a number out there and we'll see what we can agree on."

Dame wasted no time in answering. "Well, you've got to respect my position right now Tyrone. From where I'm sittin', we looking pretty damn good right? We got the best thing that happened to music since Michael Jackson. With the numbers we did independently with the mixtapes and the single and video that we have waiting on deck, I think we can pretty much write our own ticket. Like you said, it's all about the numbers homie."

Tyrone agreed. "Since I'm the one calling you, I'm not even gonna argue the point. Why don't you just give me some idea of the type of situation you're looking for and I'll let you know if we can get you there."

Dame lit a cigar and stood to look out his window to the bay. "I've already had three calls this week from other distributors who wanna do business with us. But again, like you said, it's all about the numbers. And I ain't heard the right one yet. Once I do, I'll sign a deal rather it's with Nationwide or somebody else."

Tracy came storming into the office looking irritated. Dame held up a finger telling her to be quiet and pointed to the intercom sitting on his desk.

"I hear you Dame." Tyrone said and they could hear papers shuffling in the background. "Just give me a second and I'll throw something out there and see if you can live with it."

Tracy raised her eyebrows questioningly and Dame smiled while rubbing his thumb and index finger together. She sat on top of the desk and let her gaze settle on one of the expensive African pieces hanging on the wall.

"You still with me Dame?"

"Yeah I'm here."

"Okay look. First of all, I agree with you about Spits being the best thing to happen to music for the past couple of decades. The way you guys put Northern Cali on lock so fast is a testament to his marketability." Again they heard papers shuffling. "What do you say we go ten million for a two album deal. We'll handle the distribution and help with the promotions and we do a fifty-fifty split on the back end. You've already done an impressive job in putting your music and the Paper Chasin' brand out there independently. But just imagine how more much exposure you'll get with us behind you using our muscle to push your music."

Dame and Tracy shared a smile and high five. Sitting back down and puffing on his cigar, Dame told Tyrone that he'd have to run it by his team and get back at him in a couple of hours.

"Okay. Why don't you take my cell number and hit me as soon as you make your decision and I'll have my attorney fax you the paperwork."

Dame took down the number and hung up the phone smiling. "Cha-Ching." He said with a kool-aid grin plastered across his face. "We did it Trace."

"You dang right we did." She stood and begun talking animatedly about what this meant for the label. "We've got some muscle now. We can push him out there in a big way with Nationwide on our side. Ten million dollars for two albums. We can't beat that Dame. We did it."

Dame stood and looked out his window at the boats docked at the wharf just across the street and wondered how long it would take for him to cop the yacht he'd always wanted.

"Five million. I'm fixin' to go big on 'em for realz now. They thought I was stuntin' before, just wait till we get that check."

The smile left Tracy's face at hearing this. She was confused as to what he meant.

"What you mean five million? He just said ten."

"I'm the one who put up the money for this crap." He answered. "It's only right that I get a bigger piece of the pie."

Had he been facing her and see look of disgust on her face, he would have thought better about finishing that sentence.

"You know what? You are one, no good, thirsty old guy Dame."

The rage in her voice more so than the words made him turn to face her and he found her staring daggers at him with murder in her eyes.

"I won't sit by and let you do those boys wrong Dame." She shook her head violently. "I won't!"

"Tracy ain't nobody trying to-"

"I won't dangit!"

She slapped her hand down on the dark desk causing the intercom and phone to fall. She walked to him pointing, stopping inches from his nose, her eyes fiery-green and full of anger.

"I swear to God that I will never in life speak to you again if you don't do right by those boys. What in the world is wrong with you? Don't you have any loyalty to anything besides money?" She shook her head. "I can't believe you."

Tracy spun and stomped to the door, slamming it so hard on her way out that one of his paintings fell and crashed to the ground. Dame was left standing there in shock at how angry she'd been and scared of losing his only real friend. After regaining his composure, he took a deep breath and walked through the side door connecting his office to the conference room where everybody was waiting on him to start the meeting.

When Dame opened the door and walked in, all eyes were on him as he went straight to the window with his back to the room. Spits and Mash shared a look. Tracy stared straight ahead to the label's logo.

"What's up unc?" Mash looked to Tracy as he spoke. He wasn't used to them fighting and it scared him. "Tracy, what's up?"

She kept staring at the logo.

They'd all come today to discuss the upcoming V.I.P only album release party and concert at the Fox California Theater in Old Town Salinas two weeks from now. They were all excited that their hard work had paid off. The Central Coast and Bay Area loved Spits. And everyone in the room was proud of the work they'd done to make it so.

Or they had been before Tracy had come in slamming the door. Dame turned around, his hurt eyes sweeping the room, stopping on Tracy and noticing the veins in her neck throbbing. He took his seat and stared down to the other end of the table at Spits.

"I just got off the phone with Tyrone at Nationwide Records. They offered us ten million for two albums and a fifty-fifty split of the profits."

Mash stood smiling at Spits, all thoughts of Dame and Tracy's attitudes forgotten. "We did it homie. What did I tell you? Didn't I tell you that you had it chief?!"

They met each other half way and hugged.

"Thank you homie. You were right. You changed my life for me chief. Thank you." Spits whispered in a voice full of emotion. He'd known from the start that Mash was the main reason his life had went from filth to fabulous overnight but until now there had always been the fear that it could all disappear just as suddenly as it had materialized.

Spits looked at Tracy and the joy she saw in his eyes made her smile. 'We did it.' He mouthed and she nodded her head while wiping the tears from her eyes. She was happy for him most of all.

"Okay look." Dame said getting down to business. There was too much emotion in the room he wanted it put aside so they could discuss the Nationwide offer. "We need to decide what we're gonna do. I-"

"Ain't nothin' to decide unc. Ten million dollars decides for itself. I say we take it."

"Me too." Spits agreed.

"Me too." Dame said smiling. "I'll call Tyrone when we're done and have him fax the contract to Frank so he can go over it."

Dame looked to Tracy and she looked away.

"Now what? Do we stick to the script. Or do we do somethin' different?" Spits asked.

"Why should we?" Mash asked. "Everything's in place. KDON's announcing the concert, the street teams working the Bay, all of the invites done went out. We all good."

"Naw we better than good." Spits corrected.

This deal changed everything. They'd gotten themselves into just the position they'd mapped out and on schedule. They could go big now and really move the crowd.

"I say we make some moves. Bigger moves than we'd planned to." Spits said.

Janet scooted to the edge of her seat and picked up a pen. "What do mean?"

Spits shook his head. "I don't know. I haven't thought that far ahead. But now that we got all this money we should stunt. We should show everybody that we chasin' paper, you know."

Janet nodded her head. "You're right. That's what our name's about and we should turn our swagger all the way past one thousand just like you be doing in your songs."

"How about a block party?" Tracy suggested. She was all business now. "We can get a permit from the city and set up jumbo screens outside of the Fox and treat the people who supported us from the gate to a free concert."

"Now that's a good idea." Janet said as she began writing on her legal pad. "We can provide food and drinks and announce it as a thanks to the Central Coast and Bay Area."

"We only got two weeks to put the word out and get everything together." Dame reminded them.

"I think that as long as we handle the security, the city will give us the permit. They ain't gonna want to miss out on the all that tax money. I'll call Robert at the security firm and have him draw up a plan to present to the city." Tracy said not quite meeting Dame's eyes.

"And I'll get with KDON when we're done here." Janet said.

"What about me and Mash?" Spits asked.

Dame threw his head back and laughed. "Y'all just stay yo behinds in that garage making that music. We got this."

"How are rehearsals coming?" Janet asked

"We good." Mash answered and smirked at Spits. "He's still hecka uncomfortable on stage but we'll be ready though."

"How's the album coming along?" Tracy asked him.

"I'm almost done mixing it. Don't sweat that. We already got all the tracks we need and then some." Again he looked at Spits. "There's something else though."

"What is it homie?"

"We need to be trying to talk Margarita into signing with us. If I can get her in the studio for a month, we'll have two back to back multi-platinum albums."

Dame's eyes turned to dollar signs. "Is she really that good?"

"Better." Mash assured him. "That hook and verse she did for 'Take a Chance on Me' wasn't a fluke unc. She's a bona-fide star, even if she don't know it herself."

"Are you sure?"

"Come on unc. You don't trust me yet? I wasn't wrong about Spits was I?"

Dame looked at Spits and back to Mash. "But he's different. He's-"

"Nope," Mash shook his head, "same stuff. She got it too. Whatever you wanna call what he got; talent, skill, expertise, whatever. We can't lose with her."

Dame looked to Spits who had stood and was staring out to the ocean with his back to the room.

"I don't know if she'll do it." Spits said.

"What do you mean?" Dame asked him. "She's a singer ain't she? How could she not want a recording contract?"

Spits turned and explained how hard it had been to convince her to do what she'd already committed to.

"She doesn't like the limelight. She's real private." He shook his head with a look of hopelessness on his face. "No. I don't think she'll do it."

Everybody looked to Tracy.

"What?" She smiled. "She's his girlfriend. What do you want me to do?"

"Make her butt sign the contract." Spits suggested and they all laughed. "You sure don't have no problem making everybody else do stuff."

"Okay. I'll go out there and talk to her when we're finished here."

Dame stood. "Then you better be going because we're done. I gotta call Tyrone and get this deal signed."

"And me and Spits gotta get back to the Blue Room and make us some more money." Mash said smiling at Spits as he stood and made ready to leave.

ULTERIOR MOTIVES...

TRACY HAD OTHER reasons for rushing out to Salinas besides trying to convince Margarita to sign with Paper Chasin'. She was going to talk to her about Spits. She knew that he liked Margarita a lot and after having met her, Tracy felt that she was just what Spits needed in his life. A good down to earth female to keep him away from the hundreds of groupies who would soon be throwing panties at him every time he stepped outside.

When they'd first met, Tracy had been a bit skeptical of her, finding her a bit too timid for her taste. But in watching her deal with the homeless drug addicts in Chinatown during the video shoot, Tracy realized that what she first thought was a weakness had more to do with Margarita being wary of strangers than her being fearful of them.

Spits was taking too long as far as Tracy was concerned. He'd finally told her about their little lunch date and from what he'd said, he hadn't gotten any closer to getting with her.

I got a little something for him though. She thought while giggling as she pictured the look on Spits face when he found out what she was about to do. Tracy got to the block and found the street jam-packed with homeless drug addicts, drunk's and the vultures who came here to prey on them. The time she'd spent here during the video shoot had did little to prepare her for the utter hopelessness she saw in these people's eyes. She got the feeling that these lost souls were standing around waiting on something, not sure what, like newly freed victims of a holocaust.

After parking in front of Dorothy's Place and getting out, she stopped in her tracks. Her gaze was drawn to the group of addicts sitting on old milk crates smoking crack like it was perfectly legal. Watching the group, a chill went through her as she fully understood just what her little brother had escaped from.

"Do you need anything?" A scraggly looking, clearly drunk forty-something year old white lady asked her.

"No, I'm okay." Tracy said and hurried through the door. She couldn't help but laugh at the shocked look on Margarita's face as she saw her from the office. Tracy waved and made her way to the office breathing through her mouth so she wouldn't have to smell the heavy body odor in the air.

"What are you doing here?" Margarita asked hugging her when she stepped inside the office. "Is there a problem with the video?"

"No. The video's fine. I came to talk to you about something else."

Confused and curious, Margarita offered her a seat before sitting herself. She sat nervously wringing her hands as she waited for Tracy to tell her what this was about.

Tracy dug through her purse. "Just give me a second girl. Let me find this damn granola bar real quick. I ain't ate nothing all day."

"It's okay."

Margarita's heart pounded in her chest. She knew why Tracy was there. She had been expecting for them to ask her to sign a recording contract. Truthfully, she'd expected for Spits to be the one to ask but wasn't all that surprised that he'd sent Tracy since she had given him such a hard time about doing the video.

After having listened to 'Take a Chance on Me' and the other songs her and Mash recorded, she was convinced that she was good enough to be a pro singer and had been thinking of little else the past few weeks. The dilemma she found herself facing was that she really did love working at the shelter, it fulfilled her like nothing else did. She knew that the her work mattered here, that she was making a difference in these people's lives and this allowed her to sleep really good at night.

But music was her passion and when she sang, she went to this beautifully blissful place within herself. Music was how she expressed herself best, how she quieted the storms which threatened to rage within her. And so she hadn't been able to decide how she would react when they got around to asking her to become a part of the Paper Chasin' family.

"You know why I'm here don't you?" Tracy asked at seeing how nervous Margarita was. "You're sitting there about to snap one of your fingers out of socket you're so nervous." She smiled and took one of Margarita's hands in hers. "Spits told me that he didn't think you'd want a music career. Does fame frighten you that much girl?"

"No. I-well-I can't leave-I-"

Margarita laughed at herself and let out a deep breath as she sat back in her chair, her eyes looking to the ceiling.

"I'm not scared of fame. Do I want to be famous? I don't know. I do love singing, but I can live without the fame."

"But do you love singing enough to sign with us? I just left from a meeting and Mash was pushing us to sign you."

"He was?" Margarita smiled. She liked Mash. They had vibed at the studio session and if she were to take the time to put in the necessary hours, she'd be an unstoppable force.

"Yeah, he did. He told Dame that he thought you had just as much talent as Spits and that we'd basically be fools not to sign you to a contract. So here I am."

Tracy watched Margarita closely as her face became a mask of concentration. Her silky dark hair framed her face giving her an angelic appearance as it flowed gently onto her shoulders. Her dark, thick eyebrows were drawn up as she decided what she would tell Tracy.

"Okay." She said opening her eyes and nodding her head. "I'll do it. I've been dreaming of being a singer all my life and although I never really thought that I ever would be one, that opportunity is in my face. I'd be a fool to let the chance past me by."

A knock on the door got their attention and Margarita stood to answer it.

"Hold on Tracy."

"They're ready for you in the kitchen Margarita." The tall, skinny white guy told her when she opened it.

"Okay, I'll be there in a sec." She closed the door. "I've got to go and help prepare lunch." She looked at her watch. "We feed in an hour and there's about three hundred sandwiches with my name written on them. Can we talk about this later?"

Tracy stood smiling. "How about I help you make those sandwiches? We can talk about you signing with us later but I wanted to talk to you about something else too."

"You do? What?"

"You and Spits." Tracy said in all seriousness. "I want to talk to you about you guys' relationship."

"What relationship? We're just friends. Who told you that we were in a relationship?"

Tracy gave her a devious grin. "Nobody told me nothing. I just wanna make sure my little brother's happy and I think that you're the right girl for him. So I'm playing matchmaker today." She paused and brought her hand to her chin as if in thought. "You do know that he has a big ol' crush on you don't you? Do you like him too? And why ain't Y'all together?"

Margarita laughed. "Now I see what he was talking about. You are a piece of work."

"I sure am. And I guess he told you that it was a waste of time trying not to tell me what I want to know then too."

Margarita laughed again. "Come on. We've got to make those sandwiches." She opened the door then turned to Tracy smiling. "But we can talk about me and Spits while we're making them."

A TOAST TO THE FANS...

SPOTLIGHTS SCREAMED 'SPITS! Live in
Concert' into the night sky, calling out to Central Coast rap
fans like a beacon and drawing them to Old Town Salinas by
the thousands.

Some five thousand fans from Sacramento to Seattle
had come invading the downtown area, leaving it bursting at
the seams and filling the air with an electric buzz. They were
packed shoulder to shoulder in the Steinbeck Center's
parking lot where the three jumbo screens were set up. There
were also booths set up where free food and drink's were
being given away. Janet had hired thirty girls to run around
with skimpy shorts and shirts passing out Paper Chasin' party
favors to the fans.

Banners hung from the light posts all throughout Old
Town with pictures of Spits and the Paper Chasin' logo,
flapping in the gentle springtime wind. The restaurants, bars
and clubs were doing brisk business on this night. Old Town
had never seen the likes of an event this special. Paper
Chasin' Records had went all out tonight sparing no expense
in making sure that the concert would be one for the ages.

The fans were proud of having a homegrown rapper
good enough to finally shine the spotlight upon the Central
Coast. For tonight everybody put their differences to the side
to enjoy this historic moment. They were anxious to see Spits
perform for the first time.

Fat Daddy, Spits' and Mash's big homie, stood center
stage in the Fox playing MC in an all white tuxedo.

"Y'all should meet my nephew Mark." He said
pointing to the balcony and the spotlight found Mark standing
against the railing smiling.

"That boy right there's a trick for realz. But he's cold
with his trickin' though. Ain't no shame in his game. He'll
pop at your broad right in front of you like it's cool. The
other day I watched him ask this square ol' white boy if he

could sleep with his girl for a hundred dollars. And he was serious as heck."

The crowd laughed and broke into applause when Mark pulled out his wallet and waved it in the air while pointing at different women and nodding his head.

Backstage in the dressing room, Spits sat with a jittery Margarita and a fussy Tracy counting down the seconds before the show was to begin.

"Don't worry girl." Tracy gave Margarita's shoulder a gentle squeeze. "They're gonna love you out there. You guys have been rehearsing everyday for the past three weeks. You'll knock it out the park. And you look lovely."

Margarita wore a white flower print summer dress and sandals, her hair fell freely onto her shoulders and she had on little makeup.

"Yeah you do." Spits agreed thinking that she looked as beautiful as he'd ever seen her. "You look like an angel girl." She looked to him and smiled. "Plus, this is what we been dreaming about all our lives. Tonight's about making our dreams come true."

She nodded her head at the truth of his words and promised them that she would be okay.   "I'm just a little jumpy that's all. But this is about you anyway so stop worrying about me. Tonight's your night. Enjoy it."

Margarita still couldn't believe how far he'd come so fast.

Tracy looked at her watch. "I'm 'bout to go and ruin that smoke-fest Mash and his no good friends are having. We go on in forty-five minutes."

"He'll be here in a minute." Spits told her, not wanting her to spoil his homies party. "They just doin' them right now. Go somewhere and do you."

They all laughed.

Tracy looked at them and knew they needed to be alone. "You know I will too." She waved on her way out.

"You do look good Ma." Spits told Margarita when the door closed. She blushed and turned to the mirror fussing with her hair. She was extra nervous now that it was just them.

"I am so scared!" She brought her hands to her cheeks in a panic.

He laughed. "That's how I felt when Tracy and Janet rushed me with them cameras for the YouTube site. You gotta ignore it and just do it though." He counted out on his fingers. "You did it for the video, we've been rehearsing, and you look like Madonna."

She laughed in the mirror.

"We got this Ma. Just do it."

She smiled at him as she kept fussing with her hair in the mirror. "You think so?"

"Yep, we just practicing for your stuff. You got next like the Women's NBA remember."

Mash and his home-boys, F, Chill, Half-a-Chicken, and Boy Blu, along with ten white groupies had it crackin' outside in the stretch Benz limo. They were smoking on Girl Scout Cookies, some of Cali's finest green and the back of the limo was heavy with the smoke from the blunts being passed around.

"Mash. Will you sign your name on my breast so I can show my sister when I get home?"

The blonde cutie pulled her piece of a shirt off and hopped onto his lap burning her butt on the blunt he held.

"Dang girl, watch yourself." Mash let her settle on his lap while staring at her chest. She handed him a marker with a steamy smile on her face.

Boy Blu, at nineteen, was the youngest of the three rappers that Mash planned on releasing as a group. He followed Mash's lead and pulled one of the girls into his lap as she pulled off her shirt also.

"This it right there! I'm tryin' to live like this all the time big homie. This it right there!"

"Stay messin' with ya folks then." Mash told him, "We chasin' paper 'round here chief!"

"That should be our name right there!" Chill, who the oldest member of the nameless rap group, said thinking the name a perfect fit. "The Paper Chasers!"

Half smiled and Boy Blu got juiced. "Yeah! That's what we do! We the Paper Chasers. That's it right there chief!"

A knock on the window reminded Mash of his commitments. He looked at his watch seeing that it was thirty minutes till show time. Mash cracked the window and seen that it was his homie and personal bodyguard Yak.

"Give me like five minutes Yak."

"Okay but Tracy called and told me if you didn't hurry your yellow butt up she was gon' crash the party."

Mash laughed and rolled up the window. "Pass me some cookies chief. I gotta get up out of here before Trace start flashin'."

Dame had had Janet buy twenty bottles of Louis the 13th for the ten label owners and their guests he'd invited to join him tonight on the theater's balcony.

Loco sat at one of the choice tables closest to the rail drunk off the Louis with a big grin on his face. He looked across the table to his two brothers and he threw up Cabrillo Street's hand sign.

"Mob!" He screamed.

Janet sat below the balcony in a front row seat along with the media reps. These were the people they were trying to impress most. The fanzine writers, television producers, and DJ's had millions of people reading, watching, and listening to them. Their opinions were priceless. Everyone else was just part of the celebration.

"You guys put together one hell of an event Janet." Paul Ray, the editor the Hip-Hop weekly magazine 'Rap Biz' said. "If your boy pulls off his performance, the rap world's gonna have to take notice."

"They better take notice then." Janet answered confidently. She was certain that Spits would set the roof on fire tonight. These past few weeks she had been attending the rehearsals and witnessed Spits go from being uncomfortable to cocky on this same stage. This was his house now and she had every reason to believe that he would give the five thousand people exactly what they'd come for.

Janet smiled when she saw Tracy come from back stage and make a bee line for Anthony at the sound booth to pester him for the ninety third time tonight.

"How we doing Anthony? Is everything good?" Tracy asked him.

"Stop worrying Tracy. Listen to how good the music sounds. It's going to sound just as good when Spits performs. Just like when we did the sound check earlier." Anthony patiently explained. He knew how important tonight was to her and so understood her concern. "Go up there with Dame and enjoy yourself. You deserve it."

Tracy smiled and looked to the balcony where Dame stood at the rail puffing on a cigar. "I think I will." She winked at Anthony. "Remember when I told you to take a chance on us? Now do you believe me?" She said and turned to wave at Janet before making her way to the stairwell leading up to the balcony.

Mash walked into the dressing room smiling like a fat kid in an ice cream shop. "You guys ready?"

He went to Spits and gave him a hug and winked at Margarita.

"Heck yeah we ready. This is it right here. This is what you tried to tell me the first time I came to the Blue Room remember?"

"I told you chief. You got that gas. After tonight, ain't nobody gon' be able to tell us nothin'."

Spits got a little choked up, unable to find the words to tell Mash how much he appreciated all that he'd done to get him here. "Thanks homie."

"Naw." Mash said shaking his head. "Thank *you*. I'd still be posted in the garage listening to all the homies come in with that watered down crap if you wouldn't have came through."

Passing by security at the bottom of the balcony stairwell, Tracy went up and headed to the rail next to Dame. "You ready?"

He smiled and nodded his head. "What you think? We 'bout to be all the way on after tonight. Heck yeah I'm ready. What's up with Spits and my nephew?"

"Spits is in the dressing room with Margarita. I just called Yak and told him to tell Mash he got five minutes to climb his butt out of that smoky limo before I come mess up his little chick party."

Dame's deep chested laugh could be heard over the music.

"Is he still mad that you told him to keep all that stuff in the limo and away from Margarita?"

"I don't know. If he is, he'll get over it."

Tracy saw Eric come from backstage and hold up his fingers signaling to his camera crew that the show would start in five minutes. Mash came from the side of the stage and took his place onstage at the raised platform. He looked up to the balcony and waved at his uncle and Tracy. Tracy waved back and Dame pointed at him with his cigar. Anthony cut the music when Fat took the stage again bowing dramatically.

"Ladies and Gentlemen, on behalf of Paper Chasin' Records, I'd like to thank you all for coming out tonight. We hope that you've all enjoyed the party so far. But the best is yet to come. Are Y'all ready to see Spits?"

The roar from the thousands of fans down the street at the Steinbeck Center could be heard inside the theater and Spits felt the rush of energy from the side stage.

He was ready.

"Without further ado, I give you all Spits, the legend in the making!" Fat Daddy hurried off the stage as Spits took to it. The beat from a song from the first mixtape pounding crisply from the theater speakers.

He stalked across the stage like a caged lion in a pair of light blue True Religion jeans and a white wife beater holding the mic in his left hand. The swoosh tatted on his elbow was on full display.

I'm a soulja. Trick! I'm a bona-fide soulja, trick!
I know you lonely when I'm gone so I'ma hold ya trick.
When I get home tho', right now I gotsta get these chips,
'cause I'm a hustla.

It was obvious to Tracy that most of their guests knew the words to the song as many of them sang. She looked at Dame who was smiling as if he'd just thrown the winning touchdown in the Super Bowl.

"You know I want a raise don't you?"

Spits was in a zone with his swagger turned way past a hundred. He was just as cocky as he sounded on wax. This was his moment. He owned the theater as he went through six of the most popular tracks from the mixtapes and the crowd loved it.

Down the street at the Steinbeck Center, the crowd was in an uproar, loving every minute of the performance. It was official. Spits was the new prince of the Central Coast, heir to the rap throne and he was up there on the jumbo screens letting the world know it.

He finished the last of the songs from the mixtapes and brought the mic to his mouth. "This next song I'm about to do next is the first single off my album, 'Legend'."

On cue the theater lights went out and Spits left the stage, leaving only the spotlight shining in the center of it.

Margarita was standing next to the curtains smiling when he came off stage. "You were wonderful!" She hugged him. "You did it! You did it man!"

"Don't get too happy Ma. It ain't over yet." He warned, though he was no longer worried. Not after he'd rocked the house so easily.

"How did it feel?" She asked as Mash threw on the 'Take a Chance on Me' instrumental.

"You're about to find out." He told her with a smile and a push. "That your cue right there."

She threw him a smile over her shoulder and headed to the waiting spotlight. "Wish me luck."

"You ain't gon' even need it. You're a star already Ma." He whispered to her back.

She stepped into the light and a gasp went up inside the theater. As planned, she looked the very picture of innocence and it was obvious that the crowd thought she was beautiful. She stood slowly swaying to the rhythm with her eyes closed and head down as she hummed into the microphone.

Shocked at seeing Margarita blossom right there before her eyes, Tracy managed to pull her attention away from the vision in the dress just long enough to check the crowd's reaction. She nudged Dame.

"They love her Dame. Look how into her they are."

It was if Margarita's understated gracefulness had the crowd hypnotized. As she sang her song she stood there lost in a world of her own. A world where love ruled supreme.

"It looks like we're about to have one hell of a year don't it?" Dame asked pleased with how the night was shaping up.

When Spits joined her onstage, the crowd went mad. The two looked like royalty up there. He looked in her eyes as he said his verse and saw the raw pleasure in their green depths and knew that there was nothing in the world which would make her give this up.

She loves this. He thought as he finished his verse and watched her turn from him to sing to the crowd.

Tracy grabbed Dame's hand and pulled him towards the stairwell. "Let's hurry up and get backstage before they finish."

She waved for Loco to follow knowing that Spits would want him there to celebrate his brilliant success.

When they finished the song and hugged center stage, a thundering roar went up from the crowd down at the Steinbeck Center. The fans were screaming their appreciation and making enough noise to rock the very foundation of the Old Town building.

After having popped a couple bottles of celebratory champagne in the dressing room, they all followed Janet back to her table where the media types sat.

Janet made the introductions. "Spits this here is Michael Owens from '*Rap Now*' magazine. Paul Ray from 'Hip-Hop Biz', and Janet de'Marco from 'The Script'." She beamed proudly. "Guys, this is the man himself, Spits"

"How you guys like the show." Spits asked as he shook their hands.

"It was great." Paul answered quickly, wanting to be the first to engage him. "You sounded even more cocky on stage than you do on record. If that's possible. Are you really as arrogant as you act?"

"I'm a rapper, not an actor Paul." He reminded him smiling. "What you see is what you get. But you'll have to ask my team if I'm arrogant or not. I don't think of it as arrogance, but truth. When I came out saying that couldn't none of these rap cats see me, I meant that. So if that's arrogance then I guess I'm guilty as charged."

"What did you think of the crowd's reaction?" Michael asked. "Was it more than you expected?"

"No, not really. This is how we planned it. So no, I wasn't surprised. It's all part of the plan. When we set out to do this, the feeling in our camp was that we would come out throwing rocks at the throne and to do that, we had to be on point. The fans reaction to the performance tonight just validated that we're right on target." Spits explained.

"I've got a question for Margarita." Janet de'Marco said winking her eye at her. "But before I ask you, I wanted to tell you that you look lovely tonight."

"Thank you." Margarita blushed, once again shy now that she was off stage and amongst strangers.

"Now for my question. What's the deal with you and Spits? Are you just friends, or are you his girl? Sparks were flying up there when you performed together."

119

Spits threw his head back and laughed at Margarita blushing red.

"Shoot Janet, I can answer that for you. We're just friends. I been trying to get with her since we met but she think's I'm a bad boy."

"I do not!" Margarita looked shocked at his words. "I've never thought that about you. I thought you were a little lost when we met. But never bad." She looked to Tracy and they shared a secret smile. "But that was before. You've changed your lifestyle and I think that I might be willing to take a chance on you now."

"Aw shoot chief." Loco said and brought a fist to his mouth, "You must done blew up If Margarita's stuck up butt is giving your lame behind some play."

CHART TOPPIN' AND STATE HOPPIN'

"HEY Y'ALL WELCOME to another episode of Rap Down, where we count down the ten hottest rap albums in the nation." The light complected, dread locked hostess said and waited patiently for the applause to die down. "My name is Sweet."

"And I'm Dre." The bald, slim co-host added. "And today we have a very special treat for Y'all"

"That's right. Today we have here in the studio the man who's currently taking the music world by storm." Sweet said.

"Coming all the way from Seaside California, the one who currently has the number one song in the nation. Spits!"

The crowd erupted.

Dre held his hand up for quiet. "This will be his first time performing here in New York and we are honored to have the privilege of being the first stop on his East Coast trip."

He went on to explain about the meteoric rise of Spits and Paper Chasin' Records and the release of 'Legend'. The album critics were hailing as the most important West Coast album since The Chronic 2001.

"But before we bring Spits out to set the stage on fire. Let's get into the countdown." Sweet said and looked at the screen to her left where a video had come on.

"New on the countdown today is a group we all know and love. Coming in at number ten…"

Backstage in the dressing room, Margarita sat staring in the vanity mirror at the flat screen hanging behind her. Spits and Loco lounged on the couch eating chicken from the buffet set up along the wall.

"Watch," Loco said in between bites. "I'm 'bout to holler at Sweet's fine behind."

Margarita laughed. "That girl ain't thinking about you."

"She will be once I shoot some of this raw game up under her though." He promised.

"Go on with that crap Loco." Spits met Margarita's eyes in the mirror and smiled. "You always be on some crap. You ain't gonna even say nothin' to her when she gets here."

"You got the Loco jacked up. You the one who be on some shy stuff. I got game for a chick. Watch when the show's over and see if I don't knock her."

Margarita shook her head in disbelief and received a sharp look from the make-up artist.
Rap Down was the hottest music video countdown show on television and they'd all grown up watching it. The single had been at the top of the charts for three weeks now and they had been crisscrossing the country doing shows. But being here in New York on Rap Down was real big and they were all a little star struck.

For Spits, this was what made him finally feel that he was a bona fide star. He remembered well all the times he'd watched the show in CYA and San Quentin fantasizing about being with Sweet. Now here he was getting the star treatment on the very exact show.

A knock on the door caught their attention. The door opened and one of the show's producers entered wearing a headset and carrying a clipboard.

"You're on in ten minutes Spits." The short, feisty Puerto Rican man announced. "Just like I explained earlier, You'll go out and do the interview by yourself before we go to commercial break. Afterwards, we'll take questions from the audience and then you and Margarita will perform 'Take a Chance on Me'."

Margarita kissed Spits on the cheek before he left with the producer. "Good luck baby."

"You too." He said and left to the interview.

Watching Spits sitting on the couch between the two hosts as if he were the king of the universe without a care in the world and the studio audience loving every minute of it, Margarita realized that a part of her was jealous and that this strange place within her longed for the attention people had been giving to him.

"Oh my God." She mouthed not understanding these unfamiliar feelings.

What's happening to me?

"So tell us Spits. How's it feel to be sitting at the top of the charts?" Sweet asked him.

"Man." He answered with a million watt smile. "It feels good and at the same time it feels right. This is what we had in mind when me and Mash stepped into the Blue Room and started on the album."

"And what's with this Paper Chasin' movement that we keep hearing about?" Dre asked looking to the audience who were sitting on the edge of their seats. "You first made mention of it on the mixtapes you guys put out and now that you're at the top of the food chain, we're all waiting to see what's next for you and your label."

Spits nodded his head at the question while smiling at the audience. "What the Paper Chasin' Movement is about is us taking over the rap game. We on a mission to do just what our name says, chase paper. I'm trying to take my label to the top of the mountain and we have a line-up that we feel will allow us to do just that."

"Okay." Sweet said. "We can feel that. With you coming out the gate dropping a chart topping single on us like you did, I'm not about to be the one to doubt you and your team."

Spits laughed. "Yeah, that wouldn't be the right thing to do Ma. I'm at this." He pulled the sleeve of his shirt up exposing the swoosh. "You see this? This is my motto. Just do it. That's how I get down with everything that I do. It's what I'm thinking when I step into the booth to spit out a soprano."

He went on to explain that when he recorded, his mind was empty of all thoughts except for proving to the world that he was the best to ever do this.

"Not to sound big-headed or nothing, but there just ain't nobody out there who can see me. And if there Is, I ain't heard him yet."

"I've listened to the album myself and I gotta agree with you." Dre said. "You're definitely in a class all by yourself. What do you think it is about your music that separates you from everybody else?"

"My realness." He answered immediately. "Everything you hear from me is straight from the heart. When I freestyle my songs, you're getting it raw and-"

Sweet and Dre shared a look and she brought the mic to her face. "Did you say when you freestyle?"

Spits laughed remembering Mash reacting the same way that first day in the garage. "Yeah, that's what I said and that's what I do. I freestyle all my songs."

"Wow." Sweet said with another look at Dre. "If that's true then I don't think anyone can dispute your claim that you're the best to do this"

"It's true and I am the best." He turned and looked behind the couch. "Where's my trophy at?"

The audience laughed.

Sweet stood and went into the audience and choose four fans to ask Spits questions then they went to commercial break so that the crew could get the stage ready for them to perform.

Loco stood just behind one of the camera men when Spits came from the stage.

"These New York beezies are hecka jazzy huh? Too bad Margarita been playin' defense on you and stopping you from getting any play."

Spits laughed on the way to the dressing room for Margarita. "Let's do this baby."

She was bending down touching up her hair in the mirror when he opened the door. He laughed. "Get out of that mirror girl."

"Okay. I'm ready." She spun around with a wide grin. "Let's do this."

INFAMOUS REPUTATIONS...

MASH WAS IN the studio with five females, the Paper Chasers, and plenty of bottles.

"Trick watch! I'm 'bout to put Hood Life on the Map." He promised his homegirl Brenda.

She went wild. "Who the heck you callin' a trick? Trick!" She looked at her sister, who sat next to her nephew Boy Blu, before walking to stand over Mash on the couch. "Fool, I know you ain't just call me no trick."

"Chief you better get your Auntie or somethin'." He warned Blu.

Blu stood and grab Brenda by the waist easing her back towards the kitchen. "Come on Auntie. The homie just drunk."

"His punk butt must be, callin' my all out my name. He got this girl messed up. Come on Nae, let's get up out this fool's house."

The sisters left leaving Mash, the Paper Chasers and the three Mexican beezies from Salinas alone just like Mash had intended.

He laughed. "Your aunties were in the way. They had to go."

Blu didn't hear him. He too busy trying to hit on the short, thick girl. "What did you say your name was again Ma? Maria or somethin'?" He asked her. She was wearing a pair of shorts that barely hid her behind.

"Yeah something like that." She giggled when he grabbed her butt.

"I got somethin' I wanna show Y'all." Mash said and stood up. "You beezies hold up for a minute." He headed for the garage with the Paper Chasers following. He reached behind the washer and pulled out a camouflaged duffel bag laying it atop the washer with a thud.

"The homie hooked me up with some fat ol' choppers." He unzipped the bag, reached inside and pulled out a camouflaged SKS assault rifle. "Look at this chief."

125

Chill looked at Mash like he was crazy. Blu also received a look from Chill when he stood from the couch to see what else Mash had.

"You got some pistols in there?" Blu opened the bag wider. "Oh snap!" He pulled out a camouflaged 50. Cal. and smiled at Half before turning to aim at the Bob Marley poster." I'll smoke Bob up in this piece. HoodLife! Bab-bab-bab" He yelled as his arms jerked like he was shooting.

Mash looked pleased with himself. It reminded him of the funk, when the homies use to run around the hood with a gang of straps.

"Put that down 'lil boy. You ain't gon' bust on nothin'." Mash told Blu.

"You got me jacked up." Blu said waving him off and reached into the duffel to grab a clip to put in the gun before sticking it into his waistband. "Everybody in the Side know what time it is wit' Boy Blu." He reached for the assault rifle, "Let me see that SK."

Chill remained on the couch watching Mash and Blu act like fifteen year old gangbangers.

These cat's trippin'. He thought. At thirty-two, he was the oldest of the four and also the most laid back. As a veteran of the Central Coast rap scene, he'd pretty much seen it all but never got the chance to blow up.

Tall, slim, with walnut-brown skin and eyes of the same color, Chill was a nice looking man. It was him who, out of all other local artists before Spits, had come closest to making it in the industry. He'd dropped the indie album 'Seaside Talks' five years earlier and had created a strong local buzz moving some twenty thousand units in two months. Bay Area record labels came calling and eventually he signed a three album contract from hell.

With every reason in the world to think that his next album would sell big, Chill had locked himself inside of the studio with his new label's in house producers for two months anxious to drop a follow up album. A week after the album was complete, the feds had arrested the CEO of the label on racketeering charges leaving Chill and his label mates in limbo, unable to sign with another label.

So the last thing he needed was this crap Mash and Blu were on. "What's up with that song we was working on yesterday Mash?" Chill asked.

"Forget all that. Let's take this heat to the beach and bust some caps." Blu pulled the 50.Cal from his waist and pointed it at the Biggie poster. "bab-bab-bab."

Mash noticed that Half was extra quiet and looked at him. "What's up with you Half? You scared of burners or somethin'? I know all this peace treaty crap ain't turned you soft chief. You use to be with it."

Half didn't say anything for a moment. He picked up his brush from the table and started brushing in his waves. His name was actually short for Half-a-Key, he'd gotten it at fifteen when him and his brother had bubbled selling work in Hood Life and started copping kilo's within two months of jumping into the game. He was the first artist that Mash worked with when he'd come home from school. But Half had been getting money for so long and much like what Spits said at first, he wasn't about to waste his time making music when there was so much money in the streets.

Known throughout the hood as a stand up guy, the the last thing that Half was was scary. And so Mash's question meant little to him on the surface. But just underneath, he was angry. Out of the three group members, he was who had been doing just fine when Mash had come calling. His money had been as right as rain and he had few cares in the world. It had been the amount of money that Spits and Mash were on the verge of making that had convinced him to leave the streets behind. And now Mash was on this hood crap.

"Ain't nobody scared of nothin' homie." He said after a long moment. "I just ain't with the dumb stuff. When you got at me about gettin' down with the Paper Chasers, you told me that it was my chance to get out the game and now you and Blu sittin' in here actin' like you 'bout to go put in some work or somethin.'" He shook his head. "So naw, I ain't scared. But I am wondering if we gonna get back to work on our album. 'Cause if not I'm fixin' to bounce and go chill with my baby-mama. I ain't got time for this."

Mash put the 40.Cal on top of the dryer smiling. A strong part of him wanted to check Half and let him know who was running this. But a much stronger part of him respected him too much to get at him like that. Plus, in his heart he knew that Half was right. He knew that he was tripping. He had known it even before he'd copped the guns.

Born to a single mother, Mash had learned at the age of five that negative behavior, like temper tantrums, got him the attention that he craved. By the time he was a teenager, his mother was at a lost as to what to do with her only child as he had began hanging in the streets with his no good friends.

By the time he was seventeen, Mash was a full-fledged bad boy and his mother knew that he was headed to prison or the morgue. Knowing how much he loved to make beats on the beat machine, she'd taken a second job in order to get him some more equipment, hoping that maybe his love of music would do what she'd been unable to; keep him from running the streets.   Luckily it had, and eventually it was the very thing which had made him go off to college. During funk season when Mash and the rest of the homeboys from Hood Life were on some ride or die trip, music had been there for him. When he was coming up wishing his father was around, music had comforted him, and when he'd come home from school, it had been music which had managed to quiet the furor within him just below the surface.

He smiled at Half and Chill. "Y'all act like you ain't wit it no more." He laughed and went to his chair. "It's cool though. We gon' get with this music. That is what I put Y'all on the team for."

"When we done with that, we gon' go to the beach and bust these though." Blu said still clutching the 50.Cal.

Mash laughed liking Blu's enthusiasm. "Yeah 'lil homie, we gon' bust caps later on. I wanna see how this SK gets off." He scrolled the computer screen for tracks and remembered the females waiting in the living room. "Half. Go tell them broads that we gon' be in here recording. If they want, they can wait for us to finish. If not, then get rid of them."

REALLY BIG THINGS IN SMALL PACKAGES...

LOCO HAD A wide grin on his face as he floored the 2011 Audi A8 passing cars along 101 north as if they were standing still.

"Slow this car down 'fore you wreck it!" A scared Spits told him from the passenger seat. "You gon' get us pulled over." He looked at the speedometer and saw that they were doing over a hundred and ten and climbing. "Slow down chief."

Loco eased up off the gas. "Shut your scary butt up. I just wanted to see how it handled." He looked over at Spits and chuckled. "It got a gang of heat though."

"That's why I bought it." Spits checked the speedometer again, seen they were only doing ninety and relaxed. "I saw one of these on the Transporter 3 when I was in the Pen and wanted me one."

"You better let me use it too."

"Why? So you can wreck it?" Spits laughed.

"If I do, so what? You ballin' like heck now." Loco pointed out. "Shoot. You need to be buying me one too while you playin'."

Just getting back from New York where Spits and Margarita had performed close to thirty shows, he and Loco were on their way to San Jose so that Loco could see this female that he'd met at San Jose State.

"Don't for forget what I told you chief." Loco reminded Spits for the fourth or fifth time since he'd picked him up from his grandma's house. "Once I go in the room with her give me like ten minutes and then start calling me. When we come out say that you have to go."

When Spits had called asking Loco if he wanted to go to Frisco to watch a Giant's game in the owner's box, Loco told him that he did but he needed to go and see this female in San Jose first.

"You the homie so I'm gon' shake baby but I wanna stop by for a minute though."

Ever since the concert, Loco had managed to think up hundreds of ways to use Spits' fame to get females. But this one took the cake. "How you gon' use me to get some play and shake ole girl?" He asked then added "That's some cold crap."

"Forget all that. You let her blow your socks and you won't be sayin' that. She be givin' it like she got a battery in her neck or somethin." He inhaled as if shocked. "Oh yeah, I forgot. Margarita got you on restriction." He shook his head. "You hecka dumb. All these broads tryin' to give you the panties and you sprung on Mother Theresa's daughter."

When Spits didn't respond, Loco took it to mean that he was right and so explained what he thought the problem was.

"You did it to yourself by checkin' into the game playin' defense. She had the ball from the gate. That's why she keep striking your retarded butt out."

Spits cried tears of laughter. "Naw, I'm straight. "Margarita's wifey material. She the type of female I can see myself with till I'm old. And she 'bout to be gettin' money too. You and Mash can have the groupies."

Loco stopped laughing at hearing Mash's name. "Dude's a trip."

"Why you say that?"

"I don't know. There's just something about him that I don't like."

Spits turned to look at the scenery of Gilroy as they passed it rather than respond. He owed Mash too much and didn't want to hear anything bad about him. His phone rang, it was Tracy so he put the call through on the car speakers.

"What's up sis?"

"You in Frisco yet?" She asked.

"Naw. We stopping in San Jose first."

"For what? You told me that you were gonna pick him up and go straight there."

"Why you always be on him like he on parole an' crap?" Loco asked. "Shoot. He the one making all the money anyways. You just be talkin' crap to everybody on the phone."

Spits died laughing.

"Shut up Troy. Don't let that big head boy get you in any trouble Spits! Bye." She said and hung up.

"Tracy's butt be trippin'." Loco said and hit the gas.

"Naw. You be trippin. But don't get up here and get to actin' stupid or I'm gon' leave yo behind in San Jose. You got ten minutes and we out. I'm tryin to catch the beginning of that Giants game."

"I got this. Let me do the Loco, just stick to the plan and we all good."

Spits was shocked at how fast they got to South San Jose. Loco had pushed the A8 over a hundred and fifty just past Gilroy, reaching the Berryessa exit in less than four minutes.

Loco called his friend after exiting the freeway. "Diana. We just pulled off the exit."

"Stop lying." She said through the car speakers.

"For real. I just got off on Berryessa. We gon' be at Oak Ridge Mall in like five minutes."

"Girl, they on Berryessa now!" They heard her tell somebody.

"Who's that?" Loco asked.

"That's just Peaches. She stays in the complex next to mine. I told her to come over and meet your friend."

Spits shot Loco a look and shook his head. He just knew that some crap was about to begin.

"Alright. I'll be there in a minute." Loco told her and hung up.

"Here we go." Spits said.

"Just remember the plan. Forget Peaches. We gon' do us and get up outta there like I said."

They pulled up to Diana's complex and Loco punched in the access code for the security gate, found a spot and parked. "Come on." He said as he climbed out. "Don't mess this up neither."

They reached Diana's building and climbed the stairs. Loco knocked and the door swung open to reveal a tall, curvy, light-skinned girl with green eyes and gold dreads.

"It's about time your good fakin' butt came to see me." She said with a smile. "Always talking about you out of state or busy." She stepped close to Loco and hugged him.

"I do be busy. The homie Spits be begging me to go on tour with him when he got shows."

Diane pulled back from Loco and looked at Spits for the first time. "Oh my God! That is Spits!" She put her hands to her mouth in shock then turned to Loco and swatted his arm. "Why didn't you tell me you knew Spits? You should have told me."

"You got the Loco messed up trick. I ain't 'bout to be ridin' the next fool's stick bragging that I know them." Loco told her before grabbing her by the waist and taking her to the back. "Let me talk to you for a minute."

She pulled out of his grasp and spun around.

"Peaches!" Diana yelled running down the hall to bang on the bathroom door. "Peaches! Girl guess who's here!"

Spits stood by the front door enjoying the show. He usually didn't like it when people started tripping like he was extra special but since this was Loco's little thing he went with it.

A short chocolate girl wearing a pair of black biker shorts, a T-shirt, and running shoes came storming out of the bathroom. "Chick, what's your dang problem?"

Diana pointed to Spits. "It's Spits! Look girl!"

"And you couldn't wait for me to finish using the bathroom before you told me he was here?" Peaches demanded with hands on her hips. "What the heck is wrong with you banging on the door like you crazy or something?"

Spits stared at the vision in shorts.

Now that's a bad chick right there. He thought.

133

Tony Clincy

Dark as milk chocolate, Peaches stood five-foot-four with a body as graceful as a statue of a Greek Goddess. She wore her hair close to her scalp in a jazzy cut and wore no make-up nor jewelry. She looked at him and caught him staring and laughed when he diverted his eyes in embarrassment.

He wanted her.

He tried to tell himself that he was tripping, that he was into Margarita, that the two of them were meant to be together, that they had a bright future together. But try as he might, he couldn't get rid of this overpowering urge to possess this little wisp of a woman staring at him as if daring him to acknowledge her.

"Spits!" Loco's voice brought him back to the here and now.

"What's up?"

"What's up with your weird butt? Didn't you hear Diana? She said this her home girl Peaches."

"Oh, Hi Peaches. My name is Spits." He offered her hand and managed not to meet her eyes.

"It's nice to meet you." Peaches said sweetly.

Diana, still in disbelief that Spits was standing in her living room, began her groupie routine. She hit him with a barrage of questions and as he was preparing to answer them Loco stepped in.

"I need to talk to you about something Diana." He said grabbed her hand and pulling her towards the bedroom while giving Spits a look to remind him of the plan. Loco and Diana disappeared into her room leaving a nervous Spits alone with the seductive coal black eyes of a stranger. He sat on the couch and Peaches followed him, her sensuousness hanging in the air like a cloud of thick smoke.

Sensing his discomfort and finding it cute that a famous rapper was afraid of little ole her, she scooted closer to him. "Why are you afraid of me? I don't bite."

He tried to laugh and choked. "I ain't-ain't nobody-I mean, I'm not."

134

She laughed. "Then why are you stuttering. And are you shaking?"

"You trippin'."

Peaches scooted back to the other side of the couch. She wasn't concerned with his fame in the least. She knew that she was a bad female and had gotten used to men clamming up in her presence though this was the first famous one.

He's really scared of me. She thought and smiled to herself.

"Why do they call you Peaches?" He asked after a moment finally working up the courage to turn to her.

"It's a name my father gave me when I was a baby and it stuck. Why they call you Spits?"

"Because I spit my raps like I'm spittin' game at a female."

"Well, I guess you must rap in silence then because you dang sure ain't spittin' no game." She teased.

"Oh you got jokes huh?"

"Yeah I got a few."

They shared a laugh and began telling each other about themselves. She told him that she was an only child of Jamaican immigrants and that she had been born and raised right there in South San Jose.

"I'm single with no children and I'm graduating from San Jose State this summer."

"What are you studying?"

"Fashion. I'm a designer." She said proudly. "I hope to one day have my own women's line."

"That's good. You seem like you got a good head on your shoulders and know what you want out of life." He said.

"What about you? I know you're all famous and everything. But what drives you? Do you want more out of life than what you already have?"

He nodded. "Of course. I want it all. When I walk away from the game I want it to be said that not only was I the best rapper but the best at making power moves too."

"So you want to be a mogul like Diddy then?"

"Naw. I'm gonna be bigger than Diddy and all the rest of them cats." He told her. "Now that I got my foot in the door, I'm gonna go for it all."

"Wow. That's amazing. Here it is you own your own record label and have a number one song on the radio and you're still hungry. I can't even imagine the work it's going to take you to turn those dreams to reality."

"I've got a good team behind me. We've been working hard the whole way through, so all I have to do is stick to the pace and I'll be good."

She found his drive and certainty about what he wanted attractive if not a little intimidating.

"I wish I had that much drive." She admitted. "Not that I'm lazy or anything. But damn, you've got so much of it."

She asked if he was single and he hesitated. He wanted so bad to tell her that he was but didn't want to start off lying to her. Seeing his hesitation, she told him that whoever his girl was she was a very lucky woman.

"She's gonna have her hands full trying to keep up with you though. I hope she knows what she's in for."

He knew that he should end the conversation and quickly get away from this enchanting specimen sitting across from him. But he couldn't. His attraction to her was just too strong and he found himself unable to pull away. His desire to posses her was more than he was able to resist.

"Look Peaches. I probably shouldn't be asking you this since I do have a girl. But there's something about you that I can't walk away from. I don't know what it is and I'm not one of those habitual cheaters but I want to get to know you better. So can I get your number?"

She turned towards him and tucked one of her legs under her. She closed her eyes for a moment and when she opened them again he saw the indecision in them.

"I don't know. You seem like a really nice, down to earth person. But I don't do other women's men. It's a rule of mine, and even though you're this bona fide big shot famous rapper, I won't be one of the females you keep in every city that you travel to.

He shook his head at this. "It's not even like that. I don't get down like that. I don't be doing the whole groupie thing Ma. I know that's probably hard to believe but-"

"Not really." She told him smiling. "You weren't exactly the most talkative man I've ever met when you first came in. So I can see you as not being a dog like most of you men are."

"I think I'll take that as a compliment."

"It was."

A loud crash came from the bedroom followed by Diana's yelling.

"Well it looks like Loco done wore out our welcome." Spits said and stood just as Loco came hurrying out of the bedroom pissed.

"And don't bring your no good behind back either!" Diane yelled at his back. "Sorry ol' fool. I don't know who the heck you think I am but you definitely got the wrong chick."

"Come on homie." Loco said as he hurried past. "Baby's trippin'."

Spits look to Peaches with a question on his face, she nodded her head then told him her number before he left following Loco.

IF ONLY FOR ONE NIGHT...

THE THICK, RICH aroma of cooked beef hung heavy in the condo Spits had bought last week in Carmel Valley. Since the furniture had arrived yesterday, tonight was sort of a housewarming. So Margarita, dressed in a black and white strapless evening gown, was in the kitchen cutting the vegetables for a salad and keeping an eye on the pot roast in the oven. Spits was busy at the office going over paperwork and would be home shortly.

They'd been a together for just over a month now and she couldn't be happier about the way their relationship was going so far. He had been nothing but the perfect gentleman from day one. He made sure to give her the time and space she needed when she needed it. When she'd agreed to be his girl, she made sure to let him know that she was still a virgin and had every intention of saving herself for marriage. To her delight, he respected her for that and said he was willing to wait until they married since he was sure that one day the would be. And he held true to his word.

All during their trek across the country performing, he'd been practically attacked by shamelessly loose groupies at every stop. And knowing that he was a man needs and desires, she couldn't do nothing but respect him even more for waiting on her. They'd begun sharing hotel suites when they traveled and as he held her in his arms at night she would sometimes feel his hardness pressing against her. So she knew full well just how hard waiting was on him.

She scooped the cut vegetables into the salad bowl and checked on the roast before taking a sip of wine from the half full glass next to her.

"Tonight's the night." She sang with a private smile. She was ready. Tonight she would give to him what she could only give one man; her virginity. Even though she wanted to wait till marriage, getting to know him intimately these past months made her feel safe in the fact that he was the man she would spend the rest of her life with.

As she was placing the candle holders on the table her phone rang and she put the phone on speaker. "Hello?"

"What's up Ma?" Spits asked.

"Nothing. I'm just getting dinner ready. I hope you're hungry because I cooked a big meal for you." She responded.

"I am. I haven't ate since this morning I've been so busy."

"Good. And I have something special for dessert."

"Okay. I'm leaving here in about ten minutes so I'll see you in a little while."

"Alright baby. I love you."

"Love you too. Bye."

She sat down with a smile on her face thinking about how much their lives had changed since he'd had started making music. Sometimes she had to remind herself that this was real and not a fairy tale because most times it felt like one. She'd found that the dream of this life could never compare to the reality of it. The lights, the cameras, and the screaming fans gave her a high which she knew nothing else ever could and the more she experienced this high, the more she came to crave the limelight that she'd once shied away from.

In the beginning, she had thought herself too frail to deal with the pressures of a music career. But after getting used to the hectic pace and demanding fans, she found that not only was she strong enough, but she actually thrived on it all. She felt more alive now than she ever had before.

Her and Mash had been hard at work recording tracks for her upcoming album and the closer the album came to completion, the more anxious she became on what she would do next. Being featured on Spits single was all fine and dandy but in her heart she knew that she wanted to step to the fore front and be her own headliner.

The door slamming brought her back from her thoughts. She looked up and saw Spits standing there with his mouth hanging open in shock at the sight of her in the clinging black dress with her hair gathered at the top of her head like royalty.

"Hi." She waved and gave him a sexy smile as she stood. Turning slowly for his inspection, she shot him a look filled with all of the passion she felt for him.

"Dang Ma. You said we was having dinner but looking at you in that dress I'm in the mood for some dessert." He smiled. "You look good enough to eat."

She went to him and gave him a kiss and told him in a low suggestive voice. "Dinner is served." She stepped back from him. "Go and wash up and I'll set the table baby."

When Spits left to shower, Margarita took the bottle of wine out of the refrigerator and opened it to let it breath. She turned on the stereo and Maxwell's 'Embrya' filled the room with soft sensuous music. She handed him a glass of wine when he returned and he sat at the place she'd set for him.

"You look better and better every day. Especially since we started doing the shows. It's like you done found yourself all of a sudden." He saw how her olive toned skin glowed and told her that being famous agreed with her. "Everybody keeps telling me that I was meant to be a star but I think they got it wrong. You're the one who was born to be famous."

She blushed as he'd known she would. He'd learned long ago that she grew embarrassed whenever he complimented her and it had become one of his favorite things to do.

"Oh yeah!" He said and brought a hand to his forehead. "I almost forgot. I got brought you a present."

Her eyes lit up and he laughed.

"You did? Where is it? What did you get me?" She asked excitedly.

"You always turn into a little girl when I get you presents." He teased. The past couple of months he had learned that she became as excited as a child on Christmas morning from the mere mention of a present.

"Stop laughing at me. Where is it?"

He was tempted to play with her but with the romantic vibe she'd went through so much trouble setting decided not to. He scooted his chair back and stood. "I left it in the room. I'll be right back."

When he returned he held a black velvet jewelry box which he handed her before returning to his seat. She opened the box to reveal a diamond Cartier wrist watch with a panda outlined in diamonds on its face. Her eyes grew wide and she brought a hand to her mouth.

"Oh my God! It's beautiful baby! Thank you."

"It's called The Cirque Animalier. It's part of an animal themed line Cartier makes." He explained as she put the watch on her wrist.

She smiled and held her wrist out to admire the watch. "I love it Papi. Thank you." Margarita said standing up to walk over to him. She bent down to kiss him and all her tenseness left when their lips met.

"Are you sure?" He asked her, knowing no other words were needed. They both knew where this was headed. She nodded her head and bent to taste his lips yet again. Her eyes turned coal black momentarily and he saw Peaches before their lips met again.

2011. YEAR OF THE APPLE...

THE PLANE LANDED and the five security personnel exited first, alerting the paparazzi that lurked in the LAX terminal waiting for the chance to snap pictures of the famous.

Loochie, the highest selling artist in the history of rap music and sole owner of Get Money Records was aboard the plane. After coming into the game sixteen years ago with what many called the greatest rap album of all time, Loochie had used his newly found star power to build himself an empire. Six months after the album, he started Get Money Records and released a string of multiplatinum albums and firmly cemented himself in the driver's seat of the rap game.

Many referred to him as 'your favorite rapper's favorite rapper' since he was the undisputed King of Rap and he effortlessly outdid all competition. Loochie went on to prove to be a savvy businessman in this shark infested music business and sold some sixteen million albums from his label's roster during a four year stretch. With his own albums moving thirty million units over the past ten years, he was sitting firmly at the top of the pile. He held the rap game by the throat and took pride in it.

"Looch, it's all clear outside." The head of his security team told him.

"I hear you yo. Let us finish this pinochle hand and we out." Loochie responded then laughed at his cousin Spank. "I'm 'bout to set you folks."

On the dark green teak wood table sat the thirty thousand dollars they'd been playing for in a best of seven series. Loochie scratched the scar on his chin then pointed at the cash.

"I'll buy Justin this bike he wanted to ride out to Texas and back with this folks. You know I'm the pinochle champ. I don't know why you wanna bet me at this yo."

They played out the hand which Loochie won, and then exited the plane. Loochie, his cousin, and two childhood friends followed security through the bustling airport while being followed by the paparazzi who were hitting him with a gang of stupid questions as they took their pictures. When they exited the terminal, Loochie stopped and let his eyes roam the vehicles waiting at the curb until he found what he was looking for. Parked behind the two black Expeditions was an all white 2011 Jaguar XJ.

Leaning against the Jag with a smile was Jane Whitman, the first black woman to run a major Hollywood studio. Dark as mahogany with a figure that left men gawking and women green with envy, Jane gave off the impression that she was a woman used to having others do her bidding.

"Well if it isn't Mr. New York himself." She said with a smile meant only for him as he stood staring at the sight of her in the tight fitting pantsuit.

"If I would've known something as bad as you would be waiting when I got here I would've came a long time ago."

She ran and jumped into his arms while laughing. "I missed you baby. You gotta stop staying all the way in New York." She whispered in his ear. He kissed her, for once not caring about the paparazzi snapping pictures of him during a private moment.

"You know I be missin' you. I just been too busy to fly out."

"Whatever." Her lips turned to a pout when he put her down. "You always bragging on TV and magazines about how you're your own boss and preaching to everybody how they need to be owners so that they don't have to jump when somebody says jump. But when I call and try to get your yellow butt to fly out here to be with me, you tell me you you're too busy."

He laughed and opened the passenger door for her before walking around to the driver side. "So what's new in the movie business? You still got everybody at the studio scared to death?" He teased as they pulled onto the 505 following behind the lead security truck.

"I heard a rumor that you fired one of the in house producers for going fifty thousand over budget on a hundred and fifty million dollar movie. You need to learn how to control that temper of yours woman. That's why you ain't got no husband."

She laughed and smacked the back of his head. "First of all. Don't believe everything you hear. Secondly, I don't have a husband because a certain rapper I know is too scared to commit his yellow butt to being with one woman."

He knew better than to respond to this so he stayed quiet. She was watching him for a reaction and laughed when he ignored the statement.

"Smart guy." She pointed out.

He smiled. "A lot smarter than that producer that you fired."

She rolled her eyes at him. "Speaking of rumors. I heard that you have some kind of beef brewing with a new rapper. My girlfriend called last night and when I told her that you were flying out she told me that she saw an article online about you dissing a west coast rapper."

"It's nothing. Just this youngster talking a little too much. That's why we're heading to KRAP. I'm doing an interview with Slim about it."

She turned to him looking worried. "Are you telling me that you're about to get into one of those rap beef thingies? I thought that you were too big for that. They've been calling you out for years and you've ignored it. What's going on baby? What's so different this time?"

He shook his head. "It's nothing'. Just a little something I need to handle."

She wanted to push him but knew his moods well enough to know that she'd best leave him be for now.

"Good Afternoon Los Angeles. This is the slimmest, slick talkinest DJ on the radio comin' to you live from radio station KRAP, the soundtrack for the streets. Today I have a very special treat for our loyal and lovely listeners. If you are listening to KRAP right now then you're about to be witness to hip-hop history right before your very ears."

The skinny Hispanic twenty something year old disc jockey turned to Loochie with wide excited eyes. This was an exclusive live interview with the rap behemoth himself. The ratings would go through the roof.

"That's right LA. I have sitting next to me, the most significant artist in the history of rap music and he's brought along a new unreleased track for your listening pleasure." Slim looked to Loochie. "Why don't you say hello to our listeners and tell them who you are."

"What's going on Cali? This is none other than Loochie the don getting' atcha live and direct. I just flew in and wanted to stop by the hottest station in the west and drop a jewel on Y'all." Loochie said into the mic hanging before him.

"You heard it yourself LA. We have Loochie here in the studio with us and let me tell you it must be true what they say about how long this boy's money is because I swear it smells like Fort Knox up in here."

Loochie laughed. "Yeah, you know Slim. That's what we about in the Get Money camp, getting that Loochie. That smell your smelling that's called success. That's what it smells like when you start seeing that big boy money."

"I hear you man." Slim said. "And let me be the first to say that it dang sure smells good on you. All I want to know is how can a brotha be down? You know I got skills on the mic and they ain't paying me near enough money here. How 'bout you sign me to one of them big boy contracts so I can be smellin' successful for all these beautiful California girls."

"Just have your people call my people and we'll hook that up Slim. You know how we do."

"I'll definitely do that. But on another note, there's a rumor floating around industry circles that there's a little problem between you and one of Cali's own. How true are those rumors?"

Slim sounded thrilled at the possibility of a rap beef involving Loochie. It was well known that Loochie didn't participate in rap beefs since he'd gotten stabbed sixteen times in a Harlem park after he'd served three neighborhood rappers in a late night battle. Somehow he'd survived the life threatening injuries and went on to release his ground breaking album six months after getting out of the hospital. The ugly scar running along his chin was a reminder that he'd come close to losing his life to rap music.

"The rumors are true." Loochie admitted and then went on to explain. "You've all been knowing me for years and know that I'm the one who goes out of his way to avoid the whole beef thing. But I feel like this boy Spits is being very disrespectful to the rap game that I love so much. I mean, come on yo. He came out with his little mixtape series and one album and now he's screaming he's the best that ever did it. I take offense at that.

"After all I've done in this game I feel like I wear the hat he's been speaking on. What's this Paper Chasin' he's talkin'? I'm the one with all the paper, Slim. And I don't think he wanna try and chase me, 'cause I'm kinda of fast." He paused for a second. "And Where's he from anyway? Sunnyside or somethin'? I ain't never seen him out here in all the times I've came to this beautiful city of yours."

Slim had the most pleased smile ever on his face. "You heard it first Los Angeles, right here on the soundtrack of the streets KRAP. What's that city you said he's from Looch?" Slim laughed. "Was it Sunnyside? What's up with that Los Angeles? Isn't that an orange juice company or something? Holla at us Spits. The soundtrack of the streets is waiting. We'll be right back LA."

146

WHEN THE WORLD IS WATCHING...

MASH WAS THE most upset and his silence said it all as he stood with his back to the room looking down upon the wharf. Dame sat at the head of the conference room table with a worried look on his face puffing a cigar and wondering why everybody here seemed on edge but Spits who sat with Margarita to his left as calm as a can be. Loochie's interview had aired two hours ago and that's why Dame called this emergency meeting. Tracy, the last to arrive, had just walked through the door after racing there from Frisco in her new Benz. They didn't need this kind of large scale attention right now.

Things were better than great for them. 'Take a Chance on Me' had stayed in the top ten for three straight months and was still hanging around the top twenty five. The second single was set to drop on Tuesday and it would be off to the races again.

"Okay." Dame said ready to begin the meeting. "Now that Tracy's here, we can start." He paused and let his eyes scan the room. "We all know what happened so we won't waste time talking about that. We're strictly here to decide what our response is gonna be. I think-"

"There ain't but one way to respond. We go at him! Me and Mash go in the studio and serve that fool for speaking up on us!" Spits said cutting Dame off.

Margarita looked up at the anger in his voice.

"Hold up Spits." Dame said holding up his hand. "I got the floor right now. Let me finish and then the table's yours." He made supreme effort in controlling his tone. This was a high stakes game they were playing and given that their plate was full already, he didn't think it wise to add a steak to it.

"In case you didn't notice, there's a lot of people eating off of this plate. So before we start making quick

147

decisions that might affect those people's lives we need to look at all of our options."

Spits smacked his lips and shook his head. "There ain't but one option for me. I'm going to the Blue Room and when I come out Loochie's gonna shut that crap up! I got this." He looked at Mash and felt the murder oozing from his pores. "Is you wit me homie?"

When Mash turned around Tracy shivered at the chilling hate in his eyes.

"Yeah. Let's do this. Ol' boy's way out of pocket for speaking on the hood like that. I'm ready right now." He said starting for the door. Dame threw his cigar to the carpet then stood and slammed the palm of his hand on the desk.

"You two hold the hell up!" Dame yelled looking from Mash to Spits as he spoke. "I've invested a lot of money into this label and I'm not gonna let you to mess up my investment! I didn't get into this stuff to sponsor no dang rap beef!"

He sat back down still staring at Spits and spoke in a deathly voice "Both of Y'all got me jacked up if you think I'm going for that."

"And how you gonna stop me?" Spits challenged. "I'm a grown man and I own part of this label too."

He heard a hint in Dame's voice and hadn't liked it. Nor did he like the statement about his money either since Spits knew that he was the one who brought the most to the table when it was all said and done.

"You guys all calm down okay." Tracy suggested in a soft voice. "We've came this far together so let's not fall apart the first time we run into a little turbulence. This is the big leagues. We knew coming into it that the show business was full of sharks. Okay, so now we find ourselves in the water with the biggest shark of them all." She paused and met each of their eyes and nodding her head. "What's it gonna be? Are we gonna swim or do we sink?"

"We gon' float." Spits said with a smile. He looked at Mash and saw the same determination to handle Loochie that he had. "Dame's right. We've got to look at all our options."

Dame calmed down some and sat thinking trying to figure a way out of this.

These lil cats ain't gonna listen to nobody right now. They already got they minds made up and if I push them, we just gon' be up in here fighting.

"Look." Dame said into the heavy silence. "I see right now that I can't stop you guys from going at Loochie. So I won't even try. But I want you to know this. I got into this for one reason. To make money. That's it and that's all. So if we gon' do this then we gonna get paid when we do."

"What do you have in mind Dame?" Tracy asked him.

"I don't know yet. But we gotta figure out something."

"Why don't we use the beef to introduce the Paper Chasers to the public?" Janet suggested.

"That's a good idea." Tracy said. "We can push up their schedule and hook them up with a choreographer so they'll be ready when we drop our response."

"And we can send them and Spits to LA to KRAP to release it." Dame added.

"And I can set up a club tour too." Janet said.

"And when we finish with this fool ain't nobody gon' speak on Hood Life again." Mash said with a scowl as he took out his phone to call his group.

Margarita sat quietly and listened to them make plans to assault Los Angeles and Loochie at the same time. Her was mind on her own project. Her and Mash had been hard at work on it the past month and prior to today, all the excitement had been about how superb the material they'd recorded so far was. The intense sessions in the White Room with Mash had awakened a lust for fame within her that she knew she'd never be able to resist.

But she knew that this situation with Loochie could quite possibly derail her career before it took off. And as much as she had resisted the lure of fame and fortune in the beginning, she wanted it so bad now that she could taste it.

CITY OF THE STARS...

BOY BLY WAS extra hyphy in the back of the limo.

"I'm at these LA chicks!" He announced for the millionth time tonight. Seated across from Spits and Half with Chill lounging next to him, Blu was living the moment for all it was worth. Janet and Tracy had worked overtime in setting up the tour of twenty of the top clubs in and around Los Angeles. They had just landed at LAX and were on the way to perform at the first show.

"This it right here!" Blu yelled waving his arms as he spoke. "Y'all gon' have to catch a cab home when we leave 'cause I'm 'bout to have so many females in this limo there ain't gon' be no room left." He laughed at his own joke and reached for a bottle from the wet bar.

"Don't even trip on that Blu." Spits told him while laughing at how pumped up he was. "I'm gonna make sure you get your little groupie fantasies fulfilled this weekend. Just stay focused on putting on a good show. The broads gon' be there lil' homie. Keep your mind on your business and let all that kiddie stuff alone. This is the big leagues so don't let no groupies make you take your eyes off the prize."

Spits had begun to see Blu as somewhat of a little brother. The four of them had been living in the studio since right after the meeting and bonded because of it. When Mash had assembled the group, Spits had been crisscrossing the country with Margarita and hadn't gotten the chance to know them. But all week he had taken the time to drop jewels of wisdom on them, telling them just what to expect once the bright light called fame cast its eyes on them.

Chill was enjoying the moment the most because he'd worked hardest to get here. He reached out to give Half some dap. "We here boy. We really 'bout to do this."

He'd been in a bit of a shock all week in anticipation of tonight. This was the level of the game he'd always wanted to play on but it was bigger than he imagined. Loochie had given them life. Their album hadn't been planned to be released for at least a year, but now all bets were off. Chill knew that if they gave it all they had this weekend then the sky would be the limit. That was the motivation they used during the week as they recorded a mixtape going at Loochie and his Get Money Clique.

Half stuck his fist out with the biggest smile ever on his face. "You right. We 'bout to show these LA cats how Seaside do it."

"And we gonna get papered up while we at it." Chill reminded him. The conversations he'd had this past week in the studio with Spits had been priceless. In all of Chill's years in the music industry, everybody he'd met with money or power had been suspect and he had to assume that they were more than likely keeping him out of the loop to fatten their own pockets. But Spits gave it to him raw. Half had been surprised at both Spit's understanding of the situation he was in and the type of money they were playing with at Paper Chasin' Records.

Spits came from the same projects as the whole team and he still acted like he was with it when he was with them. He let them know that to him the music industry was just another hustle.

"Y'all ride this beef out with me and I guarantee you'll all be millionaires within a year." Spits promised early one morning while recording. They had all stared at him as if to read whether he were serious or not and came to the conclusion that he was.

Their first performance was at Club Feva on Hollywood Blvd. Slim himself was hosting the event live for KRAP and had spent the week hyping the show on air. They'd left the airport twenty minutes ago and were headed straight there. In the meantime, Tracy checked them into the hotel that they would be staying in for the weekend. Janet had also flew out and would meet them at the club. Tonight would be the start of 'The Takeover' as Spits had named his beef with Loochie. Once he destroyed him, the rap game would be his for the taking.

The limo pulled to the back of the club and parked. Once their security team was satisfied that all was well, Spits and the Paper Chasers were surrounded and escorted backstage to their dressing rooms.

"There he is!" The suave Slim said when Spits stepped through the door. "The Man of the year. The savior of West Coast rap music himself."

Spits accepted the compliment graciously while smiling and offering his hand. "What's up Slim? It's good to finally meet you." He looked over his shoulder and waved his boys forward. "This is my crew The Paper Chasers."

"The Paper Chasers?" Slim asked with a shocked look. He looked to Janet who looked up from her daily planner and smiled. She'd been working with him planning tonight's event and hadn't mentioned anything about any Paper Chasers. He'd been expecting Spits to perform the tracks he'd made in response to Loochie's 'Who is Spits?' diss song.

He looked them over and a wide grin spread across his face. He nodded his head in understanding. "You guys are gonna go at the Get Money Clique ain't you?"

Blu answered for them. "They're as good as through. We got something for Loochie and the rest of his punk team. After we put these shows down everybody gon' be talking about Paper Chasin' Records. We takin over the game."

Spits stayed in the background and let his squad get their interview on noticing how Blu was taking the lead.

"Do you guys have an album coming out anytime soon?" Slim asked and Blu told him that for the moment they were focused on taking Loochie and Get Money Records down.

"So it's war then?"

"Heck yeah it's war! Loochie should've kept his mouth shut. He done went and messed with the wrong cats." Chill answered. "Can't none of these rap cats see Spits and after we drop this mixtape on Y'all, ain't nobody else gon' speak on the movement."

"Everybody's been wondering how your camp would respond to the 'Who is Spits' track." Slim told Spits "But a whole mixtape? I don't think anybody saw that one coming."

"Speaking of mixtapes." Janet said as she reached inside the black leather bag at her feet. "I've got one here for you Slim. It's called 'The King is Dead." She stood and handed him the CD. "I was waiting for them before giving it to you."

Blu excitement got turned all the way up from the dozens of bad females he'd seen in the three minutes they'd been here. His head moved from side to side like a traffic cop. "You see this?" He said swatting Half on the chest and pointing at one of station DJs. She was a tall, dark, sexy sista with a short close cropped do that did her high cheekbones much justice. Blu stepped to her and pulled away from the crowd by her elbow.

"What's your name home girl?" He asked.

She stopped walking and pulled her arm back. "Home girl? Little boy you better go somewhere. I ain't your home girl." She said in a raised voice with a hint of a laugh in it while looking back towards the crowd. "Somebody come and get this child and teach him how to talk to a woman. He called me home girl."

"I know how to do that already. Why you think I pulled you and that sexy haircut over here?" His eyes roved her hips noticing how there wasn't an inch of space to spare. "Shoot, I know how to do some other stuff besides talk too."

The room laughed.

"That's my lil' homie." Spits announced to the room. "He's the youngest in the group." He smiled at Blu who was cheesing from all the attention. "He hecka hyper too. After tonight, he's gonna be famous."

"You have thirty minutes before you guys go on." Slim reminded them. He looked at his watch then the door.

"I need to go out here and do what I do." Spits said. " I'll see you guys after the show. Good luck."

GOING AGAINST ALL THAT'S RIGHT...

MARGARITA STOOD SINGING her heart out into the mic as Mash watched her from outside the booth. They stayed home to record rather than go to Los Angeles with Spits and the crew. She came yesterday at noon and they'd planned to just record the three songs she had been arranging for the last week but they've been feeding off of each others energy so much that they were still going hard at eight thirty in the morning.

From the jump, Mash had felt a certain closeness with Margarita that he really didn't understand himself. Their personalities were totally opposite and they didn't share any traits or interests outside of a strong love for music. They both noticed that each brought out the others best and both started looking forward to these recording sessions.

She finished laying down her verses and came from the booth smiling. "That was good. I love the rhythm you came up with. You're the best."

Smiling at her praise, he told her that it was her that brought it out of him. Having only produced rap songs before Spits had brought her here, he'd learned since working with her that he had a knack for making the slow and sensual work too. "I can't wait till we drop your album on 'em. You're gonna be the biggest name in R&B girl." He predicted.

"You think so?" She sat on the couch with her eyes wide and full of stars picturing herself as a grand diva. "Do you think our music's really that good?"

"Stop it." He said waving her doubts away. "You already know it is. Listen to it." He played the song she'd just sang and they shared a smile. It was good. Really good.

As the date for her albums release quickly approached, she found herself becoming antsy. She'd let Mash know that she wanted to work overtime in the studio getting material for her album and Mash had agreed, promising her that she would be priority number one. And now that Spits and The Paper Chasers were done making

155

their response to Loochie, Mash was back to giving her his undivided attention and she loved it.

"Do you want to hear some other tracks I made for you and try to do some writing?" He asked her when the song ended.

She looked at her watch. "I've got to go to the office and meet with Tracy and the stylist she hired for me. I can't believe it Mash. This is all too much. I mean here I am fresh from working in a homeless shelter and I'm about to be a famous singer. Dressing all glamorous and everything, It's kind of overwhelming."

"You're gonna be alright though. I remember when we had to sic Tracy on you to get you to sign and how nervous you were that night at the Fox. Now you jump on stage like you been doing it for decades."

Margarita laughed and stood to gather her things. "When I'm done with the stylist, I'll go home and get a couple hours sleep and come back tonight okay?"

"Sounds good to me." He told her and walked her out.

On the drive to the office, Margarita found herself thinking, as she often did these days, of how blessed she was to be where she was at this point in her life. Her and Spits relationship was everything she'd ever thought she want and it seemed to only get better as the days passed. He was such a gentleman and so devoted to her that she couldn't help but feel like she was the luckiest woman on God's green earth. She found his nonchalance about other girls reassuring. He was so focused on reaching the pinnacle of the music industry that she knew she needn't worry about him being unfaithful. His mistress was music and the business which would insure him a long run in the game.

She passed the security gate and parked in the underground garage, got out and made her way to the elevator.

"Hi Candace." Margarita waved as she walked past the desk. Candace waved back with her free hand then pointed down the hall to Tracy's office as she talked to someone on the phone.

"Here she is now." Tracy announced to the fabulously gay, balding, skinny black twenty something year old man sitting on her couch with crossed legs. "Margarita, This is Fred Johanna. Fred, this is our golden girl Margarita."

"It's nice to meet you Fred." Margarita offered her hand and held back a smile at noticing the critical look he gave her as his eyes shamelessly roamed over her body.

"Lovely." He breathed sexily. He turned to Tracy. "This girl is a jewel. I see her in short tight skirts with slits on the side. We need to do something dramatic with her hair though. It's too plain. What size are you anyway?"

"What?" Margarita asked annoyed. She hadn't heard anything he'd said after he started talking about her wearing skimpy skirts. "What did you say?"

Fred looked to Tracy with raised eyebrows. "Am I missing something here?" He'd caught the irritation in her voice and knew not from where it came. He was the top stylist on the west coast and was not use to people talking to him in such a tone.

Tracy too had caught the tone and saw the anger in her eyes. "Baby what's the matter? Are you okay?"

"I will be when you tell Fred here that I won't be wearing any short skirts with slits on the side. Other than that, I'm fine." She looked from Tracy to Fred then back. They both wore matching surprised looks on their faces. They had spent the past thirty minutes going through the pictures Fred brought with him of the latest in women's high fashion and neither of them had saw this coming.

Tracy went to sit behind her desk letting out a deep breath as she sat back in the reclining chair. She silently thought of how to handle this situation. When Margarita had performed with Spits, her wardrobe had consisted of a lot of chaste looking dresses because that's what the song called for. So figuring out what kind of look they were shooting for with her own project hadn't came up. But as Tracy sat staring at her, she knew that they had made a big mistake. Margarita had always been a very conservative dresser and so Tracy could understand her reaction to Fred's suggestion that she dress the harlot.

"Look girl, why don't you sit down a second and let's talk about this?" Tracy suggested. "This is a big decision and we need to be certain we make the right one here."

Margarita remained standing with her face a mask of barely controlled rage. "There's really nothing to talk about until you tell Fred that he can get his mind off me parading around in trampish clothes because *that* decision was made a long time ago."

Fred kissed his teeth and rolled his eyes dramatically. "Tracy I didn't come all the way out here to the middle of nowhere to deal with no diva. I'm the diva when I'm in the room and I have other things I could be doing with my time than dealing with this girl's bad attitude. What kind of label is this anyway? I know you're not going to try and release her as an ultra conservative nun R&B act are you?" He laughed at his choice of words.

Tracy looked to Fred and smiled before pushing her chair back and standing up. "I'm sorry for the inconvenience Fred. I know this looks very unprofessional and I take full blame for that. I should have talked with her first."

Fred cut his eyes at Margarita before returning Tracy's smile. "Girl, I understand. You just be sure you call me when this heifer gets her little panties untangled." He laughed his feminine laugh and headed for the door leaving them alone to figure it out.

Tracy sat behind her desk and stared at Margarita in silence. "You know he's right don't you?"

"No I don't." Margarita answered with attitude. "I didn't sign up to wear skimpy clothes Tracy."

"What the hell did you sign up for then girl?" Tracy raised her voice. "We sell records around here Margarita. And in case you hadn't noticed, music fans like their stars to be sexy and glamorous."

Margarita stood there looking past Tracy thinking about what she'd said and knowing that she was right. "I guess I hadn't thought about it." She said after a moment. "I've been so focused on everything else that I hadn't thought that far ahead."

"I understand." Tracy told her with a voice full of compassion. "Neither did I. But it is what it is girl. We've gotta do whatever we can to make sure your project's successful and right now that means you working with Fred and figuring out the right look."

Margarita didn't want to dress like a tramp to sell records because that wasn't who she was as a person. But at the same time she wanted to be a star more than anything.

How can I not do what they're asking me? If I don't, they'll think I'm being childish. "Okay Tracy," She said after a moment. "I'll do it. Call him back and we can figure this out."

She couldn't help but feel that she was selling herself short and wondered if this would be the first of many times she'd be forced to go against what she felt was right.

Tony Clincy

WHEN THE EAST WAS LOST...

"HEY AMERICA, WELCOME to another episode of Rap Down. My name is Sweet."

"And I'm Dre. Today we have a very special surprise for our studio audience and those of you watching at home."

That surprise sat backstage watching the show.

"Man I wanna get with Sweet, yo." Loochie told D-Boy who was his oldest and most trusted famous friend.

"My boy from Jersey already had that. He say it's all good." D-Boy laughed and hit the gold diamond flask in his hand. "Yeah yo. I thought son was lyin' till I saw 'em all hugged up and stuff." He said drank from the flask.

The two rap heavy weights were there to premiere the video 'Not like us', another track going at Spits and his crew. A fellow New Yorker, D-Boy had got at Loochie last week after the release of 'The King is Dead' and told him that he too thought that Spits was a little too big for his britches and needed to be put in his place.

The mixtape had been met with a warm reception from coast to coast and D-Boy knew that this beef was going to go down as one of the classics. His career needed a boost and so he teamed up with Loochie to rep the East in what was quickly turning into another East vs. West.

A knock on the door grabbed their attention and they looked up to see one of the show's producers coming through the door.

"You guys are on in ten." He announced. "Is there anything that you need before we come back from commercial break?"

"Naw we good." Loochie told him before standing to check his reflection in the mirror and scratching the scar on his chin. His being there wasn't something that he hadn't foreseen when he'd went into the studio to record his first diss song. But with what seemed like the whole world talking about the Spits mixtape, he found himself in a place that he wasn't familiar with anymore. That of the underdog.

His team had shown him numerous posts on the web where East and West Coast rap fans were declaring Spits the winner of the first round and that was unacceptable. He knew that this single he and D-Boy were dropping today had to hit or his reputation would be forever damaged.

"Welcome back to Rap Down." Sweet waited for the audience's applause to die down before continuing. "Like we told you earlier, we have a very special surprise for you today."

"As a matter of fact," Dre cut in. "we have two surprises for you."

"That's right we do." She turned towards the side of the set where Loochie and D-Boy stood waiting. "All of you put your hands together for the biggest thing to ever happen to rap music. The King himself, Mr. Get Money, Loochie and his friend and fellow Hip-Hop star D-Boy."

The audience lost it and stood to give the rappers a thunderous welcome. They loved Loochie out there. He was one of them. A New Yorker who had pulled himself up from the ghettoes of Harlem to become a Hip-Hop behemoth. A man that they could look to as proof that they too could climb from the gutter and brush shoulders with the big boys.

"How are you two?" Sweet asked as the applause died.

"It's all lovely with me and Get Money." Loochie assured her with an air of confidence. "You know how we get down with ours, getting our paper up, hustlin' like always."

"I see you brought D-Boy along with you today." Dre pointed out. "When your label called our show's producer and told him that you wanted to make an appearance on the show to release a world premiere, we figured that it had something to do with your beef with Spits and his crew. What's going on with that?"

"I can answer that." D-Boy cut in. "What's going on is that, the new kid on the block done bit off more than he can chew." He inclined his head towards Loochie. "This man here is a rap legend and he was right to take offense at Spits talking about he's the best. Shoot, I took offense at it my dang self. We *been* doing this and we both take a lot of pride in our accomplishments. So the little boy out West needs to be taught some respect, me and my boy Loochie are gonna be his teachers."

Sweet took up the questioning. "We were told that Loochie had a new song for us. But what do you have to do with it D-Boy?"

"The song we're about to bless Y'all with features the both of us." D-Boy explained. "I took it upon myself to reach out to Loochie and let him know that he wasn't the only one who felt offended at all the talk coming out of the West. I planned to go in the studio to record something speaking on the situation myself and before you know it, we were in the studio together."

"Right." Sweet said with the smile of the century at knowing that she was a part of what was sure to be Hip-Hop history. "So it looks like the lines are drawn and people are choosing sides. When this first started, everybody was wondering if this would turn into a another East vs. West situation. And now it's looking as if that is the case. Loochie, aren't you concerned about this turning ugly? I mean the last East/West beef cost us two of Hip-Hop's biggest, most talented artists."

"No, I'm not worried about that happening in this case." Loochie answered. "This beef is all about who the best MC is. I mess with Cali cats and they all know that I don't trip like that. This is about the crown that I take pride in holding and have been holding for years. I don't care where Spits is from. I care about him speaking on something of mine."

"I hear you Looch and I've been a huge fan for years." Dre told him. "But even you have to admit, the boy does have talent. Many are saying that he is amongst the best to ever grace a microphone."

"But what are they basing this on?" He asked. "One album? I mean, come on yo. How many artists have you known that came out with one or two albums and then faded out? One thing that I've learned about this industry is that it's more marathon than hundred yard dash. So I think that rap fans need to remember this before they start trying to give this new kid the crown.

"I think that my record speaks for itself if you want to be real with it. I mean, not to sound all full of myself or nothing but look at what I've done in Hip-Hop. There ain't a rapper out there whose track record can stand up next to mines. Be it sales, money, awards, or whatever else you want to use as a measuring stick. I'm the standard bearer in this game we playin'."

"You've made a good point and I'm sure that the millions of fans watching are listening." Sweet said then turned to face the audience. "And I know that you guys are anxious to see the new video featuring these two iconic MC's."

Their applause was answer enough.

Dre smiled at the crowd. "Well we won't keep you waiting any longer. " He promised them. "Ladies and gentlemen, Rap Down is happy to give to you the world premiere of the latest from Loochie featuring D-Boy, titled 'Not like Us.'

The video rolled and the beef was went up another notch.

Tony Clincy

IF IT ALL FALLS DOWN...OR UP...

DAME BURST THROUGH the door like Tracy waving a rolled up magazine in the air.   "Look at this crap!" He yelled and threw the magazine at the computer screen where Mash sat. It hit the screen with a sudden firecracker like pop waking Margarita on the couch and she sat up scared.

"Have you seen that?" Dame demanded. "I told Y'all not to bite into that crap." He pointed to the still folded magazine and stared at his nephew like he wanted to slap him. Mash sat quietly looking up to his uncle and thinking how lucky Dame was that Margarita was there. Because if she wasn't, he would get up and take one to his uncle's chin for coming up in his studio throwin' stuff.

Mash swiveled his chair around and calmly picked up the latest issue of *Rap Now*, snapping it open loudly. When he saw the glossy shot of Loochie and D-Boy with the Get Money Clique standing behind them, his face lit up like sunrise. They were dressed in matching black and grey army fatigues. The caption read. 'We Declare War'. He looked to his uncle with a smile on his face.

"I don't see why the heck you smiling!" Dame took a step toward him before stopping himself.

"What's the problem unc? We been killing Loochie and his lame crew. Why you trippin'?"

"Read the article!" Dame insisted. "There's interviews in there with some more New York rappers talking stuff about us. Y'all done started that East Coast, West Coast mess again."

"Bump them New York rappers!" Mash said. "And we ain't start nothin'. Loochie started this and we tearing his butt up too."

"But it ain't just us against Loochie now." Dame pointed out. "Now everybody's taking sides. We don't need this Mash. I told you two from the gate not to bite into it. Now look."

164

Mash shook his head with a face full of confusion. Things were lovely for their camp on the beef front. Rap fans on the web were saying that Spits and The Paper Chasers had smashed on Loochie and his diss track couldn't hold a candle to the mixtape. So Mash couldn't see what his uncle's problem was.

He looked to Margarita, who sat next to him listening to them argue looking concerned, and smiled.

"Quit trippin' unc. We got this. The Paper Chasers are officially famous and we're winning the battle. Not to mention the new mixtape done went platinum too. Ain't nothin' to worry about."

But Dame wasn't trying to hear him. All he could see was this turning into another Death Row/Bad Boy situation. "I don't think you and Spits understand what we're trying to do here. We're in this to make money. Period."

Hearing this made Mash mad. "What the heck you mean 'we don't know what we're trying to do here?' Who you think been living in this dang studio making the music that we're getting the money with?" He yelled before standing to face his uncle, ready to fight. This whole record company was his idea and he took offense at his uncle telling him what to do. "You need to check yourself and let us handle our business like we been doing from day one."

"You guys calm down." Margarita stood up and got between them, seeing that they were close to coming to blows. "We're on the same team remember?"

When Mash turned to her, the plea he saw in her eyes calmed him. He nodded once and sat back down. Looking up at his uncle who was still angry, he tried to explain his point. "Look unc. This ain't the dope game where you panic when people get to speaking yo' name. This is Hip-Hop. You want your name mentioned. All publicity is good publicity and the fans love this beef stuff."

"But what about when people start gettin' shot and stuff?" Dame asked him. "Then what? We're dealing with billion dollar corporations now and I don't think they'll be too happy when the crap starts." He pointed to the magazine on the table. "And according to *Rap Now*, it already has. You know you youngsters can't fight without somebody getting shot nowadays. Y'all need to figure out some way to stop this."

"Have you talked to Spits about it?" Margarita asked him. Just last night he'd told her that he was feeling really good about the fans reaction to the beef and that if it were to end today he'd be declared the winner.

"I'm on my way to the office to talk to him now." Dame answered and shot a disgusted look at Mash. "I wanted to come talk to this stupid boy first. But I see I wasted my time." He turned and left without another word, leaving a behind a weighted silence.

"Don't you think he's got good a point?" Margarita asked Mash after a moment.

"Heck no he ain't got no good point" He said immediately. "Loochie spoke on some stuff that he shouldn't have and we handling our business. My uncle is just scared."

As far as Mash was concerned, the whole state of New York could get it if they opened up their mouths. Once Loochie had spoke up on Seaside, him and anyone who sided with him was an enemy. *Rap Now* had gotten it right, this was war and if Mash didn't know how to do anything else, he knew how to get funky when the somethin' popped off.

Seeing that Mash's mind was made up, Margarita looked at her watch and stood. "Well, I'm gonna go now. Me and Spits are going to Oakland to have lunch and I need to go home and change. I'll see you in the morning."

She drove straight home where she showered and changed into jeans, sandals and a T-shirt. The whole time she kept thinking that Dame may be right. Maybe Spits and Mash should quit while they were ahead. Her album was almost complete and she didn't want anything to negatively affect her project.

She still liked to think herself an innocent, but understood that her newfound hunger for fame was based on

166

selfish reasons and as much as she tried to tell herself that she wasn't a vain person, she had a hard time agreeing. She was just around the corner from having all of her inner passions fulfilled and this whole beef thing was worrying her.

As Margarita drove to the office to pick Spits up, she laughed at her own transformation. When Spits had come back from L.A, he'd convinced her that if she wanted fame as bad as she admitted, then she had to listen to the people whose job it was to turn her into a star.

"Tracy and Fred's job is to make sure you look like a star. Stars are supposed to look different than normal people. You can't expect to be up on stage singing about love and all that wearing the kind of clothes you wear." He'd smirked and looked at the black loose fitting Dickies and converse she'd been wearing. She had laughed. "That's the game we're playing here Ma. We sell records and we do whatever it takes to sell them. You can't be mad at Tracy. She's just doing what we hired her to do." He'd laughed again. "You hella Amish girl."

When she stepped off the elevator, the first thing that she noticed was Candace standing behind her desk with a scared look on her face. Margarita stopped mid-step.

"What's the matter Candace?" She asked looking past her toward Spits' office. "Is he okay?" Margarita started down the hall and heard the yelling.

Dame's voice boomed into the hallway. "I paid for this crap!"

She stopped and swung back around to Candace with her hand on her mouth in shock. She walked back to her and took her hands in hers. "What happened?"

Candace stared off down the hall. "Dame came in about fifteen minutes ago and they've been arguing ever since." She whispered in a frightened tone. Margarita squeezed her hands.

"What are they arguing about?"

"Loochie and Mash."

"Loochie and Mash?"

"At least I think so from the pieces of conversation I caught. I heard Dame say that Mash was stupid and couldn't handle this beef. Then they closed the door and started yelling.

"Don't forget who built this thang fool!" They heard Spits yell and then a door slammed.

When he came stalking down the hall, Margarita's heart skipped a beat at the murderous look in his eyes.

"Come on!" He yelled to her as he kept on towards the elevator.

She reached out and touched his arm. "Baby, what's the matter? Are you alright?" She had never seen him like this and was very much concerned. "What were you and Dame arguing about?"

Spits ignored her and stepped inside the elevator.

On the way down, he remained silent. She noticed that he was breathing heavily and his black eyes had grown an even darker shade. They exited the elevator and walked to her car with her shooting him worried glances. When they reached her car, she stopped and faced him, taking both of his hands in hers.

"Baby talk to me. Tell me what's got you so upset. Don't shut me out like this, we're a team remember?"

He let out a long, tension filled breath. "It's Dame man. He tried to tell me to let the beef with Loochie go. He's scared that somebody's gonna start shootin' or somethin'. When I told him that I wasn't gonna stop until Loochie stopped taking shots at me, he got mad and so did I."

They had come close to throwin' blows in Spits' office with each man feeling that it was because of the other that they were in this position in the first place. She stepped into his arms and rested her head against his chest.

"Calm down baby. It's gonna be okay. Just stay focused on doing what you've been doing and everything will work itself out."

"That's what I planned to do. Dame ain't running this. I built this record company into what it is. I'm the one on the covers of magazines and on TV reppin' this stuff. He can't tell me nothin' 'round here."

Margarita stepped back and looked into his eyes seeing that he was calmer. "You said last night that you were winning already. Maybe Dame's right. Maybe you should consider ending the beef now while you're still ahead."

"What?" He asked in disbelief as he turned to her. "Is you sleepin' Dame now or something? Don't go against-"

The smack echoed in the garage as she cursed him while pointing her finger at his nose. "Don't you dare talk to me like that!" She pushed him in the chest with the flat of both hands and he fell into the car. "I don't know what in the heck's gotten into you but don't you dare talk to me like that!" Her eyes filled with tears that wet her face. "What's wrong with you? How could you talk to me like that?"

Spits took her in his arms and spoke softly. "I'm sorry Ma. Don't cry Margarita. I'm sorry baby." He knew he was wrong for what he'd said to her and felt bad. He held stroked her hair in long, slow strokes as she cried into his chest. "I just got so much on me right now and I lost it for a minute. Don't cry baby. It won't happen again." He promised her, his heart hurting at her tears.

Tony Clincy

SHOOT FOR THE MOON...

PEACHES LAUGHED AND slapped Spits hands away as she skated away from him.

"Stop it boy!" She screamed in delight while smiling at him over her shoulder as she put ice between them. Spits took off after her, smiling like a child on a swing.

"Come here girl." He called out chasing her around the outdoor skating ring as the stars watched from above. They came to Downtown Sacramento to have dinner at an Italian restaurant that Peaches promised had the best Italian dishes in the state. Arriving an hour and a half before their reservation, she had talked him into coming here for a skate, telling him that ice skating was a lot easier than it looked since he told her he'd never been.

Since meeting her at Diana's last month, he found himself looking forward to their less than frequent phone conversations. Once they'd gotten over the initial discomfort of knowing that they were both wrong for playing with the fire of desire, they discovered they had a lot of things in common.

Spits tried not to think too much about how sexually attracted he was to her. Knowing that he couldn't cheat on Margarita because she had his heart, he vowed that Peaches would remain a forbidden fruit that he would enjoy yet never taste.

There was something about her which made him feel comfortable enough to tell her things that he hadn't told anyone. Like how much penitentiary had impacted him, and taught him just how valuable life truly was. He explained to her how he became reclusive to avoid having his mind reprogrammed by all the useless conversations surrounding him no matter where he turned behind those cold cement walls.

Surprisingly, he hadn't felt vulnerable after opening himself up to her and sharing his deepest fears and secrets. Peaches made him feel more comfortable about who he was

170

than anyone he'd ever met and it was because of this that he refused to give her up.

She also had opened up to him, telling him how hard and lonely college had been for her the past four years because she had made a promise to herself not to have a boyfriend until she graduated. After having bared their souls to each other the past month and a half, Spits began looking forward to the day when he could find time enough to drive to San Jose and hang with her for a few hours.

Laughing like two kids at an amusement park, they took off the skates and returned them to the checkout counter.

"I liked that. I didn't think I would but I really enjoyed myself." Spits told her while leading her away from the rink by the small of her waist.

"See. I told you to trust me Mr. 'Ice skating's for white people'." She gave him a smile that damn near made his heart stop. Her grey-green eyes shining with happiness.

The restaurant was right around the corner from the State Capitol Building and it took them but five minutes before he was pulling into the one story red brick building's parking lot.

"I thought you said this was a fancy restaurant?" Spits asked and looked from the unimpressive looking building to her with questioning eyes.

"You ever heard the saying 'don't judge a book by its cover'?" Peaches asked him with a naughty grin before opening her door and climbing out. "Come on and get you a little taste of heaven."

He followed her. His eyes stayed glued to her sexy bowed legs as she strutted towards the entrance to the restaurant. The inside of the place was in direct contrast to the outside. The dark lighting, red carpet and candle lit white clothed tables indeed said' fancy'.

She gave him an 'I told you so' look and he nodded his head that she was right.

"I wanna see what the food tastes like though." Spits said.

They were seated behind a white silk screen at one of the more private tables in the corner.

"We'll both have the shrimp scampi." Peaches told the dark olive toned Italian waitress. "And bring us a bottle of the house wine."

"So now you're ordering my food for me?" He teased when the waitress left them alone. "I better watch you. You're about as bossy as Tracy."

She laughed and shook her head. "From what you've told me about her, I don't think anybody's as bossy as Tracy."

"I feel good hanging out with you Peaches." He admitted. "I've been looking forward to us hanging out every since I met you at Diana's."

"Have you now?" She asked shyly, looking away to the violinist playing a soft tune across the room. She too had been looking forward to them spending time together, and knowing that she shouldn't because this couldn't go anywhere since he was already taken. "I was looking forward to it too." She admitted when she turned back to face him. "But you're so busy all the time that I didn't think you'd ever make it back to San Jose."

"Yeah, I know. It's just that since this whole thing with Loochie and his crew, everything's picked up."

"I saw him and D-Boy when they went on Rap Down. You're really in the big leagues now aren't you?"

Spits smiled wide and nodded his head. "Yep. Loochie ain't did nothing but help me get to where I'm trying to go faster. He messed up and I'm taking advantage of it." He took a sip from the glass of wine and added "That's part of the reason I asked you to have dinner with me today."

Curious about his statement, she cocked her head. "What are you talking about?"

"I need your help with a little something I've been thinking about doing for a while and wasn't in the position to be able to do until recently."

"And what's that?"

Their waitress returned with their orders before he got the chance to answer the question and he promised to tell her all about it after dinner. They ate in silence, shooting occasional smiles across the table at the great tasting Italian cuisine.

When he finished he pushed his plate away and announced himself full. "You were right. The food was great. That's twice today you told me somethin' good."

"See. You need to listen to me more often."

"That's what I'm hoping for." He told her and saw her face turn curious and cute again. He laughed.

"Stop playing with m, and tell me what you've got going on in that big head of yours."

He reached inside his jacket and pulled out a gold envelope. "I've got a little business proposition for you." He said and handed her the envelope. "I had my attorney draw up a contract making you part owner of the clothing line I want to finance in exchange for you running it."

The envelope fell from her hands to the floor and her mouth dropped open. "What?"

"You heard me. I want to start a men's clothing line and I want you to run it for me."

She sat there silently staring at him and not at all seeing him. Her heart beat triple time and her mind tried to tell her that this wasn't real, that she was dreaming and would soon wake up to find herself in her bed.

He sipped the wine and watched her, waiting for a response. When she still didn't say anything, he went on to explain. "It's kinda crazy that we met when we did. I was already thinking about starting a clothing company once my money was right. And then like two days after we met, Loochie opened his mouth and put me right in the driver's seat. We've been moving units like crazy and I don't see it changing anytime soon. So I think I better take full advantage of this situation and milk it for all it's worth."

"Do you know how much money it takes to get a new clothing line off the ground properly?" She asked him, still not believing that she was sitting here having this conversation. "It takes millions."

"I know. I had Tracy do some research for me and I think we can do it with two million to start out with. I'm in a position where I can give the line some major exposure just from having me and the other artists on the label wear our clothes."

"It sounds like you've got it all figured out." She said.

"I've been thinking about it a lot. This will help me do what I'm trying to do."

"And what's that?"

"I want to be the biggest thing that rap music's ever seen. This is just another piece to the puzzle."

She looked into his eyes as if searching for some sign that there was more to this than what he was telling her. He read her look and told her that this wasn't an attempt to try and tie her to him.

"So don't let your mind start playing tricks on you." He said and let out a deep breath before continuing. "I'm not even gonna sit here and pretend that I'm not attracted to you Peaches because we both know that I am. But this is strictly business."

"Are you sure?"

"Yeah." He nodded his head. "Like I said, I've been thinking about this a lot and one of the things I've figured is, that if we do this, we have to agree to keep it strictly business between us."

Peaches tried not to let her disappointment show in her eyes. She nodded her head that she agreed before she reached down and picked up the envelope. She opened it and he watched her as she read the contract, thinking how beautiful she was. How if things were different, there wouldn't be anything on God's green earth which would be able to stop him from possessing her.

When she was done scanning the contract, she looked up with the brightest of smiles. "You're serious aren't you?

You really trust me enough to risk two million dollars on this?"

"Knowing how set you are on succeeding, I'm pretty sure that you'll take this chance and run with it. You've been dreaming of this since you were a kid and you've spent the past four years getting the education you needed in order to pursue your dream." He nodded his head. "Yeah, I trust in you enough. You won't go to sleep until Two Eleven is a success."

"Two Eleven?"

"Yeah. That's the name of I want to use. It's California's penal code for strong arm robbery." He explained smiling. "The Two Eleven Jean Company. They gon' eat it up in the streets."

Again she looked over the contract. Her forehead creasing in deep concentration as she read the legalese. Finally she looked up, reached a hand across the table and smiled as if she'd just been given all her hearts desires. And she had, except for one.

POP CHAMPAGNE...

TRACY WORKED THE room holding two open bottles of champagne, making sure that everybody's glasses stayed full. "Drink up. We're here to get tipsy. This is a celebration." She declared for lord knows how many times that afternoon.

The whole team was there in the conference room, gathered to watch the announcement of this year's Grammy nominees. As the official party coordinator, Tracy had demanded that they all gather here today to celebrate what she knew would be another milestone for them as a team. The feeling was that Spits was a shoo-in for the Grammys considering he moved some seven million albums of 'Legend'.

"Come on you guys, bottoms up." She picked her glass up from the table, downed the champagne, and giggled to everyone's amusement.

"If I didn't know any better, I'd swear that you were trying to get us drunk." Dame, who was already drunk, said before puffing the cigar. She allowed him to light up on this special occasion.

Tracy had receive a call from the show's producer wanting Spits and the Paper Chasers to perform at the show in February. Candace and the three secretaries under her stood together by the door with their driNk's, enjoying the moment and feeling proud to be a part of the Paper Chasin' Family. The two newest members of the team, K-9 and Holly Rock, a couple of local producers who Mash knew, were drunk on both the champagne and their good fortune at having just signed contracts with the label an hour ago.

Spits stood with Margarita and Mash by his chair at the head of the table, feeling really good about all of the smiles he saw around the room. Just knowing that it was mainly because of him that they were all feeling so good about their futures, made him feel as though all the hard work was worthwhile. That this was about more than just him chasing his dreams. That his talent was allowing a lot of people to feed their families and experience the finer things in life.

"Stop trying to look all cool like you aren't nervous." Margarita whispered in his ear before kissing his cheek.

He smiled. "I am cool. I ain't trippin' off no Grammy. I can care less whether they nominate me or not."

"Yeah right. I felt you tossing and turning all night last night." She poked him in the chest and they shared a secret smile.

"Okay everybody. Let's make sure those glasses are full." Tracy instructed. "I've got an important toast I wanna make." She waited for them to comply before continuing, this time with her glass held out. "I'd like to propose a toast to the toaster. May she continue to make the toasts that keep us feeling the most." She giggled her girlish little giggle and brought the glass to her lips as they all laughed and followed suit.

Spits stood reflecting on all that had went down to get him to this point. He stared at all the faces in the room, each in turn and knew that as talented as he was, it was the hard work and sweat from his Paper Chasin' family which had played a major part in his rise to the top. He looked to Candace and the three new girls and remembered the many times he had passed them as they busily fielded calls or sent and returned emails.

He turned to Tracy, his sis, and remembered how she had pushed him to overcome what he now thought of as a fear of fame and how she had rolled up her sleeves and got busy making sure that the world knew about their movement. He saw Dame happily puffing his cigar and talking with the Paper Chasers across the room and thought back to when he and Mash convinced him to take the music route. Spits knew that more than anyone here, it was Mash who had been most influential in his decision.

Mash and the two new producers stood talking about music under the label's logo and Spits got a sudden chill when he looked over and saw that evil look in Mash's eyes that he didn't like. He watched Loco make his way around the room talking smack about how his homie was about to set a record for the most Grammys won and smiled. He knew he'd be lost without Loco's friendship since besides Tracy, he was the only one who kept it all the way real and told him about himself no matter his feelings.

Margarita stood beside him grinning from ear to ear, lost in her own thoughts. Of course she was happy for her man, but she also had her own motives for wanting him to win the awards. Because she knew that were he to win, the anticipation for the next release out of the Paper Chasin' camp would be so high that she'd virtually be guaranteed to go platinum.

Her album was almost complete and ready to be unleashed on an unsuspecting public. They were only waiting for Spits' album to run out of steam before dropping her first single. And they wanted to release it right after the Grammys.

With Spits third single still hanging around the top ten, nobody was ready to pull the plug on the album and let it die off. So she had to wait a little longer for the fame that she dreamt about nightly.

Dame felt like the boss he was as he watched his people drinking champagne and enjoying themselves. He felt real good at knowing that it was because of him that everybody here had gotten a taste of the high life since he found the means to turn his dirty money clean and do something worthwhile with it. He still had his reservations about the whole beef thing, but grudgingly admitted that Spits and his nephew had been right. Their albums were flying off the shelves because of the exposure they'd gotten from it and his bank account was growing beyond anything he'd ever dreamed of.

Spits and Mash had been leaking songs over the internet almost every week going at Loochie and his team and the fans loved it. They were getting hundreds of thousands of hits on YouTube and from the posts they were getting on their own site. The verdict seemed to be that Spits was the new 'Mr. It' of rap music. They had Loochie up against the ropes and were looking past the beef trying to figure what the next move would be now that the found themselves in such a position of power.

"Okay you guys," Tracy called out. "the shows coming on now." She held up her hand for quiet and turned the volume up on the flat screen hanging on the wall next to the logo. They all watched in silence as two famous actors took to the podium set up out front of Hollywood's Kodak Theater. I was the same place the show would be held in two months. They began reading off the nominees for each particular category and when Spits name was announced for best new artist, a big cheer went up in the conference room.

"Congratulations baby!" Margarita told him and gave him a quick kiss. "You deserve it."

"Thanks." He said with a smile. He couldn't believe it even though he knew it would happen when Margarita sang for him and Loco in Chinatown ten months ago.

When it was all said and done, they'd been nominated for four awards: song of the year, best new artist, best rap song, and the biggest of them all, album of the year.

Mash smiled at him from across the room. "Man, we fixin' to be on like heck if we win album of the year. I told Y'all we could do this."

"Come on you guys. You already know what time it is." Tracy said happily. "Let's get those cups filled and make a toast." She popped two more bottles of Dom and this time they all rushed to her to have their glasses filled. They'd done it and were more than happy to toast to their success. Paper Chasin' Records was on the way to the top of the heap and they all felt it. It was about to be on for real.

Tony Clincy

WE GOT NEXT...

THEY WERE HARD at work at the new studio which was five minutes west of the office. There were three state of the art studios in the one story white brick building and all fully equipped with the best equipment that money could buy.

Blu was on his hype as usual. "Forget all that candy coated stuff!" He yelled at K-9. "Let's use the hook I came up with. You tryin' to have us in some shiny suits and all that crap. Forget all that. "

"Naw Blu." K-9 answered shaking his head. "We bout to stick to the plan. This ain't the 80's and ain't nobody tryin' to hear that old bangin' on wax stuff. We're trying to get our stuff on the radio so we gotta make radio friendly songs."

"Shut your radio friendly butt up fool!" Blu told him. His angry brown eyes were hard as rocks. "It's Hood Life PJs with us. That's where the heck we from and we fixin' to give it up for it fool!"

"Shut your young butt up Blu." Chill said with a laugh to calm his hot headed little homie. "We trying to take advantage of this situation. Ain't nobody trying to bang! We tryin' to get this money and you on some crap!"

"You don't be sayin' that stuff to Mash. Watch when-"

"Mash already got his money stupid! His stuff got on the radio already and he's papered up. You need to sit your little young butt down and rewrite your lyrics!"

Blu looked back down at his notepad and hushed up knowing Chill's words spoke truth. Chill looked up and saw the anger leaving his Blu's face and nodded.

"Don't trip though. You always screamin' how you in it for the broads. Watch when we get our paper all the way up. The little four or five hundred thou' you got now gon' be play money."

The Paper Chasers found themselves standing on the brink of becoming big stars in their own right. When Mash

180

had put the group together, it had been understood that it would most likely take at least two years to develop them and release an album. But thaNk's to Loochie, all timetables were thrown out the window. There album would drop a month after Margarita's and the workers at the label were preparing to push it.

Mash was down the hall in 'The Blue Room 2011', as he'd christened his new all blue studio. He was putting the final touches on Margaritas' album before sending it off to NationWide. The new Blue Room had more than just one blue light bulb. The floors, walls, microphones, chairs, light switches were all blue. And Mash was extra proud of it, having come up with the theme himself.

K-9 and Hollyrock had been given the task of getting as much Paper Chasers material recorded as possible so that they could stay leaking tracks over the internet until it came time to drop their album. Though they weren't from Hood Life, K-9 and Hollyrock were from Seaside, and had been collaborating and sharing tips with Mash for years. Having come into this situation in the middle of a beef, they found the whole team in full battle mode and the feeling had rubbed off on them. This was just as big a break for them as it was for everyone else and they too had reached into the deepest and most creative parts of themselves determined that they would make the most of this position Mash that had put them in.

When Mash had been the labels lone producer, The Paper Chasers hadn't been able to get into the studio as much as they would of liked because Spits and Margarita had first priority. But now they could get in at least sixteen or more hours a day. Having worked with Spits the past six months and seeing how hard working he was had motivated them and they'd all committed to putting forth supreme efforts.

Half sat on the couch behind the control panel writing his verse to the beat playing low over the studio speakers as Hollyrock and K-9 sat playing with the hundreds of buttons and knobs. He looked up from the notepad and stared at Blu who was standing there looking down at K-9 like he wanted to hit him.

"Man sit your little bad butt down somewhere. You the one always talking that crap about how you can't wait to be big as Spits. You need to start listening to people when they telling you somethin' real."

"I'm saying some real stuff too though." Blu insisted. "I hear Y'all though." He nodded his head and shot K-9 a sour look before heading back to the couch to sit next to Half.

"What time do you guys have rehearsals?" Hollyrock turned and asked them.

"At five." Chill told him. "After today we only have a week's worth rehearsals left."

"Beezies gon' be on me for realz after this!" Blu announced. "The opening act at the Grammys? That's it right there boy!"

It took them but thirty minutes before the three had their verses written and were ready to record. Blu went first and was in the middle of his second take when Spits made a surprising appearance.

"What's up with it homie?" Half stood and embraced him. "I thought you were going out to San Jose to check on your clothing line?"

"I changed my mind." Spits answered as he went around the control room shaking hands. "Ole girl I hired to run it knows what she doing. I ain't got to sweat her. It's all lovely over there." He asked his producers if he could borrow The Paper Chasers for a couple of hours. "I need to take them out to Carmel to my jeweler so that they can stunt like they 'posed to at the Grammys."

Both Half and Chill's faces lit up at hearing this.

"That's what I'm talkin' 'bout." Chill said and held his fist out for Spits to pound. "That's some real stuff right there homie."

"Shoot Chill, If I'm eatin' everybody around me gon' eat too." Spits looked them in their eyes, each in turn. "Y'all rode with me against Loochie when everybody thought we was gon' get our hats brought to us. I appreciate that. I know it was an opportunity for Y'all too. We in this together, so we gon' step up in the Kodak Center and shine together."

When Blu finished laying down his verse and they told him that Spits was taking them shopping for jewelry, he smiled like a little boy getting ready to blow out the candles on his birthday cake.

"That's it right there. They really gon' hate it when we come through blingin' on 'em. Watch and see."

They rode to Carmel By The Sea in Spits' Audi listening to Blu talk his big talk about all that he was going to do this upcoming year as they took the world by storm. They laughed at his enthusiasm and bravado. Truthfully, Spits was doing this for Blu most of all. He felt that out of the three in the group, it would be Blu's hyper active personality which would gain the most attention.

But at the same time, he worried about him too. He knew how much of an influence Mash had on him with all that Hood Life stuff. So though he would never say anything against Mash, he thought it a good idea to show his homie the right way to go about doing this whole 'being a star' thing.

He pulled the truck in front of a two story nondescript brown brick building and parked. "This is it right here." He announced as he killed the engine and got out.

They followed him to the locked glass door and waited to be buzzed inside. When the door opened they found themselves in an upscale, red carpeted room with shiny glass display cases showcasing expensive jewelry.

"Ah, it's my new best friend!" An old owl looking white man in glasses announced with raised hands as he came from around one of the three display cases. A wide grin lit his wrinkled features.

"How are you Joseph?" Spits accepted the hug then turned to his crew. "These are the three I told you about last month. This is Half, Blu and Chill."

"It is a pleasure to finally meet you." Joseph told them, warmly shaking all of their hands. "Spits has spoken very highly of you. He tells me that you three are the next big thing in rap music."

"Heck yeah we is." Blu assured him and walked over to look down into the case full of exotic watches. "I want that right there chief!" He said pointing to a gold watch with diamonds covering its face.

"We'll take that too Joseph. Whatever they want, just charge it to my account." Spits instructed. He turned to Chill and Half and told them it was all good. "I got a surprise for Y'all too."

"Surprise?" Half threw his head back and laughed. "Fool you already surprised the heck out of me. We fixin' to step into the Kodak Center looking like brand new money!" He saw a platinum diamond pinky ring that looked like it belonged on his hand and he asked Joseph to let him try it on. When they'd each picked out a few pieces, Joseph excused himself for a moment and disappeared into the back. He soon returned with a large black velvet box which he sat on top of one of the glass cases.

"Come look at this." Spits waved them over. "I had Joseph make these for us."

 Joseph smiled proudly as he popped the latches on the box, lifted its top and revealed seven diamond platinum chains with the Paper Chasin' Records logo hanging from them.

"Oh crap chief!" Blu's eyes got big as plates as he reached down, picked up one of the chains and put it over his head. He turned to look in the mirror on the wall behind Joseph and stood smiling at his reflection. "Good looking out Spits. You a real homie."

THE WRONG PLACE...

"THANK YOU MR. Levy." Mash said as he stood and offered his hand to the short, fat Jewish attorney. "I really appreciate all the help and advice you gave me."

"Nonsense." He told Mash with a friendly smile as they shook hands. "I simply did what you paid me to do. It's my job to make sure that your production company stands on solid legal footing. This is simply the beginning of what I know will be a mutually beneficial relationship for the both of us. You just go to Hollywood this weekend and bring us some Grammys home."

Mash's face lit up at the boost to his ego. He was proud of what his vision had became.

He nodded his head. "That's what the plan was from the start. And now that you got me up on my business for my company, I can really chase that paper."

Mr. Levy laughed. "It's funny how you coined the term for how you earn your money." He walked his potentially biggest client outside to his new red 2011 Ferrari at the curb.

"How you like my ride?" Mash asked him, thinking the car was the best thing on the road.

"It's a bit too flashy for me, but it's a good look for you so I like it. It's a fine car Marcus. And you deserve it. You've worked hard for it." He chuckled. "How did you say it? You chased enough paper to cop it."

Mash laughed as he shook the attorney's hand then jumped into the Italian machine and headed for the highway.

He was taking some of his homies with him to the show on Sunday and was heading to the PJs to make sure they were ready.

This gonna be off the chain this weekend. They ain't gonna understand it when we come through LA hecka deep. He thought as he took the Seaside exit then laughed and hit the gas when he hit Broadway. He loved how the Italian engine sounded as he climbed the hill headed for the PJs.

185

Tony Clincy

They bout to trip when I pull up in this piece.

Turning right on Yosemite, he saw the dark brown wooden buildings and the youngsters sitting out front, watching Broadway for the police.

Mash hit the gas and the car shot up the steep hill like it would jump it. The youngsters and everybody in the parking lots or out front watched the red streak reach a 100 in seconds. It ran the stop sign, shot to the top of the hill past Hood Life and disappear over the other side.

Half the hood was standing out front when Mash came back down the hill and pulled into the second lot. He pulled in slow, sliding his middle finger back and touching the second knuckle of his index finger. "Hood Life!" He screamed and meant it. Mash hit the doors and they arched up like the car would fly. He swung his legs out and stood with his chest poked out.

"What's up boy?" F came to the front of the crowd.

Mash hugged him. "What it do homie? Your behind stay in this piece don't you?"

F smiled at the truth. "This the hood boy. Where else I'ma be but in here?'"

Mash looked past him to the youngsters out front watching out for the police and money. Then he looked between the two buildings across the lot where a circle of homies stood looking down at his boy Spen shooting dice. He smiled and inhaled through his nose.

"I love this. I be wishin' sometimes that I could come hang out with Y'all."

F looked at him like he was stupid and laughed.

"I know chief but I'm just saying though." Mash replied.

F saw him looking toward Spen and the dice game. "The homie just got out last night."

Why the heck he ain't call me? Mash thought as he headed for the dice game smiling. Him and Spen had been friends since sixth grade and he hadn't seen him since he went to prison five and a half years ago. He reached into his pocket and pulled out a wad. "Bet his yellow butt don't hit. What's your point square?"

Spen looked up while shaking the dice in one hand and holding a fist full of money in the other. When he saw Mash, he gave him a chip toothed grin. "I'm taking all bets baby boy. My points four."

Mash peeled of two hundreds and tossed them at his feet. "Bet two hundred."

Spin counted out the two hundred from his fist and threw it at Mash's feet then let the dice go.

"Deuces." The dice hit five trey. Spen scooped them and grinned at Mash then looked at the money in his hand. "That's fixin' to be mine if you keep betting against your boy." He threw the dice. "Little Joe from Cocoamo!" He shouted and the dice hit deuce deuce.

Hands reached across the center of the circle picking up winnings. Spen left two hundred at Mash's feet. "Bet back square. I'ma eat off some of that music money you got in your hand."

Mash accepted the challenge and threw two more hundreds to his feet. "Shoot."

Spen shot and the dice stopped on seven. Spen picked up his money and stood to leave, telling the crowd that he was through. He hugged Mash and stood back to get a good look at him.   "How you been homie?"

"I'm lovely. Stuff done changed since you left. We been out here doing our thing for real."

"So I heard. I been hearing your stuff all over the radio and seeing the videos on TV when I was down." He counted out the two thousand he'd won off Mash and tried to hand it back to him.

Mash looked at the money. "I don't want that stuff. You got lucky and hit. That's all you. If I would've hit you, I wouldn't give you nothin' back."

"Take this. I used some loaded dice." Spen shot him a devious grin and smacked the twenty hundreds against the side of Mash's head. They approached the car and saw that the hood had went back to hustlin'. Spen looked appreciatively at the vehicle.

"I wanna drive this later."

Mash pushed a button on his keychain to open the doors before tossing Spen the keys. "You can drive it now."

"Naw, I'm waiting on my broad so I can go handle something." Spen told him then climbed inside and pulled the door down before taking out a sack of trees and a blunt wrap.

"Yo butt ain't changed a bit." Mash told him laughing. He reached into his pocket, took out the rest of his stack and threw it onto Spen's lap. "You always be comin' up with some kinda swindle. Somebody gon' mess around and catch you runnin' game and-"

"Get served." Spen finished for him as he started breaking down the buds. "How long you gon' be out here?"

"Why? What's up?"

"I'm 'bout to run out here to Marina and meet with my Pisa connect. I'll be back in about an hour though."

Mash shook his head and looked at him like he was crazy. "You trippin. I just gave you ten racks. Didn't you just get out? I'm eating like heck homie. I got you. Just kick back."

"I feel you." Spen said slowly nodding his head as he brought the blunt to his face and licked it shut. He held it out and put a lighter to the tip for a few seconds before bringing it to his lips and inhaling then exhaling after a few seconds. "I gotta do me though. I feel you when you say you got me 'cause I know how we always got down with each other. But I been putting together these moves for a few months now and I gotta handle it. I'm 'bout to sow this stuff up out here. It's already in the works chief."

Mash knew there was nothing he could to say to that so he changed the subject. "Why you ain't get at me and let me know where they had you at?"

"I was good. Ole girl rode like a brand new car. I just figured I'd get at you after I got out."

"Still though homie. You already know I would've looked out. You my dude. When we was kids we use to…" Mash stopped and a huge smile came on his face. "Man I'm taking your butt to the Grammys with me Sunday!"

He told him about the nominations and how he and twenty of the homies were flying out tomorrow night. "We 'bout to set LA on fire. We got VIP and everything. I got passes to all the parties. It's gonna be live as heck."

"Yeah we can do that. Just let me handle this and I'll get with you tomorrow." Spen hit the blunt again then passed it to Mash.

As they sat talking of old times, Mash saw that Spen kept checking the time. "What's up homie? Is everythin' all good?"

"Yeah, I'm straight. Baby just needs to bring her butt on so I can get out here to meet Carlos."

"You want me to give you a ride?"

Spen shook his head. "No! You doing stuff too big to be around that stuff. She'll be here in a minute."

"Miss me with that square stuff. It's still Hood Life on mines." Mash told him with pride.

Spen held up his hands and laughed at him. "Hold on Playboy. I don't want no problems. I heard you was out here ridin' for the hood when stuff popped off."

"Forget you." Mash said and smiled.

Fifteen minutes later Spen's girl still hadn't come and he started to get mad.

"She still ain't answering." He said closing his phone after calling for the tenth time. "I'm 'pose to meet ole boy in like thirty minutes."

"I told you I'd take yo' scary butt."

Again Spen shook his head, not wanting to expose Mash to no crap. But he knew that if his girl didn't hurry, he just might. Spen had manage to track down the same drug connection he'd had before going to prison and set up a deal to cop a half kilo from him. They were to meet at Mountain

Mike's pizzeria in Marina and nothing except God or the police would stop him from making the meet.

Mash smiled at the dilemma he saw on his boy's face. "You said you wanted to drive this car. You'd better start driving to Marina and quit playing chief."

Spen looked at Mash then to his watch and started the car.

"Screw it." He said and handed Mash the money from his lap and the rest from his pockets. He took a folded brown paper bag out of his jacket pocket and gave him that too. "Make sure there's eighty five hundred there and put it in the bag for me."

Spen darted down Broadway doing sixty to highway one and headed north to Marina.

"Now this is a car boy." He said when they pulled off at the Reservation Rd. exit. Spen got a funny feeling when he pulled into the strip mall parking lot. As bad as he'd needed the ride, and as much as he liked how the Ferrari handled, he knew that they stood out like a fat girl in pink. Spen let out a breath and tried to shake it off by putting his mind to the task at hand. He parked and got out, telling Mash he'd be right back.

The parking lot was mostly empty and as he walked, his eyes scanned the area for anything that didn't look right. He stepped through the swinging glass wood doors and stopped to let his eyes adjust to the dim lighting. He saw Carlos sitting in a corner booth and straight for him.

"Ah, my friend Spen!" Carlos looked happy to see him and as much money as he'd made him before getting arrested, Spen wasn't surprised.

"What's up Carlos?" Spen said as he took the offered hand and sat. "How you been man?"

"I've been fine." The heavily mustached Spanish man assured him as he poured him a mug of beer and pushed it across the table.

Spen shook his head. "I gotta go Carlos. I got some people waiting on me. We'll have a drink next time." He set the bag on the table between them and Carlos grabbed it and sat it on the bench beside him.

"Okay Spen. Here you go." He handed him a matching bag and Spen stood to leave. "You be careful out here. Things have changed since you've been gone."

"I got this. Just make sure you answer your phone when I call." Spen turned and headed for the exit. When he stepped outside, he knew that something wasn't right. He looked towards the Ferrari and saw five or six people standing around gawking at the car.

"Dang it." He mumbled before heading over.

When he reached the car, he ignored the strangers asking him how much he'd paid for it and climbed in. "Man this car's hot as heck." He told Mash and mumbled something about knowing better than coming out here to pick up work in such a loud car. He put the key in the ignition and that's when they came seemingly out of nowhere screaming.

"Put your hands in the air! Now!"

Mash raised his hands as instructed, a tear of anger watering his eye as he stared out the windshield at the cars and cops that had them boxed in.

"Dang chief. What the heck is this punk crap?"

Tony Clincy

INTERUPTED CELEBRATIONS...

DAME, TRACY, AND Janet were in Dame's office celebrating.

"I can't believe this." Dame said for like the third time. He held up his champagne flute. "My nephew hadn't been lying when he told me that we was gonna get rich." His smile grew even wider. "A hundred and fifty million? You believe that Trace? A hundred and fifty girl." He picked her up and swung her in the air laughing. "We did it again."

"Put me down boy. Stop playing!" She shrieked but loved every minute of it.

Dame had just gotten off of the phone with Mr. Clifton Davis who was CEO of the biggest, baddest major label in the world, The World Music Group. He offered them a hundred and fifty million for a ten album deal with the promise that they'd buy out the Nationwide contract if Dame was interested.

"Once we sign with them Spits will really be in position to take the throne away from Loochie. World Music Group can get us everywhere." Janet said happily. "This is big guys. It doesn't get any bigger."

"A hundred and fifty million." Dame repeated reverently.

"We can add some established artists to the team now." Tracy beamed. "We did it baby." She smiled at her best and oldest friend and they shared a tender look. The two had been through a lot together over the years but this moment right now was definitely the sweetest. "You know I want a fat bonus and a raise right?"

Dame laughed and told Janet to go ahead and pop the champagne. "My nephew and Spits act like they can't answer their dang phones so we gon' celebrate without 'em."

The smile left Tracy's face suddenly. "Baby, you need to learn how to talk to them. They're grown. You can't be talking to them like little boys every time they do something you don't like." She cautioned.

"Well they need to start acting their age then. That's stupid, wanting to go to the Grammys with a bunch of good for nothin' gang bangers." He told her with hard eyes. He and had argued with them both them separately yesterday after confronting them about their plans to treat their Hood Life homeboys to a weekend partying with the stars. This weekend was about working as far as Dame was concerned and with dueling coasts tensions at an all time high, the last thing he felt they should do was bring their homeboys with them to Hollywood.

Dame's direct line rung and he walked around to answer it. "Yeah?..." He said picking up the handset. "Yeah, this is him. Who is this?" His dark features suddenly turned to a mask of shock and he sat down hard in his chair.

"What is it Dame?" Tracy hurried to the desk scared, thinking that something had happened to Spits or Mash. "What is it?"

He held his hand up for her to be quiet and held the handset tight to his ear. "Okay, I understand…Just give me a little while and I'll be there to sign the paperwork…Okay…Yeah. See you in a bit."

When he hung up, he swiveled the chair around to face the window. His neck muscles flexing angrily as he stared silently at the boats docked at the wharf.

"What is it Dame?" Tracy asked again. She looked to Janet and saw the same fear in her eyes she knew was in her own.

"Mash is in jail." He said after a moment then spun around and they could see how angry he was. His eyes were smoldering like hot charcoal. "His dumb behind got caught in Marina with a half a kilo."

"What?" Tracy's mouth hung open. "Mash? Are you sure Dame?"

"That's what the bail bondsman told me. He said that the jail's computers are down and that Mash probably will have to spend the night in jail. But that I could come get the paperwork done now."

Tracy heard him talking but wasn't listening. She was still trying to process the fact that Mash had gotten caught with drugs. That just didn't make any sense to her. Mash had never been into the whole 'selling dope' thing and she just couldn't see how he would start selling it now.

Tracy drove because Dame was too mad. He didn't talk on the way to Salinas and Tracy left him alone for once because she was mad herself. He tried calling Spits again as he'd been doing since he got the call and let out a frustrated breath when he got his voicemail.

"Why don't you try Margarita?" Tracy suggested.

"Don't you think I tried that?" Dame snapped.

"I don't know what the heck to think!" She snapped right back. "You're the one who's been acting like a monk since we got in this raggedy car." She back handed him in the chest. "And don't snap at me neither! I ain't the one in jail fool! You need to calm your black behind the heck down so we can figure out what we're gonna do about this!"

"If Mash screws up this deal with WMG." Dame nodded his head with certainty." I know what I'm gon' do." He nodded again. "I'm gon' jack him up like I should of done when he was ten."

Tracy looked over, scared of the anger she felt coming from him and the salty look he had in his eyes. *I have to do something before these three kill each other. They're starting to act like boys.*

Dame stared out the passenger side window and saw the fifty million dollars disappearing. "The board members of a company like WMG ain't gonna want to mess with no company with one of its owners getting caught with no half a cake. They don't need our money. They sitting on billions already."

"They will if we have a good night Sunday." She looked at him and saw the chill melt in his eyes as the truth sank in. She forced a smile and felt sick with the knowledge that he cared more about the money than Mash's well being.

194

THE STARS SHINE DOWN…

SPITS HELD MARGARITA'S hand as the two of them and Loco stepped out of their luxury cottage at the famed Beverly Hills Hotel and into a scene straight out of Maui. The Annual World Music Group Pre-Grammy Event's theme for 2011 was Hawaii and the party planners had went all out in transforming the five star hotel courtyard into a tropical paradise.   Huge tiki torches gave off orange light from the six foot stands scattered around the courtyard chasing off the night's shadows and illuminating the music industry's brightest stars on the clear California night.

The best of the best from every spectrum in the business were gathered all throughout the courtyard dressed in the finest threads money could buy. The men stood proud in their tailored suits, silk shirts and Italian leather shoes and the women were grouped in packs complimenting each other's gowns and dresses.

Margarita squeezed Spits' hand and stopped in her tracks. He looked to her and her eyes were as big as pies she was so scared. Not knowing what else to do, he grabbed a glass of French wine from a server and handed it to her.

"It'll make you feel better." He took another and drank it all down and after watching him, she did too. He squeezed her hand and she smiled that she was fine.

Tracy and Dame stepped out from the next cottage and waved. Loco stood behind Spits and Margarita with a big goofy smile on his face looking from side to side like a referee.

"Chief, I'm 'bout to knock me a breezy with a cool job and some more stuff, watch."

Margarita and Spits smiled at each other and rolled their eyes.

Loco caught the look. "Watch what I tell you." He insisted and left them to their business. "I'll holla." He said and was out.

"Girl look at you in that gown!" Tracy shrieked as her and Dame approached. "You look beautiful."

"So do you." Margarita told her and the two grabbed each other in a hug. Before Tracy and Margarita could finish hugging they were kidnapped by some other women leaving Dame and Spits to fend for themselves.

"Look at all these rich white people." Dame said with a smile. "This is the big leagues right here. We really did this."

Spits smiled. "Yeah we did. And if we win big tonight, we really fixin to go big on 'em."

A deep voice boomed from the other side of the pool. "Ah! There you are Damon!"

They turned to see a tall, stately grey-haired man in a dark blue perfectly tailored suit waving to them.

"That's Mr. Davis ain't it?" Spits asked.

"Yep. That's the man himself. Live and in the flesh."

He came around to them and opened his arms wide embracing Dame. "I've been waiting to meet you all week." Mr. Davis said as they hugged.

If Dame wasn't so dark they would've seen him blush. "Mr. Davis. I've been looking forward to meeting you too as I'm sure everybody here has. You're a legend in the business."

The man smiled and waved his pock marked hand. "Nonsense. I feel too young and alive for me to be a legend. Legends are old." He winked at Dame and turned to Spits with an appraising eye. "And here is Mr. Grammy himself." He gave Spits his hand.

"Mr. Grammy?" Spits' raised his eyebrows and the old man laughed.

"Yes. Mr. Grammy." Mr. Davis said with a nod of his head. "That's what the people with the money are calling you. I've been waiting to meet *you* for at least six months. You're an amazing young man, the way you've carried so much on your shoulders this past year."

Spits didn't so much as blink, just coolly accepted the compliment. "That means a lot coming from you sir."

Mr. Davis scanned the room with the wrinkles in his forehead deepening. "I also wanted to meet Tracy and your friend Mash too but I don't see them anywhere."

Dame coughed at hearing Mash's name. "The ladies are hostages in one of those dress circles I've been hearing about for so long." He looked to his left where Margarita and Tracy stood with smiles stuck on their faces. Tracy's loud giggle was joined by the others. "There goes Tracy loud butt right there." He said with a smile.

"And Mash?"

"He went to a party a friend threw for him." Spits lied not wanting him to know that Mash was party hopping with the Hood Life homies. "I'm sure you'll meet him later on at the show."

As an old pro, Mr. Davis knew he when to hold his tongue. He smiled and took Spits by the elbow telling Dame that he wanted to borrow him for awhile. Spits followed the old man's lead as he led him along the side of the candle lit pool. He pointed to the ten miniature canoes floating atop the water carrying orange flamed tiki torches.

"That was my idea, to use the canoes to light the pool area with the torches." He boasted, clearly proud of the idea and the effect that it had upon the courtyard.

"It's beautiful. The whole place looks like some island paradise."

"Ah, but you're wrong Spits. This *is* Paradise. And right here in Hollywood." Mr. Davis put an arm around Spits shoulder and led him along. "There's one thing that you will soon be learning."

Stopping, Spits turned to look him in his eyes because he wanted Mr. Davis to know how much he valued his wisdom. "And what's that sir?"

Mr. Davis smiled. "Simply this. That once you become powerful, you can make people and paradise come to you no matter where you may be."

Spits smiled and hid the information away like a treasure. Though his face was a mask of confidence, he wanted to pass out from the awe he felt for this music tycoon next to him. There wasn't a more powerful person in music. Even just standing next to him, Spits could actually feel the power comin' from the man.

"I'm hoping to be able to announce to the world that you and Paper Chasin' Records are a part of the WMG family soon." Mr. Davis told him with a sly grin. Spits held back his smile and looked to where Margarita was standing and found her watching him as the women standing around her cast mean looks at her gown. He smiled and her face lit up for a moment before she turned back to her new friends before downing the drink in her hand and laughing at something Tracy said.

"We should have an answer for you by the close of business Tuesday. We wanted to take the weekend to let everything set in before we made such a major decision."

Mr. Davis' body shook as he chuckled. "That's the smart thing to do. I would've done the same if I were you."

His intention had been to throw a big number at them before the show and hoped they accepted so that the value of their company went through the roof but seeing how cool and in control Spits seemed, he thought better of it.

Spits had known from the start that they'd be fools to jump on the deal so quick. He and Dame had argued over it after Mash's arrest because Dame wanted to take the money now before they changed their mind. But Spits had pointed out that they were already getting big money as an indie label and would keep on whether they signed with World Music Group or not.

"Plus, once we take the money they'll be paying for the right to tell us what to do. We our own bosses right now and I like that." Spits tried to explain at the time.

But Dame hadn't agreed and they had a few choice words before Tracy stepped in and convinced him that with so many things coming at them from so many different places, it would be better if they let the decision rest over the weekend. So hearing Mr. Davis cosign his decision now told him that those same instincts which had served him so well selling dope in the streets, were still helping him now.

"Come with me son. There's a few people here that I think you should meet." Mr. Davis told him and led him to the center of the shark tank.

Loco stood on the other side of the pool talking with Angela Jones, an industry insider, trying to talk her into creeping off with him.

"I'm from Salinas baby girl, Cabrillo St. to be exact. Where you from?" Loco asked the petite lemon toned lady in the white bare back gown and pearl necklace. "You look like you just stepped out of the Garden of Eden or somethin'." He stepped back with a mischievous grin. His eyes taking in how the silk gown clung to her waist as if it belonged there. "And I'm tryin' to bite me some apples up in here."

Her eyes grew wide in shock for but a second before she put her hand to her mouth to cover her smile. "You're too much, you know that? I'm from New York though. I'm head of A&R for Get Money Records. What do you do?"

"Bang Cabrillo St. Mob. I'm a gangster. Ain't nobody got time to be doin' all that going to school and getting a degree stuff. I be too busy doing me." He bragged.

Angela couldn't help but be attracted to the handsome cocky thug standing in front of her with the biggest smile she'd ever seen. There was just something about the way his eyes laughed that drew her to him and she soon found herself blushing at his straight forward manner.

"Are you always this straight up?" She asked with a smile of her own.

"Yep. Why play around? I think you bad as heck and I'm tryin' to kick it with you tonight, so why wouldn't I say it?" He reasoned.

"Angela!" When she heard the male voice bark her name the smile left her face and she turned towards it.

"What is it Loochie?" She asked him and tried not to melt at the coldness she saw in his and his five friend's eyes as they came closer.

"Who's your little friend?" Loochie asked her. "I think I know him from somewhere." He mugged Loco. Loco's jaw clinched. He wanted to knock Loochie out.

"Ain't nothin' little 'bout the Loco but my understanding chief. You got me messed up." He looked Loochie up and down while sneering at him like he was funny. Angela's hand touched Loco's arm and she looked up to him with scared eyes.

"Please don't." She turned to Loochie's friends. "Come on Guys. It's Grammy night."

Loco winked at her and nodded his head once to Loochie then turned to leave and didn't get too far before he ran smack into Spits and Mr. Davis.

"What up homie?" He shook Spits hand with a devilish look in his eyes then looked past him to Mr. Davis. "Oh, you the fool who threw this crap?"

Mr. Davis threw his head back and laughed deep from his gut drawing dozens of stares from his guests. "I like your friend already Spits." He shook Loco's hand and patted his back before grabbing him a fresh drink. "Come with us. I was just about to introduce Spits here to a few friends of mine. I'm sure they'd love to meet you too."

Loco took a sip of the fine French brandy and the three set off with Mr. Davis between them. "You should introduce me to one of those females who you got working for you though. I was just 'bout to knock ole girl till Loochie's short butt came through hatin'." Loco suggested and again Mr. Davis' laugh boomed.

WEST, WEST YALL…

THIS YEAR'S BAY Business Pre-Grammy Smash was being held at Club Nokia in Downtown Los Angeles and hosted by KRAP. The place was jam packed with Northern Cali's Rap royalty, partying like it was 1999 as Slim rocked the joint with nothing but West Coast classics.

The artists, producers, and label owners were shining in their freshly pressed suits, jeans, Tee's, tennis shoes, and gold and platinum pieces. But nothing or no one in the club blazed brighter, nor partied harder than The Paper Chasin Record's private section of the club. Mash, Spen, The Paper Chasers, and the twenty five Hood Life homies were getting twisted and letting the world know that they were in the house.

Mash sat in a booth with Spen next to him watching a group of sistas by the dance floor watching him.

"Look at them broads over there!" He told Spen and pointed to the group of six barely dressed females.

"Invite them over here." Spen said as he waved them over and grabbed one of the bottles off the table holding it in the air to let them know it was all good. One of the girls said something and her five friends laughed.

"Watch this chief." Mash said and took the bottle from Spen and stood onto the table while laughing and throwing up the PJs with his fingers. "Hood Life's in this piece beezies!"

He took a long pull on the bottle of the Bombay then turned to the upstairs balcony and the people staring down at them. "And we fixin' to win all four of them statues tonight! I'm telling you right now! We bout to win all four of them tonight. This Hood Life chief!" He yelled.

Blu watched Mash with excited eyes. Drunk on the gin and attention, he kissed one of the girls next to him and also climbed onto the table with an overjoyed smile on his face. He twisted up his fingers like Mash's.

"That's right! This Hood Life!" He screamed. "Paper Chasin' fool!" He stared towards the pink dance floor where it seemed a million bad females were twisting their hips to the Dre beat. "HoodLife beezies! HoodLife beezies!"

Blu hopped from the table, fell into his two new girlfriend's laps, and elbowed Chill. "Man, you see all them broads out there looking all pink an crap?"

Chill mean mugged him and turned to Half seeing the same look of disgust on his face. He swung his head back to Blu. "You need to calm your little butt the heck down Blu." His voice held a threat. "We performing at Grammys in a couple of hours and you acting like we on a weekend trip to Vegas. Is you stupid or somethin'?

"You ain't sayin' that to Mash, so shut that up fool!" Blu was in his element and wasn't trying to hear it. "Mash!" He called and when Mash looked to him smiling, Blu held up his Bottle. "Let's drink to all these bad females that came to see ya boy." He laughed and took a big drink then tried to pour half the bottle down the girl's throats.

Mash stayed atop the table, scanning the club with smile on his face. He was the big fish in the pond and he knew that everybody here knew it. That's why he'd come here instead of going to the World Music Group's party. These were the people whose music he had come up listening to and had always dreamed of flossin' on.

I told them that Seaside was gon' go big. Now look at this. They all on me now.

"Come on a dance with me Janet." Spen grabbed her hand and pulled her from her seat. "You ain't had a drink or nothing since we got here and you looking way to grown and sexy in that gown for you to be actin' like it's Easter Sunday."

She stopped not two steps from the table refusing to leave and blushed at his fiery eyes sweeping over the black silk Versace number she wore. She crossed her arms and tightened her face.

"I'm working in case you forgot and you're not making my job any easier Spen."

Tracy had made her Mash's babysitter for the night to make sure that him and his friends didn't get too drunk or get into any trouble. And try as she might, she didn't feel like she was doing a good job of it.

"I'm supposed to make sure that Mash doesn't get into *anymore* trouble," She poked Spen in the chest. "and with you around, I don't think I'll be able to do that."

"So now I'm the bad guy?" He smiled at her.

"You dang sure were yesterday when the police caught you with all those drugs."

"So what's that mean? That you ain't gon' dance with me?" He smiled and took her hand again trying to pull her to the dance floor.

"Uh-Uh." She wouldn't budge but she gave him a small smile. "I can't. I'm working." She looked to Mash who was bragging to the white girl up under him and shook her head. "Look Spen. I do want to dance with you but I really can't right now."

"So do I get a rain check then?"

Janet smiled at his persistence. *He is kinda cute.* "Yeah. We'll dance after the show. Even if you're public enemy number one right now."

Spen snickered at this. "Don't trip Ma. Everything ain't always what it looks like. Mash is my dog and I wouldn't never do nothing to get him caught up. Yesterday was a fluke. He gon' be straight though."

"Well, will you help me keep him and your friends out of trouble then? We've all got a lot riding on tonight and we don't need any more drama."

"I got you." Spen promised her. "We ain't come out here to start nothin'. Like I said, Mash is my dog and I ain't trying to see him get in any trouble. So don't even trip on that." He smiled and let his eyes roam her body again. "Just make sure that you save that dance for me girl."

WE GOT THIS...

DAME CUT QUITE the imposing figure in the perfectly cut tux which did little to hide the width of his huge shoulders and back. He had a smile for the ages plastered across his face while him and Tracy sat in two of the best seats in the house waiting for the start of the show.

"You know I want another raise don't you?" Tracy looked over and asked with a smile.

"Shoot. If we win album of the year everybody with the label's gonna get a raise." He promised.

They were sitting to the right of Mr. Davis and his wife with Spits, Margarita and Mash sitting to their left. The show would start in ten minutes and the air in the Kodak Theatre was charged with an electric current as if the building itself were alive and breathing.

"How are you enjoying yourself Damon?" Mr. Davis leaned over and asked Dame.

"This is the life I was meant to live." Dame answered. "I just hate that it took me so long to find out."

"Well, we'll just have to make sure that you have a long and prosperous career in the industry to make up for lost times then. I'm glad that you're enjoying yourself though. You deserve it."

Dame nodded his thanks wondering what Mr. Davis and the rest of these wealthy people would think of him if they knew all he'd been through to make it here. If they would still be so quick to befriend him if they knew he'd taken people's lives in his pursuit of a dollar. Or would they even care.

At the tender age of sixteen, Dame had witnessed the birth of the crack epidemic as it hit Seaside like a typhoon. To Dame, it was the start of a golden opportunity.

Growing up with his sister in a single parent, single income home had exposed him to the not so fine things in life and caused him to thirst for more for himself. When crack hit the streets and he saw his classmates hanging in the projects slingin' and flossin' at school with thousands in their pockets, he wasted little time in jumping in the game.

"What are you thinking about?" Tracy asked seeing the dreamy look on his face.

"I'm just trippin' on how I came from where I did to be sitting here brushing shoulders with all these rich folks."

She put her hand on his knee and gave it a squeeze. "You don't know how happy I am that you did this. I've been sleeping like a baby ever since you stopped hustlin'."

He smiled a smile which didn't quite make it to his eyes and turned away from her so she wouldn't notice his sudden discomfort. He looked to the stage where the technical crew ran around making sure that everything was just right for the opening performance. He didn't see them but saw the faces which had begun haunting him since they'd started on this new journey.

He had the same dream every night without fail. He saw the man and his wife's agonized faces even when he was woke sometimes and try as he might, he couldn't escape their eerie screams as he shot them dead in their living room and made off with the dope hidden behind the couch.

What was most disturbing to him was how vivid the dream was. It was if someone had recorded the double homicide he'd committed 20 years ago and was now playing it over and over in his head at the most bothersome and inconvenient times.

Not tonight! Forget that. I won't let you fools ruin this for me. Y'all gon' have to catch me later on when I get to my room or something. He told his ghostly enemies.

The show began with a rousing performance by a heavy metal group that had the fans screaming from the balcony. Mash sat watching, next to Margarita, trying not to look as drunk and high as he was while taking in the bright lights, glamorous women, cameras, and power surrounding him. This was it. The biggest moment in his life and he was nervously anticipating the announcement of one of the awards they were up for.

I did this. I made all this happen. Watch. When we win, I'm 'bout to charge fools up the yang for my beats. He told himself, knowing that this and everything else that had happened had been because he had first dreamed it.

Margarita interrupted his thoughts when she leaned over and whispered in his ear. "You look like you had a little too much fun at that party you and your friends went to."

He smiled back at her. "You know how we do it. This is a big night so I wanted to have a good time. I'm good though."

"This whole weekend's been like a dream come true for me."

"Just wait till next year when your albums up for album of the year."

She blushed at the compliment and thought how she would love nothing more than to have his words turn true. Vowing to herself that she would spend the next twelve months doing whatever it took to make it happen. "Yeah. We'll definitely be back next year." She agreed and held up a hand which he high fived.

When the presenters for the song of the year took to the podium, Spits felt as if his heart would jump from his chest, it pounded so hard and fast. He took Margarita's and Mash's hands and held his breath as the nominees were announced.

Come on. Call us. Come on, say 'Take a Chance on me.

"And the winner is." The announcer opened the envelope slowly, drawing the moment out. "Spits, featuring Margarita for 'Take A Chance On Me!" He announced to loud cheers and applause.

Margarita jumped from her seat with both hands to her mouth. "We won! We did it baby!"

Spits stood, picked her up and kissed her as if they were the only two people there and this just made the audience clap even louder. Those seated before the stage with them gave them a standing ovation. When they finally came up for air, Tracy and Dame were standing there with open arms.

"You guys did it! Congratulations!" Tracy said with tears of joy running down her cheeks.

"No. *We* did it. We all worked hard to make this happen." Spits corrected.

Mash stood smiling at Spits and hugged him when he turned around. "I told you we was gon' be famous." Mash whispered into his ear.

"Come on." Spits told Mash and took Margarita's hand and the three of them made their way to the podium to the sound of ear splitting cheers and applause.

Spits stood at the podium waving to the fans on the balcony chanting his name. He bent to the microphone.

"Thank you." He began only to be cut off by the fans up on the balcony chanting his name.

"Spits! Spits! Spits! Spits!" They screamed.

"Thank you." He repeated. After a moment, the theater quieted and again he bent to the mic. "I'd like to thank God first and foremost." He looked behind him and waved Mash forward and threw an arm over his shoulder when he stood next to him. "Next I'd like to thank this man right here, my producer and friend Mash." He looked at Mash with tears in his eyes. "Thank you for believing in me and making me believe in your dream. I know I don't say it a lot but I appreciate all you've done for me homie."

He turned to Margarita with a look so full of love that the audience again stood to clap.

"And to the most beautiful woman in the building-"
The audience clapped their agreement.

"I'd like to thank you for taking a chance on me and for teaching me what love means. You are the single most important thing in my life and I'm just glad that you've been here living my dreams with me." He pointed to the third row. "And to Dame and Tracy. You two worked your butts off to put us in this position and I want you to know that I appreciate you very much. Thank's for believing in me and forcing me to believe in myself."

Finally, he looked to the balcony and smiled. "And last but not least. I'd like to thank the fans for supporting me and the Paper Chasin' movement."

Margarita stepped to the podium and thanked God, her parents for being the best parents in the world, Spits for talking her into going to Mash's studio and Tracy for convincing her to chase her own dreams.

She then waved to the balcony smiling. "And thank you all for making our song number one because without you none of this would be possible."

Mash was next and he kept it short and not so sweet. "I didn't prepare no speech so I won't be long." He looked straight to the balcony where the homies were now chanting 'Hood Life'.

"I'd like to give a shout to my Hood Life homies who've been holding me down from day one. I love Y'all and trust and believe that it's still PJs all day." He twisted his fingers and threw up the hood and the homies started going crazy chanting 'PJs' over and over as they were led offstage.

With statue in hand, Spits followed their escort who led them through the chaos backstage and to the media room. There they found the last award winner being interviewed by reporters from a variety of magazines and entertainment shows.

"You guys will go on next." The usher informed them before handing them off to a beige suited gentleman holding a clipboard and wearing a head-set.

"We gon' win the other ones too!" Mash predicted as his eyes took in the activities going on around him. "Look! He pointed to where a small group stood around an older white gowned woman wearing pounds of diamonds. "Ain't that that famous actress whose ex bought her the biggest diamond in the world?"

Margarita brought a hand to her mouth, stunned at the sight. "Oh my God! It is! I love her movies." She tapped Spits arm excitedly. "Baby do you see her? Look, it is her. I can't believe it."

He smiled and let his eyes slowly sweep over the crowded room. "I think that everybody here's more interested in you than her. Look at how they all keep looking at you."

She looked and saw that indeed she was receiving lots of complimenting stares.

"It's just the dress." She looked at herself in the wall length mirror beside them beaming. More people had told her how beautiful she was tonight than all her life and she found herself loving all the attention.

"The dress makes me look better than I really am."

Spits shook his head at her modesty. "If you don't stop it. You know dang well that you fine as all outdoors girl."

Margarita kissed him. "I love you Papi. Thank you for giving me this moment."

"Okay you three. They're ready for you now." The man led them to the center of the World Music Center backdrop and they were immediately blinded by what appeared to be hundreds of cameras flashing.

"How does it feel winning your first Grammy Spits?" The tuxedoed host of the TV show Entertainment Now asked as he held a microphone towards him.

Spits smiled. "It feel great. This is what I saw happening when I first heard Margarita sing. I knew then that her voice was just what we needed. I knew we had a hit so it feels good just being proved right."

The host turned smiling to Margarita. "It's been declared by us within the media that you have been voted the most beautiful woman in attendance Margarita."

She gave him an award winning smile. "I wish that were true but thaNk's for the compliment. There's a lot of beautiful women here tonight that I'm sure would be much more deserving of that award if there were one."

"I wasn't kidding though." He insisted smiling. "Although it's not official but every year we media types vote on who the best looking woman and man are at the Grammys. And tonight, you've managed to outshined the brightest stars on the planet."

"And I fixed the vote." Spits added to much laughter.

When they finished with the interviews they were led back to their seats during commercial break. Tracy and Dame stood and walked to the aisle as they came down the stage steps.

"We did it!" Tracy screamed as she hugged Spits. "I'm so proud of you baby. You deserve this."

Dame hugged his nephew with an emotion filled voice as he spoke. "You were right. You called it and I'm glad that I listened."

Mash was a bit surprised by his uncle's affectionate display. "Unc you acting all soft up in here around all these white folks."

Dame laughed and wiped at his eyes before leaning in close to his ear. "Forget these white folks. We from Hood Life."

Mash's laughter could be heard in the balcony seats. "That's right unc. HoodLife's in this piece." He agreed.

They sat through the rest of the performances in a dream state as Spits name was called twice more. Throughout it all they all kept shooting secret smiles at each other, knowing that come Monday, it would really be on. All that they'd done so far had been nothing but practice for what was to come.

Spits was unusually quiet and withdrawn as the show progressed. He learned much this past weekend. In talking for hours with Mr. Davis earlier, he had learned the most important fact of his life: in order to be truly powerful he must begin cultivating relationships with powerful people. Mr. Davis had been nice enough to introduce him to some of the wealthiest people in the world and telling him that if he was as hungry as he seemed, then it was a must for him to meet the right people.

He'd also found that Dame had been right in not wanting them to react to Loochie's diss track. True enough, they'd made millions from it, but with all of the tension he'd felt from East Coast artists, producers, and label owners, he saw just how dangerous the situation really was.

Mr. Davis had made a comment that had stayed with him. He told Spits that sometimes a man must swallow his pride and make friends with those who were supposed to be enemies for the sake of winning in the long run. Although he hadn't said Loochie's name, it was clear to Spits that the man was advising him to squash the beef and put his focus on building up an empire of his own.

When the show's host announced that the time had come for the presentation of the album of the year award, the auditorium grew eerily quiet. Margarita took hold of Spits and Mash's hands and gave them a squeeze.

"And here to present the Grammy for album of the year, is a man who many have called the greatest Rapper of all time. Owner of Get Money Records-"

Spits looked to Tracy with worried eyes which mirrored her own. This had to be bad. The Grammy committee had to know that he and Loochie had been beefing for the past six months and he felt that they wouldn't have Loochie to present him with a Grammy for that simple fact.

He turned to Margarita and saw that she too was worried. "We ain't gon' win it." He whispered and saw Loochie walk onto the stage out the corner of his eye. He heard the booing from the balcony and the applause from the star studded audience around him.

"They're gonna give it to somebody else." He predicted with a grimace.

Loochie smiled as he walked to the podium holding the oversized envelope in his hand, ignoring the jeers.

"Thank you." He said graciously. He scanned the faces in the crowd. "I see a lot of familiar faces here tonight and you all remind me just how lucky I am to be involved in the entertainment industry…"

Spits wasn't listening as he sat seeing visions of somebody else taking the stage to accept the award. He felt as if he would be sick and realized that he wanted to win more than he had thought. He tried to tell himself that it didn't matter, that he'd already won three awards and that they'd had a good night regardless. But this didn't help. He wanted this one so bad he could taste it.

"And the winner is," Loochie said as he tore the envelope open and removed the card inside, pausing as he read it. "Spits for the album 'Legend!"

Caught up in his thoughts, it wasn't until Margarita jumped from her seat holding his hands that he knew he'd won. He looked up at her with a look of shock on his face.

"Baby you won it!" She pulled him up and hugged him with wet eyes. When he kissed her, the auditorium erupted and started chanting his name again. They then shared a group hug with Dame, Tracy, and Mash.

"Come on Y'all, we're all going onstage for this one. This belongs to all of us." Spits said and led his team to the podium to a standing ovation.

"Again I'd like to thank God first." He began then stopped to let the applause die down. He turned to look behind him. "And to my team, you guys are the best, I love you all." He looked up to the balcony and again they began chanting his name. He closed his eyes and let out a deep breath, finally able to let his past life go. It was here in this moment that he finally felt free from those prison walls which had once held him captive.

He breathed deep again and looked into the third row where Mr. Davis sat smiling at him. He thought back to their earlier conversation when he had told him that he thought Spits had the potential to become an American icon if he but made the right moves from this point on. He leaned to speak into the mic again.

"This weekend has not only been the best of my life to this point, but it has also been a learning experience." He turned to look over his shoulder and saw Loochie standing with a fake smile and hate in his eyes. He nodded and turned to the mic. "I'm sure you've all heard about the so called "beef" between me and this great man behind me."
The fans on the balcony started booing and he held up his hands for silence.

"This weekend has shown me that any disagreement that we may have isn't worth the coastal divisions it has caused." He turned again and waved Loochie forward. "So I'm officially throwing in the towel and ending the beef between Paper Chasin' and Get Money Records."

Loochie stepped forward and the two hugged to roaring applause as the auditorium cheered 2011's biggest winner.

Mash stood behind them with a scowl on his face watching as Spits stood with his arm around Loochie and smiling for the cameras like they were the best of friends.

What the heck's wrong with this soft fool? Forget that East Coast punk. That fool dissed the hood. What's Spits doing? He thought as he watched the sickening display.

FOLLOW THE LEADER...

PEACHES AND HER ten newly hired designers were all gathered around one of the twelve tables scattered throughout the warehouse. Dressed in an all black no nonsense pantsuit, Peaches sat at the head of the head of the table taking the time to make eye contact with each of her designers.

"When we finish here, I've got to catch my flight to China." Lisa, her best friend and second and command, reminded her from the seat next to her. She looked at her watch, worried that she'd miss her flight which left in three hours.

"I know girl. Don't worry, I'll be sure to wrap this up quick enough for you to make your flight." Peaches assured her. "This meeting's just a formality anyway."

Peaches looked around and smiled before pushing her chair back and standing. "I'd like to thank you all for not only coming but also for taking this chance of a lifetime to become a part of what I believe will be something big. Like me, you are all lovers of fashion and I want you all to know that I am dedicated to turning 211 into *The* urban fashion brand on the West Coast.

"As you all know, the West Coast rap scene has a cult like following and what I envision for 211, is that we will take on the essence of that. And Spits is dedicated to promoting the products that we here will design and create just like he has dedicated himself to becoming one of the most popular artist in the hip hop genre. I expect for 211 to become the best and most respected fashion house in the industry." She sat and gave up the floor for questions.

"Hi everybody. My name is Chanel Cook and I'm from San Diego." The brown skinned smiling twenty something year old said from the opposite end of the table. "I have a question for you Peaches. When you interviewed me, you mentioned that you wanted for your designers to think outside of the box. Do you have anything specific in mind when you say that?"

Peaches shook her head. "No. But let me clarify myself so that we'll all be on the same page. What I expect from us here is that we be trendsetters and not simply play follow the leader. I don't want for us to get labeled as radicals or anything but I do have every intention of leading the way. As I've told you all, for our first year, we will stick to jeans and T-shirts. Shoes, jackets, and accessories are to follow in our second year.

"The numbers say that jeans and T-shirts are the biggest seller in Urban wear, so we'll use these items to gain a foot hold in the industry and from there we will be able to take full advantage of our share of the market."

After answering all their questions and kicking around a few ideas, Peaches called an end to the meeting and let her team get to work. Her and Lisa walked up the stairs leading to her office overlooking the warehouse and she sat down heavily in her desk chair.

"I'm glad that's over." She laughed. "Did I look as nervous as I was feeling?"

"Girl, you did fine." Her tall, light complected friend told her as she took the seat facing the desk. "You came across like you know your stuff and ain't gon' be taking no mess." She looked at her watch with a frown and stood. "I better go before I miss my flight. I'll give you a call when I get to China okay?"

"Okay. I'll see you in a few days." She came from behind the desk and gave her a warm hug. "Good luck girl."

With Lisa gone, Peaches sat back down and smiled. She still couldn't believe that this was happening to her so soon. She'd mapped out her future years ago. Four years of college, ten years working for an established Italian fashion designer then she would start her own business. And yet here she was ten years ahead of schedule.

Knowing from whence her blessings came and wanting to share the news with him, she picked up her desk phone and dialed his number.

"Hello?" Spits answered.

"Congratulations!"

"ThaNk's. Did you watch the show last night?"

"What else would I have been doing? Of course I watched it and I'm so happy for you. Did you have a good time in LA?"

"It was cool, mostly work. But I did have a good time. I never knew that the wealthy partied so hard but I guess I should've since they work so dang hard."

"Speaking of hard work, we just had our first meeting and everything is going according to schedule here. Lisa just left for her flight to China to meet with the manufacturers that I want to work with and my designers are downstairs getting started as we speak." She heard him laugh. "What's so funny?"

"You." He told her. "I knew you were a workaholic when I met you. It's only been what, five months and you're already up and running."

She laughed too. "And look who's talking. Aren't you the same man who came out of nowhere to steal four Grammys night in less than a year in the industry?"

"Naw, that wasn't me. That was because I've got a good team around me."

"Yeah right, Mr. 'I can't come to see you because I'm travelling to all corners of the world, or recording new material'."

"You got me there. I do work hard." He admitted.

"So what now? You're officially the biggest thing in music as of last night. What's next?"

"I'm getting ready for this meeting where Me, Mash, and Dame are gonna decide whether or not to take the hundred and fifty million that World Music Group offered us last week."

Again she laughed. "That doesn't sound like too hard a decision to make."

"It's more complicated than that." He told her. "Thank's for calling and keeping me up to date."

"But you've got to go right?" She asked with a smile in her voice.

"Yeah. The meeting's starting in a few minutes and then I have a flight to catch. I'll call you when I get back in town though okay."

"Okay. You take care of yourself Spits."

"You too." He said and hung up.

She sat staring at the phone long after the call ended thinking of how her good fortune was actually a double edged sword. Because try as she might to not allow herself to, she was falling in love with him in spite of their deal to keep their relationship strictly business.

In these past three months, they'd been in constant contact and the frequency of their conversations had saw them getting to know each other a lot better. The more that she learned about him, the more she began to see just how compatible they actually were. When they'd first met at Diana's, she had mistaken him to be just another shallow rapper that believed all the bull he rapped on record. But he wasn't and she loved him for it.

In the beginning of their relationship, there had been this sexually charged energy between them. But once they'd agreed to go into business together, that energy had seemed to die and they had grown closer because of it.

Sitting here now thinking about him with a smile that didn't reach her hurting heart, she admitted to herself that it was refreshing to finally have a male friend who wasn't always trying to get in her pants. Yet on the other hand, her heart desired him as it had never desired anything before and she found herself constantly fantasizing about sleeping with someone else's man.

"Oh my God. What's going on with me? I can't let myself get caught up loving somebody that I can't have." She whispered with tears of longing in her eyes.

BIG BOYS MAKE BIG BOY MOVES...

THEY WERE ALL seated around the conference room table laughing as they passed the statues around and talked about their big weekend. The whole Paper Chasin' team was ready to discuss the next assault they would make upon the industry. They were feeling like kings of the hill at the label and everyone's energy was off the charts. As usual Tracy had popped a couple bottles of Champagne for the mini celebration before they'd got down to the business at hand.

After a while Dame called for silence. "Okay you guys, let's get go on and handle this. Play time's over. It's time to get back to work now."

"Hold up a second Dame." Spits said as he stood holding the album of the year statue. "I wanted to thank you all for all the hard work you put in to make this award possible because without you all, I would've never been in this position. So thank you."

As soon as he sat down, Mash spoke. "I've got something to say too." He looked down at his uncle and received an icy stare. "I just want to apologize to Y'all for any embarrassment my arrest might have caused anybody here. I-"

"It's cool homie." Spits interrupted him. "You already explained what happened and can't nobody here judge you chief. It's all good."

"Yeah baby." Tracy added. "WMG still wants us so you haven't done any harm to the label or anybody here besides yourself." She shot Dame a salty look. "You don't owe nobody nothin'. Let's just move on and keep chasin' that paper like you showed us."

"Thank you." He said and with a heavy voice.

Dame expression remained stony for a moment before he finally nodded his head that he was over it. "Okay then. The first thing we need to do is decide how we respond to the offer. Of course, Me, my nephew and Spits are the ones who will vote, but I'd like to hear what anybody here has to say before we do. I think you all know that I feel we should take the money and I'll explain to you why.

"We're on schedule to release Margarita's first single in three weeks which we will follow up by releasing her album a month later. I think that the deal from World Music will enhance our ability to push her album to the public. They're the biggest fish in this ocean we're swimming in and with them on the team, we can do it a lot bigger than we did with Spits' project."

He nodded that he was done and Tracy spoke up before anybody else could.

"I think we should accept too. With a major behind us, we'll look more attractive for the established artists who aren't happy at their current labels. And once we sign a few big name artists we'd be pretty much unstoppable from there."

"We unstoppable now Trace. Look at them statues standing in up here." Mash said proudly and they all smiled at the truth of his statement.

"I think we take the money and use WMG's media machine to promote our brand." Janet said. "We've already introduced Spits, Margarita, and the Paper Chasers to the public but with them behind us, there is no limit to the heights we can take this label. We can use their clout to associate our name with corporate names and really take it to the next level. This is nothing but a win-win situation for us."

Mash and Spits shared a smile knowing that it was the long hours that they'd spent in the Blue Room creating their sound was making this all possible. This was just what they'd talked about during those long hours and to be sitting here with four Grammys staring down the table at them felt better than good.

"I'm with my uncle on this one. I think we should take the money and run." Mash said to Spits. "Remember when you said that cats was gonna be arguing about how much money we had one day? If we take this deal that's exactly what they 'bout to be doing."

Margarita had her fingers crossed in her lap as the discussion moved around the table praying that they took the deal. Her album was a brilliant one and she felt that there was no way in hell she wouldn't be a household name in a matter of months with WMG backing them. But she was worried at how silent Spits had been since the morning following the show. When she had asked him why, all he would say was that he was thinking about the offer and that he was still trying to figure out how they should respond to it.

Spits sat next to her thinking of the long conversation he and Loochie had after the show at the post Grammy party. After giving his acceptance speech, the two had went backstage together and were rushed by the media wanting to interview them and take pictures of them together. They'd had so much fun doing this that Spits and Margarita had rode to the party with him and the two new friends had ended up staying up till the early morning talking. Loochie dropped jewels of wisdom on him and Spits soaked it all up just as he had with Mr. Davis.

When he had told Loochie of the offer Mr. Davis had made and the reservations he had about accepting, Loochie told him how he'd handled the same situation ten years ago and how he had used them to build Get Money Records into what it was today.

Tracy noticed that he was unusually quiet. "What about you Spits? You're the only one of the big three who hasn't spoke. How do you feel about the offer?"

"I think we should reject it." He said and forced himself to hold back the smile that threatened to pass his lips at seeing the shock on all their faces.

"You're kidding right?" Dame asked after a long stunned silence.

He shook his head. "I'm dead serious. I like it that I'm my own boss and I'm not in no rush to give up control of my company to World Music Group or anyone else." He paused and let his gaze sweep the room. "But. I do see how having them behind us will allow us to do things we wouldn't be able to do on our own. So with that said, I say we reject the offer and make a counter one."

He saw the faces around the table turn from shock to respect as he outlined his plan to offer WMG a forty percent stake in the label for two hundred million dollars. Out of which He, Mash, and Dame would split a hundred million, put ninety million into the label's war chest and give the team bonuses with the rest. It was a brilliant idea.

When he finished, there was a heavy silence in the room until Dame threw back his head and laughed. "Well it looks to me like we not only got the best rapper in the business but the sharpest too. I'm changing my vote. I say we make the counter offer."

"Me too." Mash agreed as did everybody in attendance.

PROMISES IN PARADISE...

MARGARITA THOUGHT THAT that the chaise lounge chair was a cloud and that she must be floating close to heaven as she lay on her stomach with the Indian sun darkening her back an almond brown. She had a smile on her face ever since she'd stepped blindfolded off of Mr. Davis' private Gulf Stream jet.

The two of them were watching the sun set over Lake Pichola and she was awed still at the reflection of the world famous Taj Resort's Rambagh Palace floating on the water's waves.

It was heaven on earth as far as Margarita was concerned and she was cherishing this moment.

She sighed deep and whispered. "I'll never forget this. Or that you gave me the most beautiful thing that anyone ever could." She reached over to the chaise next to her and took Spits hand. "I've been wanting to come here ever since I was-"

"-A little girl." He finished for her while checking out her sun bronzed body laid out like a present for him. "You've been sayin' the same thing since we got here Ma."

"I know. But I-" She stopped and rolled over while holding her top and turned so he could tie her up. "I just love it here so much so I keep saying it because I want you to know how much it means to me that you brought me here."

When her top was tied, she turned to him with raw, uncut love in her green eyes and he made a promise to himself that he'd never get tired of making her dreams come true for her.

"I love seeing you like this baby. This is how I pictured you when we first met."

She smiled at him and crossed her legs slow and sexy with a flirty pout on her lips. "How?" she asked. "Laying with my top off in India drinking Margaritas?"

"No" He shook his head and rolled his eyes at her, loving these special moments. "I pictured you happy." He said and went on to explain. "The first time I walked into Dorothy's and saw you smiling at this old lady, I've had this picture of you in my head with a permanent smile on your face." He smiled again. "Just like the one you've had since we got here."

She leaned over and kissed him before sighing again."Ummm. I love it here." She grabbed her cocktail and sipped on it some before laying back and staring out to the lake.

"I don't think I'm going to stop saying thank you all year Papi." She laughed. "You're so romantic. I love that about you."

"Do you?"

"Yep. And I love the Indian dishes they've been serving." She laughed." What did the chef call what we're having for lunch? Kep-pa-la-la-la fish curry?"

They shared a laugh at her constant butchering of the native language. She stuttered whenever she tried to speak it. A comfortable silence settled between them as they stared out to the lake and the Himalayas far in the distance.

Tipsy from the cocktails and calmed by the silence and serene surroundings, Margarita dozed off then woke with a jolt to find him staring off with a blank look on his face and a lost look in his eyes.

She didn't speak but lay there watching him scared at the fear she saw in his eyes yet again. Then she threw her legs over the side of the chair and knelt down beside him taking his hands in hers.

"Papi, what is it?" She asked him gently. "And don't tell me that it's nothing. You keep getting this far off look in your eyes and it's starting to scare me. You're blocking me out and I can't figure out how to not be scared about that. Let me help you baby. I love you."

"I know Ma. I-"

"Then *act* like it."

"I will. I mean I-" Spits looked away and let out a deep troubled breath. "I'm not keeping anything from you baby. It's just that I got something on my mind and since I can't figure it out I don't know how to *begin* to make you understand it."

"You begin by letting me *help* you figure it out." She told him making it sound so simple. "Aren't we a team?" She asked. "Because that's what you've been telling me all along. Don't go getting scared on me now."

He laughed remembering saying those words to her in the dressing room at the Fox. He looked at her and nodded his head.

"That's just it Ma. I *am* scared. I'm not used to not understanding what's going on with me and it's got me spooked."

She got up to sit next to him with her back to the lake. "What is it though Papi? What's got you so scared?"

"How hungry I'm becoming." He told her and instantly felt better. "It's like the more I get, the more I want. And I ain't never been like that. I think what's scaring me is not knowing if I'm becoming somebody that even I won't like when I get to where I'm going."

"But you were hungry when I met you selling crack out front of Dorothy's. You used to tell me all the time that you were hustling so hard because you wanted a better life for yourself. So what's so different now besides the amount of money you're dealing with?"

"I think that's the problem. That the amount's so big. I feel like I'm being ungrateful for wanting more. A lot more."

She nodded her head that she understood him completely and then turned away from him to stared out at the lake. "Have you asked yourself why?"

"Why what?"

"Why you want more?" She asked. "You say you've never been greedy so I doubt that a few million would change that about you. At least not this fast. So why do you want so much if not for the love of money?"

The question surprised him and he leaned back so he could see her face and saw that she was wearing a smart-alecky grin. He smiled also and laid back.

"Oh, you just think you're King Solomon around here don't you?" He pulled her close, holding her tight and stared off to the lake.

"I do have my moments of wisdom and insight." She said with a smile in her voice.

"That's a good question though." He admitted but offered no answer.

"Baby we need to talk about this. Whatever it is." He remained silent so she continued. "I'm scared too. It seems like the more I get into this, the bigger star I want to be too. I wondered the same thing that you're wondering a few months ago when Tracy told me that I had to start dressing sexy. And I'm scared now that I might keep having to make decisions that go against who I am for the sake of fame."

He nodded his head as she spoke and when she finished, he rolled off the chair and onto his knees before her. "Well, if you marry me we can figure this out together." He pulled a black velvet box from his pocket. "Will you marry me Ma?"

She cried while smiling. "Yes! Of course I'll marry you! I love you Deandre." She watched him put the ring on her finger with the biggest smile. "I love you so much for this baby. This is the most beautiful vacation any woman could want." She stood and they kissed.

"I love you too baby." He told her.

"Let's go for a walk." She suggested and they went hand in hand along the edge of the waters. The world was in the palm of their hands and they both felt that they knew the weight of what lay ahead. The pressures of the industries would be a thousand fold when they got back. All of the fame, money, power and experience that they had now as a unit put Margarita dead in the cross hairs. And their engagement, multiplied it all over again.

"Baby did you notice how mad Mash was when you called a truce with Loochie?"

"No. Was he?" Spits dropped Margarita hand and turned to her with a worried look on his face. "What do you mean?"

"He was standing behind you with that same look in his eyes that he had when we had the meeting after Loochie went on KRAP." She looked past him, remembering the moment. "With all the excitement since then, I had forgotten it until now. But now that I remember, the look in his eyes scared me. If all those people wouldn't have been there, he would've gotten violent."

"He's been trippin' with that extra tough stuff from the jump though, to keep it real."

Spits had let the swiftness of their rise to the top stop him from worrying about Mash and his kiddie crap. He hadn't had the time to with dang near everybody in the world wanting a piece of him.

"Well, you just make sure that you watch him and stay focused on climbing to the top baby." She cautioned.

"I will." He said then got that far off look in his eyes again.

"What is it?"

"I'm just thinking about this idea that I've been kicking around in my head for a little while."

"What kind of idea?"

"I'm thinking that if me and you go hard for the next few years and turn ourselves into the biggest things in the music biz, we can start our own independent label and get all the money." He explained. "I want it all Ma and I think that's the way to get there. With Paper Chasin' I gotta split my paper three ways. But if we do this, It'll all be on us."

"That's an ambitious plan baby." She told him, thinking of all the hard work that it would take to turn it into a reality. "But if that's what you really want then I'm in it with you." She gave him a winning smile. "I'm with you all the way. I want it all too Papi. Let's do this."

A BOSSY LADY...

TRACY SAT LOOKING out her office window while talking on the phone.

"No Ron. You can't get Spits and Margarita. Just Margarita. Her single's gonna do numbers like 'Take A Chance On Me' did. But why don't we throw the Paper Chasers in the mix. They were good enough for the Grammys, surely they're good enough for Saturday Night Live."

SNL's senior producer laughed. "You're a bossy one aren't you? I feel sorry for the men over there at Paper Chasin' Records with one like you around."

She laughed too. "Forget you Ron. You know I'm right. It's a win-win for the both of us. We're trying to build the Paper Chasers brand and you have enough viewers to help us do this. And you win because they bring a whole new demographic to the table for you. Thugs stopped watching Saturday Night Life when Eddie Murphy left."

Again he laughed. "I definitely feel sorry for your men. You haven't bitten your tongue one time since you called. Has anybody ever told you that you have a beautifully aggressive personality?" Her giggling told him that she'd heard something of the sort before. "You've got a deal lady. I'll book it."

"Thank you Ron. And I promise you that you won't regret it. She's nothing like the nun role we packaged her as for 'Take A Chance On Me'. She's the female version of her man, a winner."

Tracy pumped her fist in the air after they hung up and turned to stare out at the waves of the Pacific outside her window. She wondered what Spits and Margarita were doing in India. It had been her who had made all the top-secret arrangements for him. She loved him more for being such a gentleman to the woman he loved.

Janet came bursting through the door. "Tracy come on." She pointed behind her. "Dame wants you to hear this."

"What is it?" Tracy got up and followed her to Dame's office curious to know what was going on now.

"Okay Chase, she's hear now." Dame said to the intercom when she came in.

"What's up Tracy?" Chase asked on the other end.

"Hey Chase. How's life in The Big Apple?"

"You know how we gettin' it out here girl. It's real big yo."

"As a matter of fact that's why he called." Dame said shooting Tracy a wide smile. "They want to do something with us."

"Something like what?" She asked suspiciously, instinctively thinking to protect her little brother. "What have you two been talking about?"

Chase's laughter blared from the intercom at the doubt in her tone. "Don't trip Tracy, it ain't nothing like that. Loochie just wanted me to get at Dame and see what he thought about a joint album. Loochie, Spits, The Paper Chasers and The Get Money Clique. Fifty-fifty split of everything down the middle. We can get a tour out of it and everything."

Tracy looked from the intercom to Dame and he was still smiling. "How long will it take to put it together?" She asked.

"That's why Dame wanted you here. He said that it was on you. We think that New York is the best place to do this. We have everything here, from studios to producers. The best hotels and the whole nine. So it's just a matter of you getting your team in place."

"I can have 'em there tonight if you want." She said laughing. "I'll make Spits and Margarita cut they vacation short and fly into La Guardia within an hour." She waited for everyone to stop laughing. "What about Spits and Mash? We need to talk to them before we start making all these grand plans." She cut her eyes at Dame. "And since Spits ain't taking *or* making any phone calls, I know you two haven't been arguing have you?"

Again Chase's laugh burst from the intercom. "Dame, ole girls a pistol ain't she?"

Dame smirked at her, seeing the steel in her eyes. "Him and Loochie talked about the stuff after the Grammys. He's the one who told Chase to call me and make it happen." Dame told her. "I don't know what made him think I'd be with it."

The phone on her hip vibrated and she looked down at it noticing the India prefix. "Speaking of the devil". She mumbled and walked to the corner of the office. "Hello?"

"What's up Sis? How you doin'?"

"Why are you calling me? You're supposed to be getting your Casanova on. Where's Margarita?"

"Sitting right here in my lap wearing the diamond ring I gave her."

"How many carats is-" She stopped, realizing what he just said. "You gave her a what?" She heard Margarita laughing in the background. "Do you guys have me on loudspeaker?"

"Hi Tracy!" Margarita called out happily. "He asked me to marry him and I said yes!"

"Oh my God!" Tracy said. "You didn't tell me you were going to propose to her boy!"

"I didn't know I had to." He teased.

"Well you do! I'm going to kill you. You have me go through all the high security top secret mission stuff and you were keeping a secret from me too?" She turned to face the room smiling. "Spits and Margarita's getting married!"

Janet almost fainted at the news. "Congratulations!" She yelled towards the phone Tracy was holding in the air with the loudspeaker on.

"So you done went and turned in your player card huh?" Dame asked him.

"Yeah, you know. I'm in love and Margarita's my boo."

"Congratulations nephew. I hope it works for Y'all. You both deserve it."

"Where's Mash?" Spits asked.

"Him and Blu flew out to LA to kick it for a few days."

"So when are we gonna get a baby out of you two?" Janet asked and they heard Margarita laugh.

"He just proposed a few hours ago Janet. Don't try to slow me down with no kids yet ."

"I think that's so chivalrous the way he took you on a surprise trip halfway around the world to propose." Janet gushed playfully while batting her eyes as if love-struck.

"Oh yeah!" Tracy said suddenly remembering why she came to Dame's office in the first place. "Boy what's this with you telling Chase to call and talk to me and Dame about a joint album."

He laughed as he picturing her standing there with her flared nostrils at not being in on the secret. "It's perfect big sis. I know Dame's with it, ain't you unc?"

"You dang right I'm with it. Let's get this money while the getting's good."

"We got Chase on the intercom now. He called Dame and they been in here plotting." She told him. "Are you sure this is what you want baby?"

"Yeah. I am." He answered quickly. "Dead sure."

"Okay baby. We gonna make sure it happens then. You two get off this phone and enjoy your vacation. And congratulations."

"Thank you." They both said before hanging up.

"Okay Chase." Tracy said wasting no time. "Let me get a look at everybody's itineraries on my end and arrange everything. Give me a few hours and I'll give you a call."

"Sounds good to me." He said. "And Dame, our attorney will fax yours the contracts in a couple of minutes. Let me know what you think after you talk it over with your team."

Tony Clincy

"Bet. I'll get with you in a minute homie." Dame promised as he reached into his shirt pocket for his cigar looking at Tracy as he did so. "There's about to be smoke in the air up in here. So anybody who's got a problem with it better get to moving around."

He had a triumphant smirk on his face as he kicked his feet up onto the desk, leaned back and lit the cigar, happily puffing and making his face disappear in a thick smelly cloud of smoke.

Tracy smiled and shook her head. "Don't nobody wanna be in your crusty office anyways punk." She spun around towards the door and spoke over her shoulder on her way out. "Forget you and your big headed butt. We've got work to do. Come on Janet."

BLOODY APPLE…

SPITS, LOOCHIE AND Mash sat at the controls with one of Loochie's engineers listening to the Paper Chasers, and The Get Money Clique sing the hook to their posse cut.

"That beat ain't to be messed with Son." Loochie told Mash.

"Naw chief," Mash shook his head and spun his chair around looking like he was in heaven as he looked around him. "this studio ain't to be messed with. How you gon' have see-through walls all through this place? I thought the Blue Room was tight. But this right here?"

Spen, Loco, Yak and Chase sat on the couch smoking some of New York's finest as they waited patiently for the marathon recording session to end so that they could head to Loochie's nightclub in Harlem. They had flown in from Cali at eight this morning and drove straight there to begin recording on the joint album which would be titled 'Friend or Foe'.

For the past two months, Spits and Loochie had become as close as brothers and being the business minded men they were, they had no problem hammering out the details to make a joint album possible.

Tracy had them staying at the Trump Towers for while they completed the album. Both camps were amped, especially Spits and company. They were all playing this game at its highest level and loving every minute of it.

Margarita had the hottest album in the country now and the media were hailing her as Ms. 2011 and she was doing all she could to live up to the title. As Tracy had promised, the music world loved her drop dead gorgeous looks as well as the stunningly sexy costumes Fred picked out for her to wear. Her and Janet were across town getting ready for her performance on Saturday Night Live and would meet up with them at Loochie's club afterwards.

They were all zoned in on building the Paper Chasin' Records brand into a powerhouse within the industry. With both Mr. Davis and Loochie having taken an interest in him and his career, Spits found himself in the perfect situation to learn how to play this game with the big boys and was taking full advantage of it.

When the hook was sung to Mash's satisfaction, he announced that they were done for the night and everybody piled onto the elevators to head to the basement garage where a limousine waited to take them to Loochie's club The Mint.

They pulled up to the front of the club and found the line out front stretching down the block and around the corner.

"Man look at all these broads!" Mash said with his face to the tinted window. "I'm 'bout to be up till the sun rise 'round this piece."

Blu gave him dap at and promised that he would be doing the same thing. "This is liver than LA and we ain't even went inside yet."

They were escorted inside to cheers from the crowd outside and led through the pink lit, loud club to the VIP section on the top floor of the four story building. There they found at least a hundred of what had to be the finest women in the city.

"They love you out here Looch." Spits said as they sat in the corner booth impressed at the love and respect he'd seen the party goers give their to host as they'd made their way through the energetic mass of dancing bodies.

Loochie waved his hand like it was nothing. "I came from this yo. I grew up right here in this neighborhood and I ain't never forgot it. So my people respect that." He smiled his crooked smile. "Plus, I got the livest club on the East Coast."

"Man you ain't never lied." Loco agreed in an awe filled voice as he stared open-mouthed at the topless dancers gyrating to the bass heavy music in the cages hanging throughout the club. "This ain't to be messed with." Loco back handed Spits in the chest. "Look at them broads homie. I'm 'bout to go get my mack on. I'll get with your square butt later." With that said, he left to scout the club and see what he could get into.

"Your boy Loco's crazy as heck." Loochie laughed.

"Yeah, that's my dude right there. You don't know the half of it though. You should've seen him when we was out hustlin' on the block."

"Say Spits." Mash said as he stood looking over the rail to the dance floor where all eyes seemed to be on them. "Let's go show these cats how we do it in Seaside."

"Man, I ain't fixin' to do no dancing in this hot ol' club." Spits told him while laughing at the lustful look on his boy's face.

Mash didn't even hear him. He had his eyes on what had to be the biggest behind in the world down on the dance floor. He licked his lips in anticipation. "I'm 'bout to get my gangsta boogie on Y'all." He said and started off.

"Hold up!" Blu said and scooted from the seat to follow with a bottle of Remy in his fist. "Now we gon' show you how the West Coast rock!" He yelled.

Spits and Loochie laughed. They enjoying seeing everybody have a good time.

"Do you know what's gon' happen when we drop this album on 'em Looch?" Spits asked as he poured himself a drink. "We bout to go like fifteen times platinum big homie. The world ain't ready for this this."

Loochie laughed. "I don't know if I'm ready for it myself to tell you the truth. This is gonna be big. I been doing this for a minute and this is the biggest move I've made. I think we gon' set some records. Especially when we go on tour. How they 'gon compete with us as headlines and your girl and our crews opening up for us? Cats can't mess with us yo. We 'bout to screw the world with this one."

Spits nodded in agreement.

"You know, you remind me of myself lil homie." Loochie told him before taking a pull off the blunt Chase passed him. "When I was twenty three, I was hungry and thought I was the coolest thing since Ice Berg Slim."

"So you think I think I'm cool then?"

"Heck yeah yo. When I saw you hanging with Clifton at his party, I almost laughed at how calm you was trying to act while standing there with all them stuffy white folks."

Spits smiled and turned to look at the dance floor where he saw Mash holding onto some girl's butt with both hands as they danced close. He laughed and pointed to him.

"Look at Mash with that big ol' smile on his face. He looks like he's in booty heaven or somethin'."

Loochie looked down and broke out laughing before something wiped the smile from his face and made him frown suddenly.

"What's wrong?" Spits caught the look and followed his gaze. He saw the problem standing to the left of where Mash and Blu were dancing. It was a group of five thugs in all red staring at them with threatening looks on their faces.

"Oh crap!" Spits stood and started for the stairwell waving for Yak to follow him. Mash saw nothing but the fine red bone in his arms smiling at him with a look that promised a night he wouldn't soon forget.

"What's up blood!" A voice yelled over the music at Mash's side. Mash turned and caught a blow to the jaw as somebody swung on him. The punched knocked him back and one of the thugs reached out and snatched the chain from his neck.

Mash stumbled and saw one of them reaching to his waist for a gun. He pulled his own pistol from the small of his back and started shooting, catching a bullet to the shoulder as he did.

Spits stood watching from the balcony. "Mash!"

The gunshots sent a panic through the club as the music suddenly stopped to be replaced by screams and a loud stampede of bodies rushing for the exits.

Spits fought his way against the tide and reached Mash just as Blu did and found him on his back with his eyes closed.

"Mash!" he yelled while shaking him, scared that he was dead. "Mash! Are you alright? Mash!"

His eyes opened and he smiled. "Did I get that fool homie?"

"Come on, get up and let's get up outta here." Spits told him as he and Blu helped him up just as Loochie and his security team came up.

"Follow us yo." Loochie instructed with a look full of rage. He picked up the pistol Mash had dropped and gave it to one of his boys to disposed of. Then he led them to the rear entrance where their limo waited.

Loochie told the driver to take them to his penthouse and told Spits that he would have a doctor meet them there. "If we take him to the hospital, the police is gon' get on him. It looks like it just hit him in the shoulder so he should be cool."

Spits didn't speak but sat across from Mash with a-murderous look. "What the heck is wrong with you? Have you gone crazy or somethin'?" He yelled, seeing all the hard work and his dreams crumbling because of Mash's stupidity.

Shocked, Mash's eyes filled with a rage of their own. "What! Them punk fools rushed me. They got what they had coming. What the heck you talking about?"

"Did you forget that we ain't street thugs no more? You worth over thirty million dollars fool. How the heck you gon' shoot up a night club like that?"

"'Cause I'm from Hood Life, that's how I can. Just 'cause you done forgot where you from, don't get at me with that soft stuff. They know what it is with the Mashster."

Spits let out an false laugh at hearing this. "You wasn't talking that crap when stuff was funky in the hood and you bounced to Florida fool. So miss me with that-"

Mash came from his seat before Spits finished and rushed him, paying no heed to his hurt shoulder.

"Chill out yo!" Loochie tried to pull Mash off and got punched as the two swung wildly at each other. Flashing lights suddenly lit up the limo through the back window signaling for the driver to pull over.

"Crap!" Loochie said dreadfully and shot Spits a look as he and Mash broke up to look behind them. "This 'bout to get real ugly yo." He predicted.

Spits gave Mash a look of pure disgust as the limo pulled over. "You is about one stupid fool you know that?" He told him. "You just messed it up for all of us." He shook his head and stared outside to the dark New York night with angry tears building in the corners of his eyes as he saw all that they'd built come crashing down in the patrol car lights shining through the back of the limo.

TO BE CONTINUED...

HoodLife Books Order Form

Title	Quantity	Shipping	Total
Rap Star 1 $15.00			
Rap Star 2 $15.00			
HoodLife Books T-shirt $20			

Send money orders, cashier checks,
and institutional checks to:
HoodLife Books
1643 Flores Street #A
Seaside, Ca 93955

Rap Star

Kambino1@gmail.com

241